UNMASKING
THE
MARQUESS

A HOLD YOUR BREATH NOVEL, VOLUME 2

A THOUSAND REASONS TO HOLD YOUR BREATH,
AND ONE TO LET IT GO.

K.J. JACKSON

First Edition: August 2014
ISBN: 978-1-940149-06-6
http://www.kjjackson.com

DEDICATION

– FOR MY FAVORITE KS

CHAPTER 1

LONDON, ENGLAND
JUNE, 1820

"You cannot do this."

Killian Hayward, Marquess of Southfork, had hoped for a reprieve from the Duchess of Dunway. But she hadn't even bothered with the usual polite pitter-patter of conversation after walking in. No. She jumped right into her latest nagging session.

"You cannot do this," the duchess muttered again as she paced on the blue, spiral-patterned Persian rug before him. Back and forth. She had been wearing down the carpet for the last five minutes, and her steps had only quickened.

Arms crossed, Killian leaned against the doorway of his study. If she wasn't the wife of his best friend, and, he allowed, a beloved friend to him in her own right, he would have cut Aggie off days, nay, months ago.

As it was, he would have to wait her out. Only fourteen more hours to go.

His eyes went down to the thin line of brandy in the bottom of the short glass he held. Thank goodness he had swallowed several pours before his friends arrived.

She stopped in front of him, green eyes flickering between disappointment and desperate persuasion. "Killian, I am serious. You do not have much time left. You cannot do this to Miss Halstead."

Taking a deep breath, Killian sidestepped her small frame and walked to the sideboard. "I do not see why your concern has reached such a monumental pitch, duchess." He forced ease into his tone, even as his throat tightened. "You have had plenty of time to come to terms with the wedding."

Aggie followed him across the room, a terrier on a rat, not letting him escape. "I have not come to terms with it and you know it. I had hoped I could convince you to alter your course by now. It is not right to do this to her. Reanna is an innocent and you are being a blazing idiot."

"It is not Reanna I am concerned with, Aggie. You know that." He picked up the decanter of brandy, his thick hand wrapping around the cut glass. He paused, pondering the streams of light fighting the angles of the glass. A design he had never cared for, except for the show of expense. It was good he could still recognize show from reality. He was beginning to wonder.

"Killian—"

"I can," he cut her off, "and will be moving forward with the plan as decided."

Her hand went gentle onto his forearm as her voice softened. "But Killian, you are giving no thought at all to what this will do to Reanna."

He halted his pour, the amber liquid kissing the lip of the decanter. He looked at her. "Do I need to?"

She pulled her hand back as her nose crinkled in disgust. "Do not be an ass. You are being the worst kind of cruel if you go through with this." Her voice lost all softness and Killian could feel her anxiety explode, uncontrolled, into the room. "There is still time to call it off. I will tell Reanna myself, explain the situation to her. Please, Killian, you need to do what is right."

"Aggie, the wedding is tomorrow. I will not call it off. Not after all the work that went into it. Not for what is at stake."

"The work has nothing to do with it." She went back to pacing. "You are being a stubborn ogre and you know it. You have long since achieved what you needed to out of this. He is done. Destroyed. The wedding need not happen. Reanna should not be brought into your revenge."

She paused in her movement to stare at him, hands shaking. He could feel her struggling for words.

"Killian, you know I adore you, but how many names do I have to call you before you will listen to reason?"

He turned to her, contemplating the flush in her forehead and on her cheeks. "You have been lecturing me for too long, I agree to that. And since I have yet to yield to your wishes, you should have some clue as to what my actions will be between today and tomorrow. You continue to waste your breath on this subject."

"I am not wasting my breath, and I will not give up on getting through that impossibly thick skull of yours. I know somewhere in you, there is a shred of decency that is listening to reason and agreeing with what I am saying—you just have to stop ignoring it."

Killian's attention went back to the mahogany sideboard to pour a second glass of brandy. Skirting the duchess, he walked across the room. "Devin, can you please call your wife off?"

He handed the glass to the Duke of Dunway, who sat easily on the crisp sofa, his large form swallowing the delicate vine pattern on the silk.

A hollow chuckle escaped the duke. "Do not even try it, friend. I am not getting into this one. I have been hearing about it from both of you for too long, to be stupid enough to stick my neck in the middle of your swinging axes. No thank you." He raised his glass to both of them. "I will decline any involvement in this conversation. I am merely here to safely remove my wife from the room should you decided to throttle her."

Killian sighed and turned back to face his pint-sized adversary. She was decked out prettily for this duel; a coral silk evening gown hugged her curves and complemented her softly coifed blond hair.

It rankled his pride, but Killian admitted to himself that he did want her to understand. He hated the growing disappointment he had seen in Aggie's eyes over the past weeks. But he knew she would never fully understand what he had been through. She hadn't seen first-hand, as Devin had, the destruction that had been his life. How he had to scrape from nothing to rebuild everything that had been lost.

He also realized understanding was even more difficult for Aggie now that she had grown to count Reanna as a close friend.

Damn that the only two people he actually cared about were in this room, and one of them was Aggie. The whole of his life would be a lot easier had Devin never met Aggie, never married. And damn that she had become just as important to him as Devin was. He opened his mouth one last time to try and sway her.

"I assure you, Aggie, there is not one shred of me that agrees with you on this subject. The wedding will complete all that I have worked to achieve, for all these years. All that both of you have helped me achieve." His eyebrows rose pointedly. "Do I need to remind you that you were the one who discovered Reanna's almost-engagement to Lord Hiplan? I will not stop now, not when I am so close."

Aggie's hand flew up. "Stop right there. Yes, I was the one that started the whole damn thing, but the second you began to court her and push Lord Hiplan out of the way, I knew it was a mistake. And since then I have never supported you in this particular venture. I do not think I have to remind you that I have been fighting you for months."

"You do not."

"This is not decent, this is not right, and this is certainly not honorable."

Devin coughed.

"Too far, Aggie. Too far." Killian couldn't stop his jaw from openly clenching. "You dare to call honor into this? Have I ever been dishonorable to you, Devin, or even to anyone of consequence to us?"

He stared at her hard, the question hanging in the air, demanding she answer it.

Aggie bowed her head slightly, chagrined, and shook it.

He gave her a curt nod. "Thank you. Honor is exactly what has driven this. You knew that when you first agreed to help me."

"And I agreed to help you because of what he did to your mother…God…" She closed her eyes, a visible shiver running through her. "I still cannot bear to think on it."

She opened her eyes, pinning him, even as her voice was soft. "But this—when did you become such a cutthroat that you are willing to sacrifice an innocent?"

"She is not an innocent. Not with her father."

"Killian, how many times do I have to tell you? She is not her father. She has no idea what her father is. What her father has done. So, yes, that makes her an innocent. An innocent you will be destroying if you go through with this marriage."

"We all lose our innocence, Aggie."

Sighing, Aggie sat down next to her husband, grabbed the glass of brandy from his hand, and took a swallow. Suspicious. Aggie did not drink brandy.

She scooted closer to Devin, tucking herself under his extended arm.

Killian's eyebrow arched at her. "Are you exhausted or cowering?"

She didn't look up at him. "Both."

"You need to tell him, Aggs," Devin said.

"Tell me what?"

She took another sip of the brandy, face contorting at the burn. "I called on her today."

"You went to see her?"

Aggie nodded.

Hand wrapped around his glass, Killian's knuckles turned white. "What the hell did you say to her, Aggie?"

She handed the brandy back to Devin and looked up at Killian, defiance in her chin. "She was talking, glowing, going on and on about how happy she is. But then she asked me what your favorite color was—it was about something her aunt said regarding her trousseau and the colors she chose for the materials. She did not know what your favorite color was. She was so worried. She wants to please you and had chosen blue, but only because you wear a lot of blue. She said she actually did not know what your favorite color was."

"So?"

"So that is the point. She does not know anything genuine about you. I have never seen someone so in love, and at the same time, so misguided in that emotion. It is heartbreaking to watch. Have you ever had a real conversation with her?"

"Enough that she fell in love with me."

"Ass. If you had done so much as that—an actual conversation with her—in the past three months, you would know she is nothing like her father, never will be, and she deserves so much better than what you are going to do to her tomorrow. Maybe if you knew her in the slightest, you would actually be hearing what I am telling you."

"I know who her father is. That is the only thing I need to know about her. Maybe you should have left it at that as well."

"Stop. I like Reanna. I consider her a true friend. But I have never met such an innocent soul. She knows nothing of her father's dealings. She knows very little about the world. You are going to crush her when she finds out, and she has no resiliency, no way to handle such cruelty. She loves you deeply and believes you return the sentiment."

"What did you tell her, duchess?"

"Nothing. Nothing about your plan. But I did tell her to protect her heart."

"You what?"

Aggie tucked further under Devin's arm. "Her heart. I told her to protect it. I wanted to create a sliver of doubt in her, so that when she finds out what you are doing, it will not be such a shock. You went too far with her, Killian. She loves you."

"What difference does that make?"

"You did not just make her want to marry you. You made her fall in love with you. That is the difference. That is why this is vicious. You could at least tell her the truth about her father. She deserves that."

"You know exactly what will happen if she knows the truth." Worry invaded his face. "You are not going to tell her, are you?"

"I have a good mind to, if my conscience is to remain clean."

"Aggie—"

Her tone dropped, mirroring her shoulders as she interrupted him. "Do not worry. I will be silent. This is your decision. Even if I think you are an imbecile."

"Again, the rudeness."

"It is only because I have run out of things to say to make an impression on you." She sighed, weary. "I hate everything about this. I just cannot believe you have this cruelty in you."

Killian's eyes shifted to Devin. If his friend was worth his salt, he would have clamped his wife's mouth shut minutes ago. Instead, the duke's lips remained solidly closed, one eyebrow raised at him. Devin was probably enjoying this haranguing his wife was delivering.

His attention went back to Aggie. "Why do you continue to insist this is cruelty? If anything, I am getting her away from her bastard of a father. And saving her from being whored out to some overweight, over-old, bumbling cad with a few coins to his name."

Aggie's voice shrunk to a whisper as she shook her head. "It is cruel because she loves you, Killian. And she believes you love her. There is nothing crueler than falsely believing you are loved. Falsely believing you are important to someone."

Aggie's words rang true, Killian couldn't deny. He had given false impressions to the girl. In all that he had done to her father over the past years, it was the lying to Miss Halstead that his conscience hadn't been able to shake clean.

But Aggie couldn't know that.

Killian's voice hardened. "She will get over it in no time. Once the marriage is consummated, she will be off the market for good, and the last chance her father had to gain coinage by selling her will be gone forever." Killian swallowed the last of his brandy. "She will have an enviable life as a marchioness. A life of comfort. And I will have no demands on her time."

"Killian, that is what you do not understand. It is not about the life she will get. She wants you. You. You could be penniless, and she would defy her father for you. You can tell her. She would choose you over her father in a second."

"I am not about to take that chance. You put too much emphasis on love, Aggie. Yes, you and Devin found fortune in each other, but I do not think I need to remind you that loveless marriages are the norm, and you are the exception. You do no good arguing about love with me."

She stood up, arms flying in the air. "But that is exactly why I argue. Why can you not have the same as us? Maybe that is why I am adamant. Why can I not hope for more for you as well?"

"Aggie, I have never cared for, nor wanted the love you speak of in my life. I do this, go through with the marriage, my revenge is done. I am at peace. We are done discussing it."

Aggie went silent.

Killian's shoulders relaxed for the first time since his friends arrived. Whether or not Aggie understood, he was doing what was necessary to destroy the man that had ruined his family. The bastard had run away from the death Killian had planned, so crushing him into insignificance would have to do.

Devin understood such a duty. But he couldn't expect the same from Aggie. She was a woman, and there was too much forgiveness in her.

Aggie stepped in front of him. "It will be done, but at what expense?"

Killian's grip tightened on the glass he was holding. "So, ultimately, are you saying you will not support me on this? Will you be at the wedding?"

Aggie turned from him and sat wearily on the couch next to her husband. Devin's arm immediately went around her shoulders.

Killian's gaze went to the duke. "Devin?"

Devin didn't waste a moment. "You know where I stand on the matter. I will be there."

Killian nodded, grateful for his friend's unwavering support. "Aggie?"

She took a deep breath, hands clenched in her lap. "No, I do not support your decision on this matter."

Killian turned away from the two of them, hand clenching the edge of the black marble mantel above the fireplace.

"Killian, no, do not get disgusted with me," Aggie said. "I cannot support your decision, but I do support you. I will be there tomorrow."

He turned back to them, approval, but not a smile on his face. "Thank you. Your presence means much to me, even if you do not agree with what I am about to do."

~ ~ ~

Poised before the gold gilded mirror in her rooms, Reanna Halstead tugged at a tangled piece of long, near-black hair. The scent of the jasmine from her bath escaped as she pulled the tortoise shell comb through her wet locks.

The Marquess of Southfork loved her. And they were getting married tomorrow. How had that happened?

She never dreamed her short foray into London society would have gained her such a wonderful man. She was years older than the brightest lights of the ton, so when her father had finally allowed her aunt to present her to society, she had little hope of attracting attention from a man as young and vibrant as Lord Southfork.

She had seen so much beauty during this first trip to London, that she still had a hard time placing herself in it without self-comparisons to all the exquisiteness surrounding her.

Twisting on the stool, she forced herself to stare hard at her reflection. Her light blue eyes—too light for her hair color, she knew—searched the contours of her face. Why had he chosen her?

She wasn't worldly. Wasn't a wit. She guessed she looked enough like her mother and aunt, and they were both great beauties of their time. But she would never label herself thusly. Her cheekbones were a little too high. Bottom lip too swollen. Nose and chin passable. Her dark hair, glossy and strong, was her best asset. That, she had to admit.

Her eyes veered off.

She was uncomfortable with looking at herself for such a spell. Even if her aunt had drummed into her the importance of acknowledging exactly what looked back in the mirror, in order to harness it to the best effect.

Reanna pulled the comb through the last snarl, then forced her eyes to the mirror. She was determined to look her best tomorrow. She needed to. For Killian.

Just saying his name in her mind sent a tingle down her spine. He was a man. A true man. Killian was exciting to be around and people gravitated toward him. So how she had caught his eye, she did not know. There was always laughter where he was. And when her hand was in the crook of his arm, she was always surprised by his muscle. Even through her gloves and his crisp jackets, she could feel strength resonating from him.

Her breath caught at the thought of his body. What would it be like to really kiss Killian? Sure, they had stolen a few all-too-short pecks several times.

And when he told her that he loved her and asked her to marry him, their kiss had lasted a bit longer than a peck. But before Reanna had even realized it had begun, Killian had pulled away. He said he would not succumb to ungentlemanly behavior, no matter the depth of his feelings, at least not until they were properly wed.

A true gentleman.

Reanna pushed her hair atop her head, crooking her neck at all angles, imaging how it would look tomorrow. She needed to be perfect.

"You will look presentable, no need to worry on that." Her Aunt Maureen entered the room, sans knocking, for it was her home.

She walked to stand behind Reanna, reeking of statuesque elegance. Her aunt gave a quick glance to Reanna's reflection in the mirror, and then her eyes immediately wandered up to study her own aging face. She tucked a non-existent stray hair back into her perfectly coifed hair.

Aunt Maureen pulled Reanna's hands from her dark locks. "You will crimp your hair if you keep playing with it. Miss Melby will have a devil of a time getting your thick hair in place as it is. Let us not add to her misery."

Reanna's posture stiffened as her hair fell back down past her shoulders. "Thank you for the compliment, Aunt Maureen. I do want to look most presentable for Lord Southfork tomorrow."

"As you should. That will soon be your only duty, to look presentable for your husband."

Aunt Maureen walked over to the dresser, straightening the few objects—tin of ribbons, mirror, brush, locket—into an even line. Her characteristic neatening stretched out, almost to the point of stalling, but then she turned back to Reanna. "Child, there is no easy way to say this, so I just will. Your father will not be attending the wedding tomorrow. I just received confirmation."

A weight fell onto Reanna's heart. "Are you sure, Aunt Maureen? Are you sure there is no way he can attend? It is just that…well, it is my wedding and I so hoped that he would be able to be there, even though—"

"Do not quiver about it, child. No, there is no question. No change of plans. He will not be attending the wedding. He is still in Suffolk, and after his ruin, he believes he should not be a presence. I agree."

"But it is my wedding day."

"Which is precisely what we do not want him to ruin." Aunt Maureen's crisp tone told Reanna there would be no swaying of the situation. "It is a wonder we are getting you married off at all, what with the scandal he caused on the way out of London. I was, frankly, surprised when I came back into town and found out his ruin was so complete."

Reanna's ears perked. Sure, she had noticed the removal of trinkets and artifacts and furniture and eventually, staff, from their estate in Suffolk. She knew the changes had to be money-related. But her father had downplayed it all, reminding her she didn't have a mind for numbers, nor should she be questioning his choices. All she needed to know was that everything would be fine, he'd maintained.

"You are extremely lucky to have attracted a man such as Lord Southfork, who could overlook your father's transgressions. Very few men would. Even that list of men your father provided as suitable was suspect. At this point, if your father were to appear, there is no telling what society's—or your fiancé's—reaction would be."

Reanna's nose wrinkled at the mention of the list. Her father had sent with her to London a list of possible suitors. Lord Hiplan had been the most interested, and, Reanna had to admit, the least offensive of the bunch. Even though he was near thirty years her senior, he at least had good manners and took a bath on occasion. She had resigned herself to a dutiful marriage only a day before Lord Southfork inquired about an introduction. Thank goodness she had never said yes to Lord Hiplan's marriage proposal.

"Was my father's ruin really as bad as that?" Hand wrapping around the gilded arm of the stool, Reanna scooted forward and turned to her aunt. This was the first time her aunt had even mentioned her father's ruin, of which Reanna knew nothing. She had only heard snippets of whispered conversations in the corners of drawing rooms.

"Yes, it was. Is. As I have said, it is a wonder that you managed to snag the marquess. Far above what I would have expected you could accomplish. Your looks warred a penniless, ruined father, and apparently, you have honored the Vestilun line." Her face turned soft for a split second as she mentioned her family's long tradition of beauties.

"I owe you much, Aunt Maureen. This certainly would not have been possible without you."

"That is true. But my sister's child deserves better than what your father brought upon his family." Maureen picked up a locket from the dresser and opened it. The haunting engraving of Reanna's mother looked up at her. "It was the only proper way to honor your mother's memory."

She clicked the locket closed. "But your father is an imbecile. We should be grateful he will not be attending the wedding. It makes the production much easier. It is, after all, no secret that I despise the man."

"Aunt Maureen, you must not say such things," Reanna said, her hands fidgeting with the comb. "He is my father."

"A father who never gave any true regard to your mother. Your defense of him is uncalled for with me. I will continue to loathe the man for my time on earth."

"Why do you dislike him?"

"It is of no concern to you, especially on the eve before your wedding. Past is past, even if it always informs the present." She set the locket onto the dresser, edging it into line with the other objects. "I do have one thing that I need to discuss with you before your wedding."

Resigned she would get no real information from her aunt, Reanna turned the stool fully around to her. "Yes?"

"I have waited to do this until you were married, for I was not about to chance your father's ethics on the matter. You know after the wedding I will be returning to Spain."

"Yes. I will miss you."

"I do not intend to return to London. So it is a good time, now that you will be outside of your father's greedy grasp, to pass along this home and a tidy sum to you. The marquess is wealthy in his own right, so I have no concerns about him. But things can change. They did with your father. The money and the home are in a trust for you for sole and separate use, should you ever have need of it. There are monthly limits on it, of course, but it will keep you and any children in comfort should the need arise."

Reanna's mouth dropped open. Her aunt looked as near to nostalgia and emotion as she had ever seen her. "Aunt Maureen, this is too generous. There is no need."

"No, child. Far from it. No woman should ever have to be at the mercy of fate and greed when it comes to food and shelter. Only you will have access to the money and home, and I sincerely hope you will never have need of either."

"I will not. I trust Lord Southfork will take care of me."

Her aunt smiled at her, wryness in her wrinkled eyes. "It will be yours to pass along to the next generation, then." The smile disappeared. "Now continue to prepare for bed. I do not wish to present a haggard-looking Vestilun tomorrow."

Bluntness aside, Reanna knew her aunt had her best interests at heart. "Thank you for all that you have given and done for me over the past six months, Aunt. This has been a wonderful dream for me."

Aunt Maureen looked momentarily uncomfortable with the heartfelt words. "You are welcome." She smoothed the already smooth mix of dark and grey hairs going into her chignon.

Reanna cringed at the discomfort her words seemed to cause her aunt. So she attempted to dispel emotion and changed the subject. "Are you prepared for travel to the continent following tomorrow?"

"Yes, a day or two more, and I will leave. It will do no good to dally here in London, now that my work is done. I will, of course, keep in contact."

She turned to walk out the door, then paused at the entry. "You will go to sleep soon, I trust. I will not have a tired Vestilun at the altar."

CHAPTER 2

Hand tucked into the crook of his arm, Reanna leaned her temple against the upper arm of her new husband. Strong, immobile, but her cheek somehow managed to find softness in it. And if she kept her head tight to his jacket, the bumps of the carriage couldn't separate them.

The whole day was a blur, and now the countryside whizzed past as they rode from London to Killian's nearest country estate, Curplan Hall.

Reanna sighed, sheer joy flooding her. "This is all so wonderful Killian. It was—is a dream for me."

His hand went over hers and he gave it a squeeze. "Did you think so, Lady Southfork?"

"Yes and yes. It was more than I could have ever hoped for." She shifted so she could see his brown eyes. "Thank you for making it so perfect."

"Anything to make my new bride happy. What was your favorite part of the day?"

"It was…it was all so grand…" Reanna faltered, trying to decide which of the thousand details of the day she liked best—impossible, for it had all been beautiful. But then a random moment popped into her mind. "Oh, but there was something peculiar. I had a brief moment alone with the duchess when I was freshening up before the ceremony, and she said something odd."

Reanna thought she felt Killian tense, but then it disappeared in an instant. It must have been a bump.

"Odd? What was it she said?"

"Now that I think about it, I guess it was not so odd, it was more of her tone, something I could not quite understand in the way she said it."

"Which was?"

"She mentioned to me that if I were to ever need any help at all, that she would be there for me on a moment's notice."

Killian gave an easy shrug. "That does not seem strange. Devin and Aggie have been friends of mine for years. I am sure she was just trying to make you feel welcome into all facets of my life. Aggie knows all too well the pressures put upon a high-standing lady. I am sure she just wanted to let you know you are not alone in your future as my wife."

Reanna smiled and tightened her hold on his arm. "Yes, I am sure you are right. You know her much better than I. It was a very nice thing for her to say."

"Yes, Aggie is nothing if not caring."

Reanna thought she heard sarcasm in his voice, but then dismissed it. She had never heard Killian use sarcasm.

They rode in silence, Reanna reveling in the solidity of her new husband. Warm and hard.

"I do have one regret of the day though." She interrupted the comfortable silence.

"And that is?"

"That, until we left, I had spent hardly a spec of it with you." She tentatively laid her free hand on his shoulder, her fingertips touching the short sandy-blond hair whisking the back of his cravat.

It felt so freeing to be able to touch him without plagues of worry about proprieties flooding her mind. Her main goal in London had not been to fetch a husband, as her father had demanded. It had been to not embarrass her aunt after all she had done for Reanna. Her aunt was the stoic sort, but by far the most generous person Reanna had ever met. And getting herself ruined by an over-zealous touch would have accomplished what she least desired.

"We will have plenty of time to spend together tonight, Reanna." He placed a small kiss on the crown of her forehead.

Reanna glowed at his touch. It was almost too much to believe, that she was now married to this man, and she was quickly finding out that she enjoyed touching him.

"Killian, do not think me wanton."

He smiled down at her. "I do not think it possible for you to be so, Reanna. What do you want?"

"Would you kiss me?"

A crooked smile touched his mouth. "Have I not done that enough?"

"No, I mean a real kiss. I have been waiting so long to know what it would be like to really be kissed by you. I guess I had hoped it would have happened earlier in the day somehow."

"You truly have no patience left?"

Terror filled her and she couldn't help from catching her lip in her teeth, afraid she'd upset him.

Killian laughed. "Do not look so anxious, love. I do not think you the slightest wanton." He leaned away from her to draw the curtains of the carriage windows closed. "And if that is what my bride would like on her wedding day…"

Killian turned to her and reached out, grabbing her chin and pulling her close, ever so slowly. His eyes locked into hers, the brown smoldering with promised passion as they drew Reanna in.

The intensity hit her, and she drew in a breath that did little to steady her tight chest.

His lips met hers, and his hand slid from her chin to the small cusp in the back of her neck. He tilted her slightly, his lips beginning soft, tender, but she couldn't help her slight hesitation, even though this was exactly what she had asked for.

Painstakingly slow, his lips turned demanding, hot, as Reanna began to respond to his touch, to his hard body molding hers. She was a novice and had no inclination how to hold anything back from Killian's onslaught. Nor how to quench the fire in her belly that demanded she get as close to her husband as possible.

Without warning, and without even knowing how it had happened, Reanna had melded completely on top of Killian, her legs straddling him, her knees on the velvet squabs, cream skirts shoved up about her waist. Her hair had fallen, dark curls dancing carelessly down her back.

And still Killian did not stop. Grabbing her lips between his teeth, he sucked on the ripeness of them like they were sweet berries. His hand ran down her spine, and then came around, fully cupping the breasts that were nudging across his chest.

Reanna gasped at the touch, jerking slightly back as her eyes flew open in surprise. But it was only for a second, and she leaned back down toward him, her swollen lips asking for more, but Killian ignored it.

He was done.

He dropped his hands from her body.

"That shall do for now." His voice was crisp and short.

Her eyes flew open again, this time in foggy confusion, then in embarrassment as she looked down to find herself sitting like a common whore on top of her husband.

She scrambled off him, almost falling to the floor of the carriage in her haste to get her skirts back down and her body properly seated, this time, across from him.

Her cheeks flamed as she tried to calm her panting, and she franticly looked for a place to fixate her eyes that was nowhere near her husband. She found the spot in the corner of the carriage floor farthest from Killian's shiny black Hessians.

Reanna's breathing came under control. "I am so sorry. I did not know what I was doing. Please forgive me." Her eyes stayed averted.

"It is of no consequence," he said, straightening his jacket.

~ ~ ~

Killian stared at Reanna's shaking hands smoothing down the folds of her skirt. She was trying to hide it, but he could see her fingertips twitching.

Her eyes remained solidly stuck on the carriage floor.

He knew it was his hands that had pushed her into the spectacle the two of them had just conjured. But she had gone along with him quite enthusiastically.

She had kissed him with a passion he had never felt. Never. From anyone. Not a mistress. Not a lover. He had never felt anything like it. Unbridled passion. Unmasked. He had lost himself in it.

Hell. Maybe Aggie was right. Reanna did love him. So completely she didn't have the slightest notion of how to curb herself around him.

Aggie's niggling voice popped into his head. The many times she had told him Reanna was innocent. Naïve. That he couldn't do this. She didn't deserve to be used and discarded.

Killian's fist clenched as he shoved Aggie's voice out of his head. This had to be done. Consummate the vows. Leave no possible venue—no matter how slight—open to invalidating the marriage. Ruin her father's last chance to regain all that was lost. And when her father's ruin was solidified, then, maybe then, he could take more care with Reanna.

But not until his revenge was complete.

Reanna's hands flew to her head, quickly trying to re-pin the hair that had fallen a few moments ago, stealing the soft curls away from where they wanted to be, which was playing along her long neck and shoulders.

Her head remained slightly bowed. Killian stared at her. Her ivory carriage dress was cut square across the bodice, rising enticingly over softly rounded breasts that were not too big for her slender figure. He had just experienced that firsthand.

He thought he could detect moistness in her eyes, but no tears fell. Her bottom lip was bright pink from his onslaught and was swelled beyond its normal puffiness. Something many would see as a flaw, but Killian had never minded the slight quirk of her face. He was struck at how small she looked sitting across from him.

His gaze hardened at her. Pity could not be a part of this.

Killian pulled the curtains to his right open again, and forced his gaze onto the rolling green hills. At least she was attractive. For what he had to do tonight could have been much worse if Baron Halstead's only daughter had been a dog. He had never been one to enjoy naïve virgins, but Reanna seemed responsive, and he would be able to make do with that.

Killian's body tensed as his mind wandered to the man he was bent on destroying. It was exactly where he needed his mind to go, and he let the anger course through him, turning his blood icy. When he knew he had sufficiently built a swell of rage, he looked across to the daughter of the baron, and his stomach churned.

He could scarcely believe he had just been thinking that she was attractive. This loving fiancé farce he had been playing with her had begun to engrain into his actions, so much so that it had even seeped into his wayward thoughts. Justice. That was what he needed to concentrate on.

Killian's eyes shifted back out the carriage window. He was happy to allow thoughts of revenge rule his mind for the last part of the trip to Curplan Hall.

What he didn't choose were the nagging notions that ate away at the back of his head, though he attempted to dismiss them.

The girl he married may not know what she was doing, but Killian certainly did, and that uncontrolled, lustful display they had just shared was not sitting well with him.

~ ~ ~

The remainder of the ride to the estate was made in silence. Agonizing silence for Reanna. How had she managed to bungle things so quickly?

It wasn't until they turned up the drive to Curplan Hall, that Killian spoke to her again.

Dusk had set, but the winding granite gravel drive of the estate was lit on both sides by torches, and Reanna's first glimpse of the hall from afar took her breath away. It was just the two of them staying at Curplan tonight, but the entire structure was lit to the extent of a grand ball taking place.

Reanna leaned closer to the window, not letting the far-off main building from her sight. "Killian, it is absolutely astounding."

"Thank you. I have worked hard to make it so."

"There is no doubt you have succeeded."

Halfway up the long drive, the coach passed the stables, and Reanna's mouth dropped at the impossibly long structure that stretched outward from the gravel drive, the far side ending deep into the adjoining woods.

"Incredible." She leaned her head slightly out the open window, trying to count the openings into each of the stalls.

Killian laughed. "These are only the main stables. There are three more on the grounds."

Reanna looked at him in awe, then sat back, still searching out the window. "Why so many? I had understood that this was among the smallest of your estates."

Killian shrugged. "Land-wise, it is, but Curplan is also the most frequented by society, so the house and stables are necessities in making sure all guests are well cared for. That includes, of course, their horses." He leaned forward to look out the window. "I also keep a rather substantial collection of my own horses, some for racing, others merely for breeding and leisure."

Excitement filled Reanna. "Killian, you know I do not know how to ride. But that was by my father's wishes. I have always truly wanted to learn. There has not been any time since I left Suffolk, and I regret not making it a priority. But my aunt demanded most of my time, and then the season began, and I met you…" She looked at him, voice trailing, and momentarily horrified at what she implied. "Not that I would trade a moment of time with you for the skill of riding a horse…"

Killian chuckled. "Not to worry, your mastery of riding can be easily remedied. There is, actually, a new mare I just purchased, a docile creature that would be perfect for you to learn on."

"Thank you, it would be wonderful to learn." Reanna relaxed, grateful he was so easygoing. Especially after his earlier clipped tone. Killian was so unlike the only other man she had ever really known—her father.

She watched her husband pull on his gloves that had lain beside him for the entire ride, pleased that the silence had ended, and they were back to the easy camaraderie that flowed between them so effortlessly.

The coach slowed to a stop in front of the house. Reanna could not tear her eyes away from the glowing structure. Three levels of grey brick were warmed by the orange-yellow glow from within, even shining out the glass dome protruding from the roof above the entrance.

The footman let down the stairs of the coach, and, heart thudding, Reanna grabbed Killian's hand and stepped to the cobbled walk that met the grey gravel. Rows of servants stood in lines descending down the steep stairs that led to the home. Killian placed her hand in the crook of his arm and gave her a quick wink. He turned to the long rows of servants and nodded to the man closest to them.

The man turned to the lines of servants, voice booming. "I present to you, The Most Honourable, The Marchioness of Southfork."

Clapping reached Reanna's ears, and she realized as Killian walked her forward that this entire display was for her. Embarrassed, and heart beating even more wildly at the hundred eyes looking at her, she swallowed and managed a hesitant smile. Of course Killian would go through this much trouble for her. He had told her time and again that he wanted to make her happy.

They ascended the steep stone stairs, and Reanna was greeted with cavernous majesty as they stepped into the three-story entrance, capped off with a glass-domed ceiling. Bas-relief scenes of Greek mythology played out high on the walls, descending from the ceiling—from the flight of Icarus, to Prometheus and an eagle, to the nine muses. Mythology was the one thing her father had let her read past her studies, so Reanna instantly recognized all of the scenes.

In front of them, twin staircases intertwined up three levels, and alcoves dotted each floor in symmetrical fashion. Reanna fought dizziness as she took in the magnitude of the entrance.

After allowing her a few minutes, Killian saved her from her extensive gawking by pulling her attention to the rest of the house.

"I know you must be tired, Reanna, but would you like a short tour of some house highlights before we dine?" There was pride in Killian's voice, and Reanna was so excited, she couldn't imagine saying no.

"I would absolutely love a tour. And it can be just as long as you like."

She nearly giggled with delight at her surroundings. Nothing she had ever lived in was as grand as Killian's home, and she fought again the urge to pinch herself. How had she been lucky enough to marry him? And this. This was opulence defined. Her father had been wealthy at one time, but he had never felt the need to spend much on their surroundings or homes. At the thought, guilt panged her. She was being entirely too disrespectful of her father's choices.

Killian led her from the foyer, and what should have taken an hour, ended up taking two because Reanna lingered in each and every room. By the time they had made it to the dining hall, Killian had to interrupt the tour so they could dine. Reanna insisted they do so quickly, so as to get back to the tour. After dining, he finished the tour with the arboretum, the ballroom, his study, and the library.

The library held an exquisite collection of first editions. Two stories tall, it somehow managed to be cozy with richly lacquered wainscoting touching off from a burgundy-hued Persian rug that fit snugly to the room's size. Navy blue velvet chairs spread casually throughout the room, and Reanna decided this was her favorite area in the house.

Standing in the middle of the library, she spied several tiny figures from around the arm of a chair, and went to investigate. A chess set, with onyx and ivory pieces, greeted her. She picked up one of the figures and studied it, tracing a finger over the intricately carved face.

"Do you play?" Killian asked.

Reanna shook her head and put the piece gently back on the board. "No, I am afraid you can count chess among one of the many things that I wish I knew how to do, but do not." She smiled wryly. "You must be tired of hearing about all the things I do not know how to do."

Killian shrugged. "You are young—you have a long life to learn all the things you have yet to."

"I hope so." She turned fully to him. "I feel as though I am just coming alive. There was so much to see and do in London, that I wonder now how I ever spent my days in Suffolk. And I am so looking forward to all that you will show me."

Reanna could have sworn Killian gave her the oddest look, but it was gone before she even really noticed it, much less figured it out. He smiled down at her. "Your optimism is charming."

He started to walk to the door of the library. "So that is the short tour, which I might add, has never been so long."

Reanna laughed and fell into step next to him.

He looked down at her. "Are you ready to retire to our chambers, Lady Southfork?"

Reanna froze, while Killian took several more steps to the door. She suddenly felt miniscule in the tall room. She hadn't wanted to ask Killian, hadn't wanted to mention again what had happened earlier in the carriage, but she had to. Terrified or not.

He turned back to her, eyebrow arched at her stopping.

"Killian, before we go upstairs…" Reanna twisted her intertwined hands in front of her.

"Hesitant already, Reanna?"

"It is just that…well…" Her eyes traveled to the servant positioned by the door.

Killian inclined his head to the servant, who backed out of the room, closing the door. He stepped toward her. "What was it you wanted to say?"

Her eyes shot to his, then just as quickly, flickered away as she blurted, "Do you want an annulment?"

Killian stopped dead and stared down at her. "An annulment? Whatever are you thinking?"

She made her eyes meet his. A hot flush crawled up her neck, invading her cheeks. "It is just that, well, I needed to ask you before we went upstairs and…"

She couldn't quite make her mouth form the words, so she skipped ahead. "On the ride here, I behaved…I behaved quite scandalously, and I am sure you had no idea that you were marrying such an improper woman. So I understand, under false pretenses and all, if you would like to disengage yourself from me. You are such a gentleman, and I, I am nothing more than a common…trollop." She trailed off on the last word as tears choked her throat.

Reanna dared a look at his face. He looked like he was about to laugh, then didn't. Instead, he reached down and grabbed her chin, tilting her eyes up to his. "There will be no annulment."

"I knew you would understand." Relief flooded Reanna and she let out the breath she had been holding. "It is just that I am so naïve, I did not know—I just was not sure how to react to your kisses. Thank you so much for understanding. I will conduct myself with much more propriety, now that I know the way of it. You really are my only guide. My aunt never spoke to me of such things, and my mother died when I was young."

A slow smile crept across Killian's face, and Reanna took that as a good sign.

"There is no need to worry, Reanna. Now, if you are ready, would you like to retire to our rooms?"

~ ~ ~

Within an hour, Killian stood before the low fire burning in the wide stone fireplace. He sipped on his third glass of brandy. He wasn't about to get drunk, but he had decided that a couple of glasses might ease the nagging thoughts he was having. Nagging thoughts planted by Aggie, scolding him time and again about destroying an innocent. He refused to put any credence to what Aggie believed, but that didn't stop her voice from echoing in his mind.

Killian's eyes shifted from the fire to his empty glass, and he contemplated pouring another. A little extra fortitude against the ghost of Aggie's badgering voice wouldn't hurt. He just had to commit to this farce for one more night. And if he committed well enough, he might actually enjoy himself.

If he couldn't commit at this point, who knows what would happen. Reanna's earlier talk of an annulment had shocked him, as he had thought he was playing his part of new husband quite well. But not well enough. Imagine, a woman giving *him* room to cry off because *she* was too forward. The irony of that would stick with him for quite some time.

A sudden soft click behind him told him that his new bride had finally worked up the courage to enter his bedchamber. Not nearly as long as a virgin bride would have taken, he guessed.

He turned around to see Reanna paused by the doorway, her hand still on the knob. She didn't look scared, just uncertain… and beautiful. Her hair had been let down, the dark waves around her face a glorious onyx frame. The locks teased down the slope of her breasts to meet a silk night rail that was near transparent. Dark blue, it set off her creamy skin and brought out her blue eyes, even in the dim light of the fireplace.

The silk flowed down her body, caressing her waist and hips before falling wispy to the floor. Killian's eyes moved back to her face. Her lips looked full and ripe, while her cheeks had a slight flush, and he wondered if his unabashed scrutiny had caused it. Killian thanked himself for not having that last drink. He now realized he wanted to enjoy Reanna's beauty as much as possible tonight.

"Please, do come in, Reanna," he said as he set his glass down.

"I am not interrupting you?" She didn't move from the connecting doorway leading to her rooms. "Because I can come back…"

"Your timing is perfect. I was just hoping a vision such as you would walk from that room, and here you are. Consider me a lucky man."

She laughed as she stepped toward him. "Only if I am considered your even luckier wife." She stopped in front of him. "I really do love your house, Killian. It is glorious and I can just imagine spending wonderful days here with you."

Killian tried not to stiffen at her words. "Thank you, but there is no need to think about anything tonight except the two of us."

"Oh, of course, I am sorry. I am always rushing ahead with things. Always wanting to get to the next place without enjoying where I am. I think it is because my life was so small before, that I now want to experience everything all at once so I don't miss anything. My aunt always chided me for that, and with just cause, I suppose."

"I cannot imagine your aunt having to chide you about anything of importance."

"Oh, but she did. I have several terrible habits that she was forced to break me of."

He raised an eyebrow in disbelief. "Such as?"

"Such as, I will not tell you even one of them, for fear I will destroy all the expectations you have of your new wife."

She smiled, and Killian thought it looked almost wicked. Reanna may be an innocent, but she was turning out to be no timid mouse.

"Plus, since Aunt Maureen cured me of my worst ones, they do not warrant discussion."

"And the not-as-bad ones?"

"Do not warrant discussion, either." She smirked. "And I guess I should add 'keeping secrets from husband' to that list."

"They constitute a list, do they?"

"I have worked very hard to keep my flaws hidden from you, and I will not exploit them now for your amusement. You will discover them someday, I am sure. But until such time, you have my permission to just believe I am flawless."

Her eyes were shining in merriment, and Killian was struck at the odd shade of blue they were—the light blue glass of a tropical sea. He had never noticed that before. He gave his mind a shake. Of course, he had seen that her eyes were blue before, he had even had his valet pick out a spectacular set of blue sapphire earrings and necklace for her as engagement gifts. Blue sapphires that, in no way, he now realized, matched the color of these eyes. These eyes that looked up at him full of happiness and—hell—love.

He had best get to this.

"Flawless it is, then," Killian said, taking a step and closing the space between them.

His hand went down to hers, and he pulled it upward, placing it gently upon his neck. Her fingers needed no encouragement, and they curled into his hair, nails skimming the skin. His forefinger glided along her arm, lifting to follow her collarbone, and slid up her graceful neck.

His thumb stopped under her chin, and he could read the uncertainty in her face. Uncertainty that held fast, even as she tilted her head, curling into his hand. Killian descended gently, his lips light against hers.

She froze, stiffening, and he pulled back, looking hard into her wide eyes. Eyes full of trepidation. He went down harder, more insistent as his mouth tasted hers, his lips willing her to give in, to mold with his own as they had in the carriage. But still, he could feel her holding back, fighting against reaction. He pulled back once more.

"It is okay, Reanna, you can give yourself to me."

"But earlier…"

"Pay no attention to that, Reanna." His hand buried deep into her dark waves, and he set his lips close, but not touching, to hers. "Just open these." He kissed her, long and soft. "Open these to me, and let come what comes."

He moved his lips to her neck. "Can you do that for me?"

Her head fell back, and the slightest murmur of sound escaped as he circled her neck.

"Yes, please yes, Killian, yes."

Killian pulled up slightly to look into her face. Her eyes were half closed, cheeks flushed, and errant tendrils framed her face, taking her out of the coifed perfection he was used to seeing her in. Shifting her into something he couldn't describe, something wild and uninhibited.

Something completely unexpected.

Her hips were already pressing forward into him. She had surrendered to instinct. And her instinct was carnal. Staggered breath, ripe with passion, poured from her, and her lidded eyes caught his.

Killian lost himself.

He grabbed her lower back with his free hand as he brought his lips to hers. Predatory, he took her delicate skin hard with full intent on matching her raw sensuality.

His right hand, deep in her hair, wrapped the strands around his palm, tightening his grip and controlling the angle of her head. The scent of jasmine filled his senses, and his tongue searched out, parting the lips that had him drugged. When Reanna opened herself to him, Killian groaned and plunged deep within the contours of her mouth.

His left hand moved downward, tightening around a buttock, and he pressed her body into his, feeling every flowing curve through the thin fabric of his pants and her flimsy silk nightgown. Her tongue tentatively touched his in return, and Killian reveled in the taste, not letting her withdraw from her commitment.

A small purr, breathy, almost like a sigh, escape from deep within her throat. Killian pulled up at the sound, for he had never heard anything like it. Reanna just stood, most of her weight supported by him, her head tilted back and eyes closed, trust in every touch, every motion that Killian took, evident. Pure instinct.

No reservations, she was letting her body do whatever her body naturally demanded. Innocent passion unleashed, and Killian was no force against it. Nor did he want to be.

His lips went to her neck as he untied the six ribbons down her front that held the delicate silk together. He left no skin unattended as his mouth worked his way down with the ties.

Her fingers dug deep into his hair as he pressed aside the flowing cloth to taste a breast. She gasped and involuntarily tried to step back, but Killian would not let her gain footing, holding the small of her back to his body as he licked and suckled the pink morsel. She didn't resist his grip, and instead, arched into his mouth after the initial shock.

One nipple taut with pleasure, he moved to the next, watching the shadows from the fire dance off her smooth skin. Her purring grew guttural. Not an ounce of her was standing by her own muscle, and Killian couldn't wait any longer. He picked her up and strode over to the mammoth four-post bed, setting her in the middle of the silk coverlet.

He stepped back, removing his own clothes, his eyes not leaving her. Sprawled on the bed, her silk rail draped half open on her body. Her skin glistened with unspent desire, the translucent cloth barely covering the ripe buds that he had teased into hardness. Her hair fell above her, a halo, and she watched him with hazy eyes, lips half parted as they silently begged to be ravaged once more.

The devil. Killian shook himself. He was near to ripping off his own clothes like a besotted schoolboy for this little titan, this woman who was just a pawn in his revenge. The thought flashed through his mind, then he pushed it away, hid it, for at that moment he wanted nothing more than to ignore everything except for the salty pleasure that was her skin.

Naked, he climbed onto the bed above her.

"Killian…"

Her half-opened eyes looked downward, and he saw her wonderment mix with hesitancy at his nakedness. He was already pulsating large, hard. Of course that would startle her. In the moment, he had forgotten of her innocence.

"Just ignore it, Reanna, just close your eyes and feel what I do to you."

She glanced up into his eyes, and instantly the hesitancy was replaced with complete trust. Reanna nodded, her head arching against the bed as he descended to her lips. He continued his assault as his hands roamed her body and discarded the last of the silk covering her body.

She writhed under him, naked, hot, wanting, and Killian wanted it just as much. More.

His entire body swallowed hers, covering her, her softness filling his hard angles. His hand moved lower, and at first touch into her folds, she groan-purred, shock mingling with instant pleasure.

She wasn't at all a nervous virgin. No. She went where she was led without any reluctance, any misgivings, and she was even beginning to experiment on his body. Her fingers ran up and down the tight muscles in his back, even sloping down in exquisite motion to run across his backside and thighs.

He was hard beyond control for her, but he wanted, needed, her to gain as much pleasure from this as he would. Killian manipulated her moans with his touch. He caressed her soft, then hard, back and forth he went, and he could tell she relished every moment of it. Her body, her purrs, begging for more. Her breath quickened, became frantic, and it wasn't moments before her eyes flew open, bursting through the haze, and she looked at him in fear at what was happening to her body.

"Just let it go, love." He could barely contain himself from her writhing body. "God, just let it go."

Her eyes snapped shut, her head buckled back, and a scream escaped. Killian took the exact moment to enter her, he hoped with the least amount of pain, and sank his head into her neck, inhaling her heat. She arched under him as he plunged hard, her legs clasping his onslaught tighter to her own body.

He thrust, deep and fast, as he lost his face in her thick hair, buried into her being, until without warning, without control, he came in a black lightning he didn't know existed.

CHAPTER 3

She lay, two hours later, draped over him, asleep, and God, he wanted her.

He wanted her so much he was surprised the stiff hardness jabbing into her stomach hadn't roused her from sleep. Hell. He was hoping she would wake up.

She was the worst kind of vixen, the kind that didn't have the slightest inkling about what she possessed, much less know how to use it.

He shifted slightly on the bed. She didn't move, so he decided it was the best time to make their way to the bath he had ordered to be tempered hourly for warmth.

Moving her to his arms, he carried her across his suite to the adjoining bathing room. After a toe-test for water temperature, Killian slid the two of them into the copper tub, the warm water swirling around them. Reanna murmured, but didn't awaken.

He grabbed the soap and silently chuckled at the lilac smell that escaped. Far from the spice of his own soap, this bar smelled soft and kissed of springtime. There was a thoughtful maid somewhere in his household.

Killian slowly washed Reanna's skin, slippery and glistening in the low firelight. Beads of water clung to the skin on her shoulder, and Killian couldn't resist kissing them off. His soapy hands went down her arms to her hands, where he played with each delicate finger, half the size of his own. He soaped her body, over her breasts, her soft stomach, and deep into her, exploring every crevice he could.

Control escaping him, and certainly not what he intended, Killian was brutally hard for her again, and he wondered if the pole jutting into the small of her back was uncomfortable. He shifted her slightly so she was at a more comfortable angle to him, and then a soft voice floated up.

"I was quite curious as to where you were taking me, but this has been more than pleasant." She turned her head to look up at him, seduction in her crystal blue eyes.

"You have been awake this whole time?"

She nodded, not hiding the scheming smile playing on her lips.

He laughed at her audacity. "Hellion. Who would have guessed…" Killian splashed her, which immediately sent her scampering to the far end of the large tub. She wasted no time in splashing him back.

Killian eyed her, not quite believing that Reanna was actually such a vixen. Everything he had seen of her had been proper— proper to the point of boring—he hadn't had the slightest clue she possessed such a wicked streak. And he was quickly finding it enjoyable.

She was still grinning when she decided it was time to apologize. "I am sorry, I should not have fleeced you. But it was just so nice, the warm water, you humming—"

"I was humming?" Disbelief raised his brows.

"Oh, yes, humming." She nodded as her arms swished slowly back and forth along the water's break. Low waves rolled languidly to his side of the tub. Her nipples hid just below the bubbles on the water's surface, and at that moment, Killian would have murdered to have a bit more water let out of the tub so he could see her nipples, ripe and taut as they went from the warm water to the cool air.

"And the pretty smelling soap." The side of her face cocked up as she stared lasciviously at his chest, down to the point it disappeared beneath the water. Her blue eyes veered up to his face. "And your hands…"

Killian smiled to himself. Was she trying to seduce him? She apparently couldn't see his cock, more than ready for her, through the soapy froth. "My hands?"

"Yes, your hands. You do realize that for such large hands, you are quite good with them."

"I am?" He moved his fingers to her rhythmically moving arms, and clasped onto her wrists, pulling her whole body back to his. He could see her slight confusion as to how to position herself, so he reached down and slid his hands along her thighs, gently bending her legs until she fully straddled him.

She smiled when she was finally set snuggly onto his lap. "Yes, you are very creative with them. Flawless, one might even say."

Raw, unhidden passion flowed from her eyes. Whereas Killian had planned on holding back, within seconds, he was attacking her hungrily, and his body was screaming so harshly for release, he doubted he would be able to stop.

Minutes passed before he managed to tear back from her swollen lips, from her wet body pressing up against his.

Confusion reigned in her ravaged features. "What?" Her hands moved from his neck to his chest. "Why are we stopping?"

His fingers reached out to touch the worry on her face. "No, love, it is not you. I had not meant for this to happen. Not again. You are much too sore."

"Really?" Her face switched into understanding. "Actually, I do not feel much soreness at all. In fact, this water is perfectly soothing."

She swiveled her hips on his lap and splashed a little water on her chest for effect. Then she leaned back from him. "But if you say I am too sore…"

"Shameless—" Killian groaned as his hand dove into her wet hair, yanking her back to him, and he kissed her with harsh intensity. His hands dove down her slick body, between them, spreading her to his touch. When he finally broke the kiss, his voice was rough. "God, love, are you sure you are not in pain?"

"Killian, what you are doing to me is—" Her voice lost out to her odd groan-purr as he circled her sensitive nubbin. She gasped a breath. "Nowhere near pain."

"God help me, we do this slow, then." Killian grabbed her hips and began to guide her body onto his shaft.

"In here?" Reanna's eyes went wide.

Killian grimaced. He was just about to enter her, and the need to be buried deep within her was breaking him. "Yes, right here, right now, love."

His fingers spread her wide, and Killian brought her down atop him, not controlling his thick groan as he slid into her tightness.

Water quickly found the edge of the tub, splashing out as Killian found his rhythm, and Reanna rode, nails in his shoulders, following his lead.

His hands attacked her body, no morsel left untouched, and he continued to dive down between them, teasing her, plying her folds into pitching against him. She held nothing back, begging him with her screams.

Eyes closed, head back, her passion had Killian's eyes riveted to her every movement. Her hands had ripped from him to grip the sides of the copper tub so she could lean back and offer him better access. He took full advantage. She had not reached orgasm yet, and he doubted he could hold back another instant before he burst inside of her.

Then, just as her mouth opened to scream, her body tightening around him, Killian exploded, all sight and sound lost to him.

It was the purest pleasure he had ever felt with a woman.

The thought struck him—and didn't leave his mind for the rest of the night.

~ ~ ~

Reanna spun onto her side in the large bed, pulling the deep blue coverlet with her and tucking it up under chin. Dreams floating away, her eyes flew open when reality hit. She was married, and, good God, the things Killian had done to her last night.

Reanna closed her eyes as the memories of this bed and the copper tub flooded her mind. Her body tingled at the memories, even as she could feel her cheeks go red in embarrassment.

But there was no need to be embarrassed. Killian had taken her to those wonderful highs, and she knew he wouldn't want her to be embarrassed by them.

Killian—she rolled over, searching for him, but he wasn't in bed. Propping herself up on her elbows, she surveyed the room. She had paid no attention to it last night. Masculine. Dark mahogany overwhelmed the room, from gleaming wood floors, to the tables, chairs, wardrobe, and long writing desk scattered in the space. Several tapestries hung along the walls in muted darkness, deep rich colors played out scenes of military conquests from long ago.

Reanna swung her feet to the floor and stepped from the bed, immediately realizing she was naked. She rushed to her night rail that had been strewn across a chair by the bed. Not that it covered up much of her nudity.

Killian wasn't in the room, but Reanna knew she had slept overly long and couldn't expect her husband to lounge about, waiting for her to grace the morning with her presence.

Reluctant to leave the room that she had, in one night, grown to love, for it was where Killian had finally, after all these months, made her his own, she turned to the door adjoining the two suites.

Hugging herself, she moved into her room, intent on changing and getting ready for the day as quickly as possible. She couldn't wait to join her husband in whatever he had planned for the first day of their honeymoon.

CHAPTER 4

Killian stared at the glass of brandy before him, an ancient Egyptian flint knife flipping casually in his hand, as he debated whether or not he would down the amber liquid. The decanter was near empty and brandy had already cost him too much last night. He wasn't about to repeat that mistake. Especially not with the girl still around.

He turned his chair around and looked out the large pane of glass that ran the expanse of his study. Precise, manicured lawns rolled down the sloping hill before him, the bright morning sun and vibrant greenery of early summer doing nothing to lighten his mood. Birds chirped off in the distance, madcap conversations that only grated on his nerves.

He had slept for a few hours and woken up early, just as the first rays of light crested the horizon. Woken up disgusted with himself. Woken up disgusted at the slip of a girl beside him.

He had been down in his study since. Hours passed as he drank and contemplated what the fate of the girl tucked into his bed would be.

It was a battle he wasn't keen on having. A battle with himself over some very disturbing truths that he wasn't even attempting to lie to himself about. He had wanted, enjoyed— hell—*lost* himself with her last night. Something disturbing had happened that he couldn't describe and didn't want to think about. The other truth, and the fact that made the first so heinous, was that she was still the daughter of the man he was committed to destroying.

He didn't want her, didn't need anything like her in his life, and the whole loving fiancé farce he had produced over the past three months had grated on him. He had needed to consummate the marriage to make sure no annulment could be fought for, and now, she had served her purpose, and he was done with her.

He had originally planned to allow her to live in London, or here at Curplan. As long as their lives were in no way mingled. An occasional passing would have been tolerable, but Killian had planned to resume his pre-engagement lifestyle, including resurrecting several of the mistresses that he had begrudgingly set loose in the name of a scandal-free engagement.

But after last night. Hell. He wanted her nowhere near him.

Nowhere that he could possibly be reminded of all that he had betrayed last night when he had lost control in her arms. He had never felt so damn much in his life, and he wasn't about to again, especially not with the daughter of that bastard. Killian had betrayed his mission, his parents' memories, and his quest to honor the family name, all for one—a few hours—of pleasure.

So nowhere had to mean far, far away from London and Curplan. He could not, would not, afford such a night again.

Killian turned his chair back to the wide desk, fingertip balancing the flint knife upright on the wood, when a thought struck him. Something he had never considered.

Was it even possible that he was the one being duped? Could she have been sent to him by her father in order to fleece him? Did the bastard finally figure out it had been Killian all along who had ruined him? And then sent his daughter to prostitute herself in order to gain back what was lost?

The thought invaded his mind so quickly and fully, that the wood on the desk ripped up as he slammed the knife down. He hadn't even realized he had dug it into his desk.

A soft knock on the study door drew his attention across the room. He was not surprised when Reanna meekly poked her head in, obviously not wanting to disturb him.

"Ah, yes, the blushing bride." He waved his hand dramatically. "Do come in and have a seat."

~ ~ ~

She had been happy to find Killian so quickly, but as Reanna opened the door and stepped into the study, she looked quizzically at her new husband. His words had been said with a snap, and possibly even a little slurred. From her father, she knew well enough to step lightly around a man that was drunk. Slowly, she approached Killian and spied a near-empty decanter and full glass sitting at the edge of his desk.

Shock registered on her face. "Killian, are you drunk?"

"Drunk?" He raised an eyebrow at her. "I hardly see how that should matter to you. Sit."

Hesitant, staring at him in confusion, she sat down on the edge of an uncomfortable, smoothly leathered chair. His voice sounded biting, even malicious, and it seemed to be directed at her. That had to be her imagination. "Killian, is everything all right?"

"To the nines, or it will be an hour from now." He leaned forward in his chair, propping his elbows on the desk and clasping his hands in front of his chin. "What do you know of your father?"

Reanna blinked at the sudden change in topics, then couldn't stop the fear that gripped her at mention of her father. She couldn't let Killian see. She forced her voice light. "I am afraid not much. My father did spend more time at our home in Suffolk when my mother was alive. After she passed, he was rarely around. I have only recently come to know him more since he moved to Suffolk last year. He is a good man. He has always treated me well." She treaded carefully. "But I do know that he left London in some kind of scandal."

"Do you know what the scandal was?"

Her chest tightened. This conversation was too odd. "No. He never mentioned it, and about six months after father returned I was sent to Aunt Maureen in London. She alluded several times to his disgrace, but never expanded on the subject in front me."

Hands clasped tight in her lap, Reanna paused. She didn't want to ask the next question, but she forced the words to come out past her pounding heart. "I believed you knew about the…

the situation. I would not want anything he may have done to mar your name. If under false pretenses, you must annul—"

"I will never hear the word 'annulment' from your mouth again. We are married, and it will remain thus. Do you understand?"

Reanna relaxed, relieved. She emphatically nodded, her previous happiness flooding her once more.

Yet something in his posture was off. Was there something else about her father that was bothering him? She wanted to ask the words, but couldn't bring herself to push the topic of her family's shame. Or what she guessed was her family's shame. If only someone had told her what had happened.

Her relief quickly shifted to apprehension as Killian continued to stare at her with his sharp brown eyes. He looked more serious than she had ever seen him, as though he were weighing something of enormous consequence.

With a sigh, he casually leaned back in his chair, his hands cupped beneath his chin. He contemplated her for a long moment, and Reanna tried to hide her need to fidget away her anxiety at his odd stare.

"You will be leaving within the hour. The coach will be ready, do not be late."

She smiled at the surprise, for she had hoped Killian had planned a bridal tour. Of course he had wanted to surprise her. He was always so thoughtful. "Where are we going?"

"I am not going anywhere. You are going to Holloton."

"What do you mean?" Confusion filled her face. "You will be joining me in a few days, then?"

"No. I will not." Hands still under his chin, he didn't move.

"But Holloton…that is your estate in Northhamptonshire? Is that not days away?"

"It is."

"And you will not be joining me?" A deep fear began to ferment in the pit of her stomach, but Reanna ignored it. This was Killian she was talking to, after all. She must not understand something.

"No."

"Ever?" Her voice escaped meek.

"No."

Obviously, there was some reason he needed her away from here. "How long will I need to be up there?"

"I have not decided."

The fear that pitted in her stomach began to spread throughout her body. "But Killian, I don't understand."

"You don't need to." His clasped hands went to his lap, but his countenance didn't change. His face was an emotionless mask. A mask that gave Reanna no clues as to what he was thinking.

"What? I don't need to?" She couldn't stop her voice from taking on a high pitch. "You are sending me away and you will not even tell me why? Just tell me why, maybe I can—"

"You can do nothing."

"But is this something I did?"

"What you can do is leave quietly."

"Quietly? What..." Her hand reached out at him, grasping the edge of the desk. "But after what happened last night."

"What happened last night was nothing more than what happens in a thousand brothels, a thousand times a day."

His words cut into her, cut straight into her chest and began to smother the very breaths she took. She recoiled, gasping, her body trying to remain erect. Tears welled in her eyes. "But I thought...I thought it was...I thought you enjoyed it."

"I did, but it was nothing compared to what I can get at any street corner."

"No, no—I won't accept this—you love me."

"I do nothing of the kind, my lady. I think it is time that you remove yourself from the study and begin preparations for your journey."

She leaned forward again, both hands gripping the desk, desperation making her movements jerky. Tears streamed down her face. "No, Killian, you cannot mean what you're saying. You're drunk, or something has happened, tell me—you are not yourself—"

"I am more myself today than you have ever known of me, my lady. Now remove yourself from my sight."

Reanna sank to her knees, hands still wrapped on the smooth edge of the desk. Tears blurred her vision, dropping onto her chest and soaking into her muslin dress. The salty bitterness drowned her lips, but her voice still managed to be solid. "Killian, please…please, you cannot mean what you say."

His eyes followed her drop to the position before him without so much as a flinch. "I do mean what I say, and this pathetic display only embarrasses you. You will leave this room immediately."

"But Killian," her voice cracked, "there must be something I could—"

"As I said, there is nothing. Kindly remove yourself from this disgusting debacle."

Every cruel word he had hurled at her since she came into the study hit Reanna all at once. She doubled back from the pain in her stomach, her legs no longer supporting her kneeling position. Her arms gripped her stomach as she crumbled into a heap and began to sway, attempting to rock all the hurt out of her body. Silent sobs racked her body.

Killian's voice, if possible, managed an even icier level. "I will not repeat myself again. Remove yourself from this room."

The words sliced into Reanna, and finally, some last, very slim shred of dignity latched onto his words.

Slowly, she rose from the wood floor, still unable to control the silent sobs. Without looking at the man who had just destroyed every piece of her, she turned and picked up her lead feet.

In the long walk to the door of the study, she forced herself at every step to not turn around and plead, beg, at Killian's feet for forgiveness for whatever she had done. She would have done just that, had she even the slightest shred of hope that her begging would work.

She reached the door and paused.

In a hard fought battle between love, and a pride she didn't even know she had, she turned the knob and managed to walk out the door.

~ ~ ~

She had been gone for hours. Left the house quietly.

There was no more pleading, no crying.

He had not meant it to go that badly, but it had, and he was no force to change it now. He needed her gone. And, he reasoned, she would be better off without him.

Killian leaned back in the chair he hadn't moved from since the earlier scene. His plan had worked. He had never doubted that it would. Never doubted that he could get Reanna to marry him. And now, to complete the plan, all he needed was patience.

Her father would come out of exile soon enough, and when he did, Killian would be ready.

CHAPTER 5

It took two long days to travel to Holloton. Two days that were a blur to Reanna. A silent, tear-sodden blur.

Had it not been for Miss Melby, the lady's maid her aunt had hired for her that had agreed to stay on with Reanna after the wedding, Reanna would not have eaten or moved from the carriage the entire journey.

What did break through into Reanna's consciousness was the moment they pulled through the heavy iron gates marking the entrance to Holloton. Miss Melby drew back the curtains, and they were greeted with the sight of blackened skies and a torrential downpour. It was thick enough that Reanna vaguely wondered how the coachman could find his way up the drive. But fitting that the weather at her arrival reflected her very soul.

Escorted into the large foyer under an umbrella, Reanna did not look up at her surroundings. The house steward, Ruperton, and the head butler, Evans, introduced themselves with proper, but eager decorum, for as they explained, the marquess hadn't been to Holloton in years. Even if they weren't to see his lordship, they were delighted to have the marchioness in residence. Reanna barely heard a word they said, and quickly asked to be shown to her new rooms.

The chambers she entered were pleasant, if not stale from lack of use, and the fleeting question of who was the last to use these rooms crossed her mind. But the draw of the peach silk-canopied bed became her mind's one objective, and she crossed to it, collapsing, weary and beaten.

"Come now, my lady. My heart breaks time and again seeing you so distraught. I have not a way to ease your pain, but me mum would have told me that now that we be here, we best to make the most of it." Miss Melby went over to one of the trunks just brought in, and flung it open, busying herself with unpacking her mistress's items. She sighed as she began shaking dresses out. "It just won't do, these constant tears. I worry for your health."

No reply came from Reanna, save the silent weeping that had begun again.

"Everything will be all right in the end—you wait and see, my lady. His lordship will come to his senses and demand to have you back by his side in no time at all."

Reanna's head lifted from the now wet peach coverlet. "You…you don't know that. Everything will not be all right. You do not know what he said to me. You did not see how he looked. How he hated me. How he just wanted me to leave his sight."

"But his lordship, he loves you, anyone with two eyes could see—"

"Stop it!" Reanna sat up on the bed. "You do not know. You do not know a thing. Nothing is all right. And nothing you can say can make it any better. I have done something terrible, and I do not even know what it is. He hates me, and things are not going to get better. Do you not see that?"

Miss Melby stepped back, head down. "I am sorry, my lady. I spoke out of turn." Her head tilted up slightly, eyeing her mistress. "But you are a beautiful woman, my lady, and I may be simple, but I wish more for you. I wish for you to find a way to make the marriage with his lordship work. I saw how happy you were. How you glowed. I wish for you to be happy again."

Sarcasm bit heavily into Reanna's words. "And just what do you suggest I do?"

"I am not sure, my lady." Miss Melby's eyes flew around the room. "There, maybe there. There looks to be a sizable stack of stationary on that desk."

She pointed across the room to a desk carefully positioned under one of the four large windows in the room. A tall stack of writing paper sat neatly in the corner atop the delicate rosewood desk. "Maybe you could start a correspondence with his lordship. Maybe that would help?"

Reanna eyed the desk from the bed. She looked at it, wary, as though it meant crossing a desert to reach the desk. She glanced back at Miss Melby, who held such hope in her eyes that Reanna didn't think she could crush her hopes.

Slowly, stifling a sigh, she rose from the soft bed and crossed the room.

With one look back at Miss Melby for support, Reanna sat down at the desk, and picked up the top sheet from the stack of stationary. The Southfork seal was emblazoned at the top of the crisp cream vellum. Evidently, Killian's mother's, or even grandmother's personal stationary, waiting for the day when there would be a marchioness in residence again. The exquisite paper was almost translucent in her fingers, so delicate was the vellum. She searched the desk and quickly found ink and a quill.

Reanna sat for a long time, staring at the blank piece of paper in front of her.

After a half hour, she swept her fingers across her face in effort to wipe the wetness away, in effort to see clearly, and picked up the quill. Slowly, meticulously, she put ink to paper.

Miss Melby scurried to and fro, and hours passed before she finished setting up the suite of rooms with all of Reanna's belongings. She slipped out of the room, leaving Reanna still sitting at the desk, occasionally writing, but predominantly allowing silent sobs to rack her body.

~ ~ ~

Reanna looked at the final sheet of paper sitting before her. Six months ago, that stack of stationary had seemed bottomless. And she had requested it be replenished several times before she was ever near the bottom.

Now, one thin sheet sat squarely in front of her.

The quill in her hand was motionless, and she ignored the black splotch of ink that had stained her finger over the many months and hundreds of letters. Unseemly, but a small price to pay, she kept telling herself.

Minutes clicked by on the longcase clock that she had requested to be moved into her room months ago. Having never given time much thought, over the past six months she had become obsessed with the way time moved. Obsessed with seconds as she watched the clock steal away moment after moment.

It was hours before she had the words set, just so in her mind, to put pen to paper.

My husband,
I have begun to think that maybe your hatred of me is not my fault. Is not something that I did. But I will never know.

Maybe someday you will find it in your heart to forgive whatever my transgression was. But until then, I can no longer afford the tears that come daily, nor the way my heart aches every morning and every evening.

This is the last letter I will write. Please forgive me for not having more faith in what I thought was our love.

Yours forever,
Reanna

For six months she had tried to convince him. Convince him to forgive her. Forgive her of what, she was never sure. She had examined every moment of their time together. But she never found answers.

She had stared at that stack of paper six months ago, certain that within a few sheets, Killian would come for her. Halfway through the stack, she told herself that soon, soon he would at least send for her. But when she finally let the stack dwindle to a thin pile, Reanna forced herself to acknowledge the reality she had been trying desperately for six months to ignore.

Killian was not coming, and he was not going to send for her.

She caught Ruperton in the hallway and gave him the letter.

Within a half hour, Miss Melby bustled into her room without the pretense of knocking or privacy. "I heard Joe took a letter to be posted. That's it then? That be the last one?"

Turning on her seat by the desk, words lodged into Reanna's throat. She managed a nod.

"Well good. I'm sorry I ever encouraged you to start writing to his lordship in the first place. He done you a terrible wrong and the man will pay for it—if not here on earth, then may the devil take him."

"No, Miss Melby, no. You will not say such things. He is still my husband." Reanna turned to the desk and began neatly setting the ink and quill into the slim desk drawer.

"Forgive me for saying so, my lady, but that man is no more a husband to you than Freddie the coal boy is. I'm just relieved it be done with. It is done with, isn't it?"

Reanna let Miss Melby's impertinence slide. She never would have made it whole through the past six months without her. She turned back to her maid. "Yes, I believe it is over. We may as well settle in for good."

Miss Melby smiled. "I done that three months ago, my lady—now it's your turn. Why don't you get outside for a change? It's sunny and not too cold today. Maybe go down to the stables and see what you can do about learning to ride. The stable master, Ike, is his name, seems to be a good sort and willing to help out where he can. Seems to me like he'd be an excellent teacher."

Reanna looked out the window to find it had turned into a beautiful day. A complete opposite to the grey snow that was falling when she had sat down to write the letter.

She took a deep breath and stared for a moment at the gleaming top of the desk, now bare. An errant thought that she should look for more of the fine vellum crossed her mind. But as she exhaled, she realized the truth of the situation. A trepid smile crossed her face as she rose from her chair.

"I think I will go out and meet this Ike you talked about."

~ ~ ~

Reanna sat atop the mare she had declared as her own, Ivy, and stared down at the vast estate that was Holloton. She had explored much of it over the past weeks, but this was always her favorite spot.

It was the highest point in the estate, offering unending vistas in every direction. She ended every ride here, not only for the quiet reflection this wide-open space afforded her, but because it was the starting point of the breakneck ride back down to the stables. A ride that had almost killed her a couple times. But she loved it.

Reanna stripped off her gloves and balanced them on Ivy's white mane, and then noticed the tiniest spot of black ink on her forefinger. No matter how hard she had scrubbed it over the past month, she couldn't completely get rid of it. A remnant of the six months she had pined away for Killian. And she was ready for it to be gone.

What was he doing right now, in that instant? The thought snuck into her head before she had a chance to squelch it. It didn't matter. Not to her.

She shoved her gloves back on. Wherever he was, and whatever he was doing, was of no consequence to her. He had made that perfectly clear.

She turned Ivy toward the edge of the hill, aiming for the stables a distance off. Then, thinking the better of it, she turned to head back deeper into the far woods.

Apparently, a longer ride would do her good.

~ ~ ~

"I was just about to come looking for you, m'lady." Weathered hands gripped the bridle of the panting horse. "Thought maybe you got yourself lost again."

Reanna smiled down at the Holloton stable master. "Come now, Ike, that only happened twice. And that third time I was already set in the right direction before you found me. Besides, can you blame me for the size of this place?"

"No, no, I can't m'lady. But you were out a wee bit longer than usual today." He offered up his hand as Reanna lightly descended.

"Yes, well, it was such a beautiful day—cold, but the snow that fell last night just made the day come alive. It was a shame to leave it any earlier than I needed to." She patted Ivy's spotted white neck. The mare nudged Reanna's shoulder, so she moved her hand to the horse's nose. "And Ivy did not seem to mind one bit. I think she was happy to not be captured inside today, as well."

"She loves you riding her, that's for sure. You've been an excellent student, m'lady, most certainly the best female rider I've seen in a long time, even what with you just learning and all."

"Ike, stop—no need to flatter me. There is still so much more I have to learn."

"Actually, m'lady, there ain't. The only thing you need now is practice, which you do too much of as it is."

Reanna followed Ike as he led Ivy into the stables, and stopped at the third stall in to rub the nose of Thor, a young black stallion that was growing quickly and would eventually be a magnificent creature. He reveled in Reanna's warm hand.

"Come now, I must have something more to learn from you. You have been an excellent teacher, and your patience astounds me." Reanna winked at Ike, whose due blush looked odd on his lined, leathered face. "You could always teach me to ride astride."

Ike laughed, the sound booming through the stables. "The devil in you, m'lady. I'll not be the one to corrupt you. You'll have to find that somewhere else. I wouldn't even want to imagine his lordship's face were he to learn you could ride astride."

It slipped out between them, hanging in the air for a moment. It had been an unspoken rule amongst the staff at Holloton to not mention the marquess. She knew they did it out of respect for her, and she had been grateful for their kindness.

Ike's face froze the second he realized who he had mentioned, not sure how to proceed.

Reanna forced a laugh. "Come now, I highly doubt Lord Southfork will be finding out anything of my activities for a long time." Much less care, she added silently.

Ike gave an awkward smile, clearly thankful for Reanna's transition past his gaffe. "Still, m'lady, you will remain uncorrupt if I have anything to say about it."

"And you must stand by your convictions, I imagine." The twinkle was back in Reanna's eye. "Fine then, you may remain a gentleman."

She curtseyed before him.

"Very kind, m'lady."

Reanna started to exit the stables, then abruptly spun around. "Ike, I have been meaning to ask—does anyone on staff play chess?"

"Chess, m'lady?" His eyebrows raised in bewilderment.

"Yes, chess."

"Well, actually, Ruperton and Evans have had a bit of an ongoing feud over the board for the past six years."

"Really?" A slow smile curved onto her lips. "Six years? Does anyone else ever play either of them?"

"Nope, and no one wants to, I wager. They're both such sore losers, I can't imagine anyone willing to dive into that sordid game with them."

"Thank you, Ike. You have given me a grand idea that has more than made my day."

"I have?" The earlier blush reappeared. "You're welcome, m'lady."

Reanna could hardly contain the skip in her step as she made her way out of the stables and up the snowy hillside to the main house.

After darkness had fallen and dinner passed, Reanna leaned back in the wingback chair angled close to the fire in the library. She stared down at the low table in front of her. Gleaming in the light from the flames, the finely crafted gold and silver pieces sat evenly on the heavy checkered board. She had gotten a few curious glances when she requested the set be brought in from the study, but she chose to ignore the looks.

"Samuelson, could you please find Ruperton and convey my request that he join me?" Reanna asked the footman standing by the door.

Samuelson nodded and left the room. Moments later, Ruperton arrived, starched and detached as always. "You requested my presence, my lady?"

"Yes, Ruperton, I did. I will get right to the point. I would like you to teach me to play chess."

Reanna almost laughed at the look that overtook the steward's face. Incredulous, and Reanna even thought she saw him sway a bit.

His face turned white. "Chess, my lady?"

"I am sorry, Ruperton. I did not mean to distress you." It suddenly occurred to Reanna why Ruperton reacted so, and she sank backward into the chair. "I understand chess can be a long endeavor, and you may not wish to spend that much time with me. I am not very interesting, I know. Forgive me for bothering you about it."

"Nonsense, my lady. Everyone is interesting. You just have to discover what interests you first." He stepped closer and turned the empty matching wingback chair to the chessboard. "My reaction was not what you expected, my lady. I apologize."

Reanna eyed him, then sat straight up once more, hands clasped in her lap. "So yes, chess. I would like to learn the game, and I understand that with your vast experience, you would be an excellent teacher."

His eyes shifted nervously back and forth from the gleaming chess pieces to her. "I am afraid I could not, my lady. It would not be at all proper for me—"

"You are right, Ruperton, it would not be at all proper. Regardless, I would like to learn."

"But Lord Southfork…" The steward glanced about the room, obviously praying for an escape of some sort, or maybe just the floor to swallow him up. He looked back at the marchioness. "He would not look lightly upon such transgressions."

"His lordship is not present and is not likely to be so for some time," she said with a bright smile on her face. "So I can see no harm in it. But if you feel that strongly about crossing the lines of propriety, even by my direct request, I shall have to make due with learning from Evans, whom I also intend to ask to tutor me. I had hoped to learn from both of you, on alternate nights, but I am sure Evans will be more than willing to teach me solo."

Ruperton's ire visibly pricked at the mention of Reanna learning from Evans. "You will be asking Evans?"

"Yes, I thought it best and less time consuming for both of you if I were to split up the instruction."

"That is very…thoughtful of you, my lady."

Reanna could sense victory in her grasp. "So you will teach me?" She offered him what she hoped was her most charming smile.

Ruperton paused for an instant, then, decision made, he straightened up to his full taut self. "Yes, my lady, I will be happy to teach you, if you truly believe it is not too great a transgression."

Reanna beamed. "I do. Please, I would like to begin tonight, if that is all right with you." She motioned to the chair across from her. "I believe the board is set up properly, but I could very well be mistaken."

A quick glance at the board, and Ruperton shook his head slightly.

"It is wrong, then?"

"I am afraid it is quite jumbled, my lady." He sat on the edge of the chair, moving pieces on the board. "But easily remedied. You are a smart whip, my lady. I will have you in victory over Evans in no time."

CHAPTER 6

It was what Killian had been waiting for.

The message had finally come from Baron Halstead, a fortnight prior, requesting a meeting in a week.

Killian had made him wait an additional week.

He was finally coming to beg for money.

Sitting behind the wide walnut desk in his London study, Killian straightened the pistol on the dark wood, making sure the butt end kissed the outer edge of the desk, and that the barrel of the gun was pointed directly at his own chest. He had made Halstead wait for the past hour and a half in his drawing room, and when Ludwig reported Halstead was sufficiently agitated beyond patience, Killian allowed Ludwig to escort him in.

Ludwig closed the study door, leaving Halstead standing, still angry in his agitation. Halstead took another step in, and Killian was immediately struck at how small he was—and old. His only memory of the man had been from when Killian was a child peeking through half-closed doors.

Killian leaned back in his chair, motioning to the chair opposite him. "Baron Halstead, please come in, sit."

Halstead moved forward, his hawk nose tilted down at Killian, posturing a message of disgust at his disrespectful treatment thus far. His eyes were the same ice-blue color as Reanna's. That, Killian did not remember about the man.

"Lord Southfork." Halstead gave a curt nod as he sat, wiry on the edge of the plain wooden chair. "Where is my dear daughter? I did expect to see her here."

"She is not in residence."

"No?"

"She is at one of my country estates at the moment."

"That is unfortunate. I had hoped to speak to her of my regret at having to miss the nuptials. I presume the affair went well?"

"It did. Everything that was required to be taken care of, was."

Halstead cocked his head at the peculiar comment, but said nothing.

Killian leaned forward, resting his elbows on the desk as he clasped his hands under his chin. "I have very little time today, Halstead. What is it you wanted to see me about?"

Halstead bristled, then sighed. "You know, of course, about my ruin. It is why I stayed my distance from the wedding. I wanted to afford my daughter and you a scandal-free engagement. Especially after your understanding about her lack of dowry."

"It was my pleasure."

He smiled. The opening he was hoping for. "She pleases you, then?"

"She has pleased me, yes."

"Excellent. I had hoped yours was to be a good match. I am glad you could see past the financial aspects of the marriage business."

"I did want to marry her enough to overlook a penniless father, yes."

Halstead cleared his throat. "And that is what I had hoped to speak to you about. My ruin was through a series of unfortunate incidents that were beyond my control. But I have some new investments lined up that would get me on the track back to respectability. These are delicate matters, as we are now related, but I am sure my daughter would want that for me, for my name not to taint yours. All I need is a sizable investment—not too large, I assure you—and I am sure this venture will play out."

"So, you thought to come to me, naturally." Killian tapped his finger on his chin. "Which brings me to the suspicion that you were whoring out your daughter when you sent her to London for the season."

"What? Whoring? Bloody rude, young man. I would not whore out my own daughter."

Killian's brows arched. "So it is just mothers that you whore out?"

"What?" Halstead sputtered. "What is this mad talk, Southfork?"

"My parents. You knew them." Killian leaned back in his chair once more, arms crossed over his chest.

"I did. Vaguely. Although I remember little of them." Halstead's wrinkled eyes twitched around the room, landing above Killian's head at a line of books. "That was a long time ago."

"It was. But do you think I was too young at the time to understand what you did to my mother? What you did to my father? Or maybe you just hope it."

"Whatever you may think happened, Southfork, I can assure you—"

"No. I can assure you. I was not too young. I understood everything you did. Everything."

"This is a misunderstanding, your father—"

Killian's hand slammed onto the desk. "Do not speak of my father. There is no misunderstanding. You determined your fate long ago, Halstead, when you destroyed my world."

"But...but my daughter—you knew about me and you married her?"

Killian smiled. "She was your last chance. The last thing you could whore out. I naturally could not have that, not after all the work I put into ruining you."

"You? What do you mean you ruined me?" His eyes narrowed at Killian. He was finally beginning to understand that he was sitting across from his own destruction.

"Your companies, your holdings, did you not wonder how all of them could turn so sour, one after another?"

"But you? How? We had no dealings. There were never any like investments."

"Not directly. But I have many connections. And there was great profit to be made by others at each of your failed investments."

"Inconceivable, man—do you have any idea how much wealth disappeared with those investments?"

"Yes, I do. I kept very close tabs on your outstanding debts." Killian stood, palms flat on the desk, leaning toward the baron. "And apparently, you had no idea the Duke of Dunway and I are close. Very close."

Halstead visibly paled. "The ship."

"Yes. You had everything riding on that ship. It was near comical how many debts you had against that cargo."

"You are mad, man." Halstead bolted upright. "That ship held a fortune. A fortune at the bottom of the ocean. Do you know how much money was lost?"

"I do, and better than even you. My stake was much greater in those holdings, and I lost ten times the amount you did." Killian sat, relaxed. "But unlike you, I could lose the money. You could not, and that was all that mattered. In fact, the goods on my next ship to the isles brought in double the revenue."

Halstead's blanched face turned red, fury overtaking him. His hand flickered toward the pistol on the desk, fingers shaking in rage.

Killian willed him, desperately, to pick it up. To lunge and snatch it.

To give Killian the reason he needed to kill the bastard.

His hand a hair away from the silver of the pistol, Halstead stopped, glaring at Killian. "My daughter. She would not want this for me. I am her father. You cannot do this to her. You cannot destroy your father-in-law."

"I can. She means, quite frankly, less than nothing to me." He waved his hand flippantly. "But do not think to try to remove her from the marriage. She is probably already with babe—it cannot be annulled. Your last option, whoring out your daughter, has failed you, Halstead."

Killian stood, using his height to intimidate as he glared down at Halstead. "Go back to the hole you crawled from, Halstead. Go back there and die."

Halstead leaned forward, his hand twitching above the pistol once more, but then he stood and spun, stalking to the door. Halfway through the entrance, he stopped, turning back to Killian, his voice sinister.

"Do not get comfortable in your revenge, Southfork. You think you destroyed me. You have not. And the lesson of revenge will be returned upon you tenfold. I will crush you, Southfork. You will not see it approaching, but I will wait, I will rebuild, and I will destroy you, just as I did your father. You are as weak as he was. I can already see that in you."

He disappeared through the entrance at his last word, and within seconds, Killian could hear the front door open and close.

Killian dropped heavy into his chair, leaning his head back to stare at the ceiling.

Aside from Halstead not grabbing the gun, it had gone as Killian had laid out, perfectly.

His revenge was complete, and he waited for peace to wash over him.

After ten minutes, his eyes dropped to the tall evergreen hedges outside his window. He sat for two hours, staring out the window, waiting.

Where was the peace?

~ ~ ~

Reanna took a deep breath, filling her lungs to capacity. She couldn't believe her good fortune. Finally, after days of being trapped inside by blustery winds and chilling snow, the skies had cleared and the world was fresh.

She wasted no time in getting Ivy out for a long ride and soon found herself in the rarely-used southwest corner of the estate, nudging Ivy down a narrow trail that had frost-laden trees brushing her wool cloak. Out of nowhere, her horse reared.

Grasping the reins, trying to keep Ivy under control, Reanna at first didn't see the small boy crouched before her. Ivy spun in the path, and Reanna caught sight of him out of the corner of her eye. But by the time she got the horse settled, the boy was gone from the path.

"Hello?" she said softly, feeling foolish for she was not quite sure if she had really seen a child. It could have very easily been an animal she saw that had frightened Ivy. "Hello?" she repeated, a bit louder.

Just as she was about to move on, she heard rustling.

"Hello? I can hear you. Come out."

Ever so slowly, a scrawny little boy stepped from the snowy brush beside the path.

"Please, ma'am, please don't tell."

Reanna immediately recognized what the boy was talking about, for in one tightly clutched hand, was a dead rabbit clearly taken from a trap. He was poaching.

"Please, ma'am, please. I don't want to. It's just my brothers and sisters—they need it so. Please, ma'am, please don't tell."

Reanna had never seen a child so distraught, yet so determined at the same time. The boy couldn't have been more than eight or nine, from what Reanna could tell through the dirt all over him. She had never had much contact with children—she had been an only child herself, and only occasionally did she see any of the servants' babes. She wasn't quite sure what to make of this small creature pleading with her.

"Just to be sure, who shall I not tell, young man?"

"The gamekeeper, ma'am. Or his lordship. I know poachin's a crime, ma'am, but my family, they are little, you see." He fidgeted at the edge of the trail, looking over his shoulder.

"Where is your family? What is your name?"

"Promise you won't tell, ma'am?"

"I promise. Now, what is your name?"

"Thomas, ma'am. And my family lives over by Thorn's Hill."

Reanna dismounted from Ivy, stepping to the front of the horse to talk to him. "From what I understand, Thomas, that is a distance away. Whatever are you doing in Holloton?"

"There's nothing left right round us, not that I can catch. 'Specially with the last cold days and all. I got all I could from there, but no more, and the baby needs something real bad."

"Baby?"

"Yes, ma'am, my little sister."

"Well, what about your mother, Thomas?"

The boy's dirty form froze at the question. Reanna could see tears welling in his big, clear brown eyes and recognized the struggle he was going through not to let them fall. They didn't. "She passed on, 'bout three weeks ago."

"What about your father?"

Thomas shrugged his shoulders. "Don't know."

"Has he been gone for a while?"

Another shrug. "I think I saw him 'bout four years back. Mama said I was five."

Reanna's breath caught as the boy's words hit her. And what it could mean. "Thomas, who are you living with now?"

"My brothers and sisters."

"And are they much older than you?"

His stance straightened a bit in pride. "I'm the oldest."

Reanna swayed. "And there are no grown-ups?"

"No, ma'am."

"How many brothers and sisters do you have?"

"Five, and me, course." He began to fidget again, shuffling the dead rabbit from one hand to the next. "Ma'am, is that all? Please, can I go? The young ones—I need to get back."

Reanna put on an easy smile. "Tell you what, Thomas, since I have taken up so much of your time, why don't we tie that game to Ivy, and I will give you a ride back to your place. Does that sound all right?"

"Well…yes, ma'am, but I shouldn't. Mama always said to not impose."

"It will not be an imposition at all, Thomas. I was thinking of heading over to Thorn's Hill today, myself."

Reanna watched the boy hedge, wondering at the harm in accepting her proposal. Reanna gave him a nudge. "You did say that the baby needed something, didn't you?"

That was all it took. The two were off within moments.

~ ~ ~

Riding up the small road, which was more of a rocky trail, Reanna was silenced by the desolateness of Thomas's home.

The shack was rickety, the roof sagging, and gaping holes in the walls whistled in the wind. Just then, the pair passed by a large lump on the ground, with rocks, snow, and dirt built up in a long form.

Thomas glanced over his shoulder up at Reanna and then looked back at the lump.

"Sorry, she's right there, ma'am. It was as far…as far as I could drag her."

Reanna couldn't hide her sharp intake of breath and had to swallow back the bile reaching her tongue. Her right arm left the reins to go around the little boy, squeezing him. "It is all right, Thomas, you did very well." She bit her lip, trying to hold in all emotion. "I am sure she would be pleased to know you cared so much."

He nodded, but Reanna couldn't see his face.

They reached the front of the shack, and Reanna could hear the mayhem inside. The dread that had settled into Reanna when first talking with Thomas multiplied tenfold. She dismounted and then reached up to let Thomas off the horse. She followed him into the house.

The smell blasted her the second the door opened. Unemptied chamber pots, spoilt milk, and rotted food permeated the air. Her hand went to cover her nose just as five little faces, filthy, with the same enormous brown eyes as Thomas, went silent and looked up at her.

Reanna froze, for not only did the putrid smell hang in the air, strong, even against the open doorway, but the condition of the interior was deplorable. The lone piece of furniture, a table with no legs, sat in the middle of the one-room shack. A baby sat atop the table, bottomless and crying, next to an old blackened iron pot. The other kids sat about the room, lifeless and in tattered clothing. Reanna could see bones through all of their unfed skin.

She forced herself to not take a step back. To not jump onto Ivy and ride breakneck back to Holloton and forget the hell she was witnessing.

Thomas went over to the baby, his skinny arms picking up the babe, and he tried to rock her.

"Ma'am, these are my brothers and sisters. I here got Lizzie. Then Maggie is next oldest after me." He shuffled the baby to one arm and pointed to the little girl at the far end of the room, holding on tightly to a toddler. The little girl eyed her warily. "She's got Henry there, the second youngest. Then there's Jeannie and Albert over there."

Shock subsiding, Reanna conjured a bright smile and looked at each of the children. She had decided within moments of walking into the shack what she was going to do, but she didn't want to scare the children. "It is very nice to meet all of you. I just met your big brother in the woods and was about to invite him over to my place for a big meal of duck and pudding and milk, but then he told me he had to come home."

She walked over to the little girl closest to her, Jeannie, and bent to her eye level. "I was thinking that maybe all of you would like to come with me as well?"

Thomas didn't let her win so easily, as she guessed he wouldn't. He was a proud little boy.

"No, ma'am, I'm afraid we can't. Mama always say no imposing. She wouldn't like it."

Reanna stayed bent, taking off her gloves and handing them to Jeannie. Albert scooted along the wall to investigate the treasure Jeannie had in her hands.

Reanna looked up at Thomas, her voice holding no sympathy, only kind suggestion. "I think if your mother knew you were all alone to take care of everyone, she would have been very proud of you, Thomas, for what you have done. But I also imagine she would want you to take a break for just a night and let someone else feed your brothers and sisters. I do not think that would be too much imposition, especially for just one night, do you?"

Thomas dug his toes into the dirt floor, debating with himself. His dead mother's voice fought his obviously hungry siblings. None of the other children said anything. They all just looked at Thomas, waiting. Those that were old enough to understand what food was looked at him hopefully.

But Reanna knew Thomas would have to make the decision.

"Just one night, Thomas, I cannot imagine it would hurt anything—and your rabbit you caught will last that much longer. How does that sound?"

Finally, Thomas looked at her, and the smallest smile formed. "All right, ma'am, just one night, and we be so grateful."

At that, the little girl by Reanna got her unspoken permission and clumsily stood up, falling onto Reanna, and hugged her with what little strength she had.

~ ~ ~

Reanna smiled at the bright room and grinning faces around her. Eager eyes looked at her as she went through the alphabet once more. None of the children had ever been educated, but she was quickly finding that the children who were old enough were quick learners. Easy, she imagined, now that they had food and a warm, safe place to stay. Some of them were sparks, and some were shy turtles slowly coming out of their shells.

Since convincing Thomas to let his family stay with her over two months ago, Reanna was awed by how much had happened.

The Visper children had moved into Holloton, and it had been a week before Reanna had realized how uncomfortable they all were. She should have guessed it on the first day when Thomas had said, "Buggers, ma'am, I didn't know you lived in the palace. Mama wouldn't like us bothering his lordship."

It had taken a lot of convincing to get Thomas to allow them all to stay. And while Holloton wasn't exactly a palace, to the children it was, and it was entirely too big for the tiny ones. Many of the rooms were cold and impersonal, and the children had walked around the house, jumping at every sound that echoed through the barren hallways.

Although Reanna had separated them into three bedrooms, she would wake each morning to find all six in one bedroom, heaped in a pile on one bed.

It was when she and Thomas were traveling back to his home to pick up some of the family's very few possessions, that she noticed a hunting cottage. It was in good condition, large, two stories with plenty of bedrooms. And most importantly, unused. Ten minutes from the main house by horse, Reanna was sure it would be close enough that the children wouldn't feel abandoned by her.

She had the place cleaned and ready within two days. The children moved in immediately with the nanny, Joan, that she had hired. And it soon became obvious that the children were slowly beginning to feel the blooming seeds of security.

To Reanna's surprise, the Holloton staff had enthusiastically taken to caring for the Visper children, because, Reanna secretly guessed, they were actually quite bored. Taking care of one low-maintenance marchioness had not exactly filled their days. Whether it was specially concocted treats by cook, or making toys for the children, or the several maids that spent every day helping to take care of the children, Reanna was impressed again and again by the servants' generosity.

A week after the children moved into the cottage, a knock had come on the door. Reanna answered the door, expecting to see one of the Holloton staff. So she was surprised to not be greeted by staff, but by a haggard woman with a stooped back and grey, stringy hair. A child was propped onto each of her round hips, both gripping tightly to her wool sleeves. Reanna could see several holes worn through her serviceable dress.

"Ye the lady takin' in the wee ones?" She didn't smile, but her mouth gaped open, showing toothless gums.

"Excuse me?" Reanna wiped her hands on her apron, removing the chalk dust from going over lessons with some of the older children. She had planned to find a suitable tutor soon, but wanted to get the children started right away on their schooling.

"The wee ones." The lady stepped in toward Reanna. "I hear ye be the lady takin' 'em in. I've got two more for ye here."

"What? I am sorry, there must be some mistake."

The lady peered past Reanna into the house. Kids were running back and forth. "Yep, this be the place. I've had these two since me neighbor died months back. I can't handle 'em no more. This is Sam." She shoved one of the children, a boy with curly blond locks into Reanna's arms. "And this one is Connie. They be twins, two, maybe three years. Don't know."

Reanna had no choice but to fumble the girl into her arms next to the boy, for she was sure the woman was going to drop her.

The lady turned to leave.

"Wait, just one moment," Reanna said.

The lady turned back, impatience clear on her face.

"How did you know?" Reanna shuffled the children in her arms as they began to squirm. "I mean, how did you find us? Where did you hear that we were taking children in?"

The lady shrugged. "It be gettin' 'round the countryside. Ever since the Visper kids. There be anything else?"

Reanna had to shake the shocked looked off her face. "No, no."

The woman turned and left in a rickety wagon.

Reanna could only gape after her, and would have stood in the doorway for some time doing so, if the two wiggling twins in her arms would have allowed it. But their insistence had made Reanna quickly turn and bring them into the warm confines of the cottage.

That had been five weeks ago, and since that time, three more orphaned children had made their way into Reanna's makeshift orphanage. And Reanna had also recruited several of the Holloton maids to help out Joan around the clock.

Spring had come, and with it, a semblance of normalcy for both the children and her. Reanna smiled again at the faces around her. Maggie was slowly taking her turn at reciting the alphabet, but Reanna could tell she was preoccupied by the man and woman at the big table. The couple was visiting with her younger brother, Albert, and if everything went well, they would take him home.

Reanna hated to see the Visper children broken up, but she had talked to Thomas about his brothers and sisters, and they had decided that it was more important for everyone to have a good home with a mother and father.

The Wortsons, a childless couple, had approached her about taking one of the children in. He was a miller, and from what Reanna understood, that would provide about as much stability in a family as she could hope for. Albert would eventually learn a good trade from Mr. Wortson.

After about an hour, the Wortsons and Albert interrupted the lesson Reanna was teaching.

"Did it go well?" Reanna asked.

"It was delightful! He is a wonderful little boy, and we would love to have him join our family. I believe he liked us too." Mrs. Wortson beamed.

Reanna bent down to talk to the little boy. "Albert, how did you like the Wortsons?"

"Very much, Lady Ana. Thomas says I'm to go with them."

"If you would like to, Albert. Would you?"

"Yes, Lady Ana," he affirmed, though didn't smile.

Reanna knew he was sad about leaving his brothers and sisters.

She grabbed his hands as she stood up. "Why don't you say goodbye to your brothers and sisters and then meet us at the front door."

Albert nodded and ran off.

Twenty minutes later, Reanna stood with all of the children waving goodbye to Albert. He sat in the back of a sturdy wagon as it started off down the road that led to the cottage. Little puffs of breath were visible in the chilly air from all of the children shouting goodbyes. Albert waved hard, with tears in his eyes, but a smile plainly on his face.

It was when Reanna had ushered all of the children back inside, that she saw Thomas still standing outside with obvious worry on his face.

"Thomas, you will miss him, won't you?" Reanna said as she joined him outside the closed door.

"I will. He was a good brother. I just wished the Wortsons still had other kids for him to play with."

"Other kids? What other kids?"

"Their other kids." He turned and opened the door to the house, stepping inside. Reanna followed. "They used to have two other boys."

Reanna grabbed his arm, stopping him. "What? They did? They didn't mention anything about them to me. They said they could not have children. What happened to their boys?"

Thomas shrugged. "The good lord did not see fit to make them strong enough to accept their punishment when they were bad."

Understanding, but desperately not wanting to, Reanna grabbed Thomas's shoulders and went to eye level with him. "What are you talking about Thomas? Who told you that?" She couldn't help her voice from shrieking in panic.

"I used to see them out at the stream sometimes. Their boys. We used to fish. When the older one stopped showing up, that's what the younger one said had happened." Thomas shrugged again. "Then the young one stopped showing up. I just figured he was bad too. I hope Albert's good."

"My God." Reanna stood up, heart almost stopping. Hands shaking, she snatched her shawl from the hook by the door and swung it on. "Don't worry, Thomas. Albert will not have to be good for them. He is not going with them."

She looked around the cottage, desperate for some sort of weapon, should she need it. Nothing. The riding crop she never used sat propped by the door. It would have to do. She grabbed it and started to run out the door, but then whipped back to Thomas.

She gripped his arm and pulled him through the open door, closing it tight after them.

"Thomas, you need to take the pony out back you have been practicing on, and ride as fast as you can to the stables. Get Ike and bring him back here with a rifle or a pitchfork or something. Do you understand?"

Thomas's eyes went huge, then he nodded.

"Good. Quickly. Go."

Swearing at herself, it only took minutes for Reanna to push Ivy hard and catch up to the Wortsons. Breathless, riding crop gripped in her hand, she came up alongside them, a bright smile on her face. "Mr. and Mrs. Wortson, I am so happy to catch you before you got too far."

Mr. Wortson tipped his hat. "Lady Southfork, what can we do for you?"

"I am so sorry to inconvenience you, but little Albert's youngest sister woke up from her nap and realized he was gone. We promised her he would say goodbye, and she is beyond distraught. You know how children can get."

"Do we ever." He winked at her.

Reanna's stomach churned, but she kept her smile pasted on. "Yes, well I was hoping I could just steal Albert back for a moment and bring him to say goodbye. It should only take a couple of minutes."

"Well, we can certainly turn around—"

"No, that is not necessary, turning the wagon around on this skinny road. I do not wish to inconvenience you so. If you do not mind, I will just pop Albert in front of me and run him back."

"Thank you. That would be easiest." He looked over at his shoulder at the boy. "Hop over to Lady Southfork, Albert."

Albert climbed to the edge of the wagon, and Reanna grabbed him, settling him half across her lap. She nudged Ivy a few steps away from the wagon, then stopped.

The smile left her face as she looked at the couple. "Mr. Wortson, I meant to ask you, I know you said you could not have children, but have you ever had children?"

A glance shot between the couple. Mrs. Wortson looked at Reanna, not able to hide her wariness. Her husband kept a confused smile on his face.

"Well, yes, we actually had two boys that passed away several years ago." He grabbed his wife's hand, squeezing it. Squeezing it hard, Reanna could see.

"As you can imagine, we've missed them terribly. It has been 'specially hard on Mrs. Wortson."

Reanna nodded. "I am so sorry for your loss." She tightened her hold on Albert. "How did they die, if I may ask?"

The couple glanced at each other once more. Mr. Wortson's jaw line began to twitch. He looked back at Reanna.

"I'm afraid my wife doesn't care for me to talk about the boys. Sad memories and all. I'm sure you understand."

Guilt was plain on his face.

Reanna turned Ivy so she could face them head on. "Actually, Mr. Wortson, I must admit I do not. I do not understand—if I have this correct—'how the good lord did not see fit to make them strong enough to accept their punishment when they were bad.'"

Mr. Wortson dropped his wife's hand, and his fingers fidgeted on the leather reins. He tried the confused smile again. "What are you talking about?"

"I think you know exactly what I am talking about, Mr. Wortson."

Reanna's eyes locked with his for a tense minute.

He sputtered, and his face bloated pink. "You twit. You have no right to judge how we discipline our boys. Children must respect their parents."

It was the admission Reanna needed. She breathed an inward sigh of relief while trying to keep her anger controlled. "You, Mr. Wortson, have a warped sense of entitlement. I cannot even begin to imagine the monster that you are, but rest assured, you will not have Albert, nor any other orphan within my grasp."

"You can't do that—you gave us the boy."

"Yes, and I am taking him back. Remove yourself from my property, Mr. Wortson, and never set foot on it again. If you so much as look at one of these children, my husband will not think twice on crushing you."

The man's face turned cruel, and a forced laugh came out. "I doubt that. From what people say, his lordship don't care much for you, or he wouldn't have gotten rid of you up in these parts."

Reanna's grip on Ivy's reins tightened. So much so that the horse couldn't help but rear. Grabbing Albert tightly, she regained control over the animal. Ivy's feet stilled, and Reanna looked back to the Wortsons, glaring down her nose at them as much as she could.

She didn't allow the slightest glimmer of emotion to show. "Whether or not my husband cares for me is of no concern to this situation, Mr. Wortson. Be assured that if you disobey my wishes—if you dare to come near any of these children—my husband will perceive that as a slight on the family name, not merely as a slight on his wife. And that, I can guarantee, he will not condone." She leaned forward over Albert, her next words biting and deliberate. "Would you like to test my statement, or do you understand me?"

Mrs. Wortson had begun to cry. A snorting but soft melody. Mr. Wortson finally looked away from Reanna. Silently, red rage shaking his entire being, he shifted his body to face the front of the wagon, and whipped the reins to move his horse.

Reanna didn't move until the wagon was out of sight.

"We going back, Lady Ana?" Albert was one of the children who had had a hard time wrapping his mouth around the name "Southfork" and had dubbed her Lady Ana.

"Yes, we are, Albert. You will get to be with your brothers and sisters again, and you will play like always."

He nodded. He was not a wordy one.

Reanna turned the horse and they slowly made their way back to the cottage.

"How come you shaking, Lady Ana?"

She looked down at his head. She hadn't even realized she was. Even though it did little to cease the shake, she took a deep breath before answering. "Because I just learned a very important lesson, Albert." She kissed the top of his curly, brown hair. "One that makes me question what I can do."

Disgusted, not only with the Wortsons, but also with herself, Reanna continued back to the cottage.

Miss Melby, Joan, Thomas, and Ike, confused and with rifle, were agitated and waiting for Reanna outside the cottage as she rode up with Albert.

"Good, m'lady." Ike propped the rifle back over his shoulder. "I was just trying to make sense of this story and come after you. But you are here. Unharmed? You are ghost white."

"Yes. I am fine. Thank you."

"The boy?"

Reanna squeezed him. "Are you all right, Albert?"

"Yes."

Reanna scanned the crew of them. She knew why Ike was here, but Miss Melby rarely left the main house to come to the cottage. Concern gripped Reanna.

Reanna handed Albert down to a confused Joan.

"M'lady, Albert, why is he back?" Joan asked. "Thomas was rambling on something about the Wortsons, but I couldn't make much sense of it."

Reanna grabbed Ike's hand and dismounted. "It is a long story, Joan, and I will tell you in a bit. The short of it is that I was naïve, apparently like always, and stupid because of it. But it will not happen again." She whipped to Miss Melby. "What is wrong?"

"Oh, my lady, no need to frown. Nothing is wrong. In fact, some things are going to get right around here, I suspect."

"Now you are making no sense. Whatever are you talking about?"

"He's coming. He just sent word."

A glimmer of hope flamed up in the pit of Reanna's stomach, but her next words were cautious. "Who is coming?"

Miss Melby's eyes went wide in excitement. "The marquess. He will be here in fortnight."

CHAPTER 7

Reanna jumped at the sound of another door opening. All day long, Killian's trunks had been arriving, and it was driving Reanna out of her mind. At each clunk of a door, she would take great pains to compose herself, smooth her hair and the soft yellow silk dress that she had chosen specifically because it cut nicely across her bosom. Each time, she would be disappointed when Killian didn't appear. But the first footman to arrive this morning had assured Ruperton that lord Southfork was indeed, arriving today.

Reanna shuffled slowly to the left of the fireplace in the middle of the study, eyes fixated on the chess set she'd had set up for Killian's arrival.

"There you are, my lady," Evans said as he entered the study. "You have been the devil to keep track of today, flying from room to room as you have. You must be assured that all is in order for the marquess's arrival."

"I know it is, Evans. I just cannot seem to help but worry, though. I have not seen his lordship in such a time, and everything must be perfect." She shuffled back to the right of the fireplace. "Speaking of which, do you think the chess set should be placed more to the right of the hearth? I know that is where I had it this morning, but I am debating whether it was a mistake to move it."

"Quite honestly, my lady, I think the marquess will be impressed by your play, whether you are sitting to the left of the fire, to the right of the fire, or in a bog."

That squeezed a smile out of Reanna. "Do you really think?"

"Having been one of the fortunate ones to tutor you on the game, I can say yes, your play is impressive. Indeed, both

Ruperton and I have been plotting against you since the last time you trounced each of us in our matches."

"I am sure it was just luck."

Evans cleared his throat. "Luck, my lady?"

Reanna laughed as she rolled her eyes. "Yes, Evans, I know: 'there is no such thing as luck in chess.'" She rolled off the mantra that had been repeated over and over to her during instruction. "It is each your own fault, you realize. You both taught me every trick you had to beat the other, which only ended up giving me the advantage against each of you."

"We still have a few tricks left, my lady."

Reanna smiled at the butler. "I cannot wait to see what they are."

A door opened and closed down the hall, and Reanna shot Evans a quizzical look.

"I am afraid not yet, my lady. Which is why I was searching for you."

"Is he not coming today?" Reanna didn't think she could take another day as nerve racking as this one had been.

"Actually, we just received word that he should be arriving close to an hour from now."

Reanna exhaled, relieved, and glanced out the window. "I had not realized it was getting dark. Maybe evening wear is in order…please excuse me, Evans."

"My lady." He inclined his head to her.

Reanna charged out of the study and up into her rooms. Miss Melby had been relaxing on a plush side chair and bolted upright as Reanna nearly ran into her.

"What now? What insane nugget could you possibly have rolling in that head now, my lady? You've already changed outfits three times today, and you can't possibly be thinking of changing again…"

Reanna laid the most charming smile she could muster onto Miss Melby. "It is getting dark out, and by the time his lordship arrives, which should be an hour according to Evans, evening dress will be appropriate, do you not think?"

Miss Melby heaved out a sigh for effect, and pushed her plump form out of the chair. "I am afraid you have a point. What will it be—the one you had picked out for tonight, or another?"

"The one I had chosen will be fine."

Within moments, Reanna was down to her stockings, chemise and short stays, waiting for Miss Melby to ready the gown to step into. Miss Melby wouldn't risk the mounds of fabric going over Reanna's hair, not after the amount of time she had spent getting it perfect, the dark locks twisted and plaited in intricate patterns along her head.

Miss Melby held the delicate blue silk as Reanna stepped within the folds and balanced herself.

"I am just happy this husband of yours is finally showing up. I don't ever want to go through another fortnight like the last."

"Whatever do you mean?" Reanna asked as she slipped her arms into the short sleeves of the silk gown.

"You've been running 'round like a chicken with no head and driving us all stark batty."

Guilt touched Reanna's shoulders. Miss Melby always said what others were too polite to. "Has it really been that bad?"

"Worse, and all to impress the husband that sent you up here, alone, for months and months."

"But we do not know what his reasons were. I am sure it had to have been something drastic, or he would not have treated me so. He did ask me about my father before he sent me away… maybe it had something to do with that. Regardless, he is coming now, and he would not be coming if it was not for a good reason, correct?"

"I hope so, my lady." Miss Melby moved behind her to lace the dress tight.

"I do too. I know it. And when he sees the orphanage and all that I have learned over the past months, he is sure to see that I am worthy."

Miss Melby snorted a sarcastic laugh. "Worthy, my lady? Is that why you've been doing all this? To be worthy in his eyes?"

"Well, no…I do not think so." Reanna paused and looked at herself in the mirror. A tiny stab of realization struck her. "Maybe. Maybe just a little bit." She turned back toward Miss Melby. "But is that such a bad thing? I want my husband to be proud of me."

"And I can't imagine any man not being proud of you, my lady. Seems to me that he's not the worthy one. I am hoping for the best, for your sake, but I'm just wondering if he'll feel the same way."

Reanna straightened her shoulders, shaking off the self-doubt and bolstering herself with inflated confidence. "I am sure he will, Miss Melby. I am sure of it."

A small ruckus floated upwards from the entry, and Reanna knew that Killian had finally arrived. Miss Melby nodded approval at her mistress as Reanna rushed to the floor-length mirror, checked her latest outfit, and then pinched her cheeks for rosiness. Satisfied, Reanna hurried out of the room.

When she arrived downstairs, Ruperton was waiting for her, his face an odd portrait of worry and pity. Reanna barely noticed it.

"He is here, then?"

"Yes, my lady. He is in the study. He asked for you to join him as soon as possible."

A bright smile formed on Reanna's lips. "Good. Thank you, Ruperton." She turned, aimed for the study, then spun back to Ruperton, deciding it would be good to know what she was walking into. "Did Lord Southfork mention how his travels were?"

"I believe he said they were satisfactory, my lady."

Reanna nodded. The small frown Reanna had noticed had not left Ruperton's face. She guessed it must be the stress of having the marquess back at Holloton, especially after she had run them all ragged these past two weeks. She would have to apologize to the staff for that.

Pausing outside of the study, Reanna took a moment to smooth the few strands of hair that had managed to escape and curl along her temples when she bolted down the stairs. One deep breath to calm her nerves, and she was ready to see her husband again.

She knocked and entered the study. Her breath stopped when she saw Killian. He stood next to the hearth, studying the chess set. She smiled inwardly. His body still had the same smooth lines, thick with strength, and strands of his sandy hair fell devilishly across his forehead. His hands now masterfully held a brandy glass, just as he had once masterfully held her. And then his eyes.

Reanna had saved looking at them for last, afraid, for what they might say, for what they might mean. It had been so long since she had seen the brown in them…and no, she wouldn't think about their last words.

She needed to concentrate on their wedding day—on their wedding night. Not the following morning. These last months, even as she had fooled herself into believing she had moved past her love for this man, she had nurtured the tiniest flame of hope.

Hope that wouldn't let her love die.

Had she been stupid?

There was only one way to tell. She looked up.

There they were. Brown, warm, comforting. For an instant, Reanna thought she recognized a flame of passion in them as he looked at her, but it was gone too soon to tell. Now she only read speculation in them.

"Killian…" Her voice trailed off tentatively.

He was judging her. She knew it. And in the next instant, she learned what his verdict was.

"I had rather hoped to hear news that you were with babe, duties being what they are." He threw his words out flippantly. "But do not fret. Eventually, I am sure I will get around to it. Not this trip, though."

A cruel sound flitted out behind Reanna. Laughter? But it sounded too harsh for laughter—a malicious, evil sound.

She turned around and found herself staring at the most perfectly formed woman, with skin as pale and smooth as moonlight, classic cheekbones, a small, pert nose, and a crown of wild ringlet red hair, pulled off of her face to either enhance her features or to not steal the show—Reanna wasn't sure.

Reanna's mouth dropped open. The blood red outfit the woman wore, encrusted with strands of glittering diamonds, only enhanced her proportions and creamy skin. She was a goddess. A goddess with the coldest green eyes Reanna had ever seen.

And a laugh that crushed her heart.

Reanna turned back to Killian. Her eyes questioned him, forming the words that her open mouth could not, did not, want to say.

"I had imagined we could have gotten through this without the introductions, but since you came in and it is before us." Killian walked to stand between the two women. "Reanna, may I introduce to you Miss Vivienne Von Houten." He stepped to align himself next to the woman, his hand going lightly to the beauty's arm.

Reanna couldn't move, couldn't speak, much less smile graciously at this woman. She looked back and forth frantically between Killian and the woman.

Killian wouldn't have done this to her. Surely she was jumping to the wrong conclusion.

"And yes, it is exactly what you are thinking, Reanna."

Killian stepped forward, positioning himself in front of the woman and effectively taking Reanna's stare off of her. Reanna looked up into his hard face, still madly searching for a different explanation.

Killian rolled his eyes. "Do not be naïve about it. She is here for my pleasure. You, on the other hand, are going back to London."

"London?" Reanna knew she sounded like a simpleton, but couldn't force any more words out.

The flame-haired beauty laughed again. The cruel, grating noise only intensified. It echoed in Reanna's head, so much so that her hand went to her temple, hoping to still the sound.

Killian looked over his shoulder at his mistress, silencing her. He walked around Reanna, turning her with him, so the woman was no longer in her sightline.

"Yes, London, and the carriage is waiting for you. I would like you gone within the hour."

"An hour?"

"Yes, and packed or not, I would like you gone. Your things can be sent along after you have left."

No. No. No.

Flashes of the last time she saw Killian flooded her mind. Only this time, a red-headed witch was in the room to witness her humiliation. She almost doubled over. It was happening again. No. It couldn't be.

"But for how long?"

He shrugged. "Until I decide to come back to London. You will be notified." Reanna could see him dismiss her.

Notified? Reanna nearly screamed at the word. Ripping her from her home was as easy as a "notified"?

"But, Killian, you don't understand. I have things—"

"You have nothing you cannot leave. Now please, let us not have you begging again."

The witch in the corner snorted a small outburst.

Reanna's mouth fell open again, no words escaping.

She couldn't let him. This scene was too familiar to her, too painful, and she wasn't going to repeat her past mistakes. Her body went numb, and without a further word, she turned and walked out of the room, taking careful, measured steps.

The witch's laughter trailed her, until Reanna left the study, closing the door.

She continued those measured steps down the hallway. Ruperton stood at the base of the stairs, a worried look on his face.

"My lady—"

Without looking at him, Reanna held up her hand, palm out, silencing the concern.

She walked past him, up the stairs to her chambers, startling Miss Melby when she entered the room.

"My lady, what are you doing back here so soon? Need to change again?" Miss Melby winked at her. "I always did think the marquess a romantic fellow, putting aside how he's treated you in the past, of course."

Reanna walked in silence past Miss Melby to the wardrobe and pulled out a fashionable riding outfit. She paused, head down, looking into the darkness of the heavy oak furniture. Silently still, she stood, breathing in and out.

In and out.

Finally, she looked up at Miss Melby. "I need to change and ride out to the cottage. I am leaving for London in an hour. Please pack whatever I might need, the rest can be sent. I will be back before the hour is up. And tell the staff to continue to take care of the needs of the children while I am away."

"Away? What do you mean, my lady? The marquess just got here."

"Yes, and I am leaving."

It was all she needed to say. Miss Melby began to silently scurry about.

~ ~ ~

Reanna stepped quietly into the cottage, drawing eleven happy little faces away from the song they had all been singing.

Anticipation shined bright on the older children's faces— they were the ones who knew how important it was going to be to meet the marquess.

Joan quickly stepped from the circle of children, batting away from her shoulder a blue streamer of fabric that had been hung by the children to liven the cottage up. The children had taken great pains to decorate the cottage for the marquess's arrival. In fact, the cleaning and decorating had consumed the children's lives since they learned Lord Southfork was coming.

And all with no prompting from Reanna. Led by Thomas, who wanted to make the best impression of all, Reanna had never seen the children work so hard together without any bickering.

"Has he finally arrived?" Joan asked. The same question was mirrored in all the children's faces.

"No, Joan," Reanna said in a snap she couldn't control. The excited smiles of the children disappeared, replaced with worry on every little face. Reanna took a breath, and stretched for control of her voice. She forced a smile on her face, but didn't look any of the children in the eyes. She couldn't.

"Actually, Joan, could I speak to you outside for a moment?"

"Yes, ma'am." Joan quickly grabbed a shawl and followed Reanna out the door. "What is it? Is the marquess not coming?" the nanny asked the moment the door closed behind them.

There was no use pitter-pattering about the truth. Reanna didn't have the time. "Actually, Lord Southfork is here. But I am being sent back to London. I am to leave within the hour."

Reanna attempted to squelch all emotion, and she hoped she was succeeding. "I have instructed the staff to look after the needs of you and the children, and I will make sure several of the maids continue to come and help during the day and night. I am maintaining hope that I will be back at Holloton soon. Maybe within the month, but I am not sure. Will you be able to handle the children until then?"

"Of course, my lady. Don't you worry about the children none. They will be fine until you return," Joan said, wisely asking no questions about the reasons for Reanna's dismissal to London.

Reanna nodded, swallowing the lump in her throat.

Now, the hard part.

"Good, then let us go tell the children, and I must be off."

~ ~ ~

Reanna slid open the window and leaned back against a red velvet squab in the coach. She was alone in the darkness, as she had left Miss Melby behind to oversee packing. Miss Melby would join her with the trunks, a day behind, in London. Until then, Reanna was alone.

She wrinkled her nose. The noxious perfume of the red-haired witch still hung on the fabric, suffocating the air in the enclosed coach. Reanna squeezed her eyes shut, trying to shake the witch's cruel laughter and Killian's words out of her head.

But if it wasn't the scene in the study that burned in her mind, it was the body-numbing worry over the children. She thought her quick talk with them before she left had soothed their worries from her abrupt entrance.

But leaving them unexpectedly…well, she just couldn't imagine what was running through their minds. These children had already been abandoned by those they loved and trusted, and she was just adding to that unspoken terror.

She had told them that she was needed in London by a relative, and that she would be back as soon as possible. A lie, which she abhorred having to do, but a necessary concession to alleviate the worry she saw around her.

It had taken every bit of her restraint to hide all emotion and not scare the children. But the second she had cleared the cottage, she broke. She was being ripped from her children. Her babies. They depended on her, and she was leaving them.

Heart twisting in her chest, and blinded by tears the entire way, it had only been by Ivy's good graces that she had made it back to the stables.

Reanna opened her eyes, tears drained for the moment, only to be consumed with picking at a thread on her sleeve that had torn loose during her breakneck ride to the cottage. By the time she got back to the main house, she hadn't had time to change, and the riding habit had to do.

Not exactly the most comfortable traveling attire, with the tight shoulders and cinching around her waist. At least the boots would keep her feet warm against the spring chill coming in through the window.

She would need to leave that open.

CHAPTER 8

"My lady! Lady Ana! Lady Ana!"

Reanna jerked forward on the carriage bench. It was early morning on her second full day of travel, and sunny after the heavy rain that had kept them stuck at the traveler's inn most of yesterday. They were moving slowly, the mucky roads demanded it, and she could have sworn she just heard Thomas yelling for her.

Had she been dreaming? Going crazy?

She looked out the window. Nothing.

"Lady Ana!"

She tore across the carriage to the other window.

It was Thomas. On his little pony, riding alongside the carriage on the edge of the road. Alone.

Blazing hell. What was going on? She flipped the trap door and told the coachman to stop. Reanna couldn't get out fast enough, flinging open the door and jumping down while the carriage still moved.

"Thomas. Good God. What is going on?"

He pulled up on his pony, jumping off and running to Reanna. Caked in mud, terror was in his eyes. He fell into her, clasping her waist.

"Thomas. What has happened?" She pried him away so she could squat at eye-level with him, keeping one hand on his quaking shoulders, and brushing hair away from his eyes with the other. "Tell me. What is going on?"

"He kicked us out, Lady Ana."

"What? Wait." She shifted him backward to the high side of the road and pushed him down onto some wet grass. "Sit down and take a breath."

Thomas sat, but ignored the breathing part. "He kicked us out."

Reanna shook her head, trying to understand his frantic words. "What? Who kicked you out?"

"He kicked us out of the cottage, him and his lady friend. Yesterday. She's mean."

"Thomas, what are you saying? Lord Southfork kicked you out?"

Thomas nodded and finally took a breath, his small fists clenching. "Bloody right, Lady Ana. The bleeding prig kicked us out of the cottage."

Reanna could see that all of Thomas's fear had morphed into anger, now that he had found her, and she chose to ignore his swearing. Reanna gave silent thanks that the rain had held them up. She didn't want to imagine what would have happened to Thomas if they had been even further from Holloton.

"His lady friend stumbled up on us and shrieked and hissed about. She's crazy. Red crazy witch hair. Said something about getting rid of us. So he kicked us out."

"No, he couldn't have. No. He wouldn't." Reanna was turning pale, her heart slowing. "Oh, God, no, the babies too?"

"Yep, lady Ana, that's why I came after you."

"Joan—where did she take them?"

"We went to my old house, but there ain't no room, and ain't no food, and she had to stay and take care of them, so I convinced her I could find you."

Reanna grabbed his face in her hands. "Thomas. You did the right thing, but the wrong thing. You could have gotten hurt coming after me. Did you tell the staff? Ike?"

"I stopped by the stables on the way and talked to Ike. He went running off, so I left for you."

Reanna managed a breath. At least Ike knew. The staff would take care of them for the moment.

She stood, hands on her hips, and eyed one of the four outriders that were huddled, chatting with each other.

It was time to learn how to ride astride.

"Thomas, I know you are tired, so do you want to ride back in the carriage, or—they are bigger than your pony, but do you want to ride back with me on one of those horses?"

Thomas jumped to his feet, grabbing her gloved hand. "I want to stay with you, Lady Ana."

She squeezed his fingers. "Let us go."

~ ~ ~

Reanna pulled up on her horse as the pair arrived at the stately entrance marking the long road up to Holloton's main hall.

"Thomas, will you please go on to Joan and the children, and tell them I will be arriving soon."

Thomas gave her a gritty smile, full of bitter fire. "Are you going to give him hell, Lady Ana?" He wanted justice for his family being kicked out of warmth and security, and Reanna couldn't blame him.

"Quite possibly, Thomas. I honestly do not know yet."

His horse next to hers, Reanna reached over and brushed a chunk of mud from his face. The roads were still a muddy mess, and both of them were caked with dirt and mud. She didn't want to imagine what she looked like. "You rode really well, Thomas. We made excellent time. I am so proud of you. Now go. I will be there soon."

"All right, Lady Ana. Hurry up though, 'cause Joan'll be worried."

"I will, I promise. Off you go."

Reanna sat on her horse, hands gripping the leather reins tightly, watching Thomas move on down the road in front of the lowering sun. It was true, she hadn't decided yet what she was going to say to Killian, but the anger that had been simmering in her for days was now a cauldron of boiling rage that she was having a hard time controlling.

She turned her horse up the drive, not bothering to calm down. Killian didn't deserve it. He deserved whatever she was going to bring to him.

Reanna ran up the front stairs of Holloton after tossing her reins to a stable boy that had seen her approaching. She yanked open the thick oak door, startling the footman who had been passing by. She didn't recognize the man. But it made sense that Killian would have more servants while in residence.

Disgust crossed the footman's features, and he wasted no time in putting on a haughty face. "Excuse me, miss. You are not allowed in here. May I show you the door?"

"No, you may not. I am the marchioness, and I want to know where my husband is."

Shock sucked the haughtiness off his face. "My lady, it is… it is good to see you…to meet you. My apologies. We had not expected you."

"I imagine not. Where is he?"

"He is in the dining hall."

Reanna stalked by the man.

"If you would wait just a moment, my lady, I will announce you."

She didn't turn back to him. "No need, I will announce myself."

Reaching the engraved double doors that stood between her and Killian, Reanna contemplated for a moment that maybe she should wait several minutes and collect herself. At least wipe off the mud that had dried onto her face and hair.

But the thought disintegrated in an instant as the image of her kids stuck in that awful shack flashed in her mind.

Rage renewed.

She reached out, whipping the doors open, and stomped into the long dining hall.

Stopping in the middle of the room, she heaved, her hands on her hips. From the far end of the dining table by the fireplace, two pairs of eyes stared at her.

One set glared at her, the witch's green eyes reflecting their superiority, along with amusement. Reanna knew she would be here, but had foolishly hoped she would be absent.

The other set of eyes, ones that she had once adored, showed mild annoyance and a touch of curiosity.

Neither one looked shocked to see her.

There was no turning back.

She stepped forward, feet aimed at Killian. "How could you do that?" The anger threatened to turn her voice screechy.

He ignored her question. "Do tell me there is a reason for this unseemly interruption."

"Interruption? Damn you, you bloody ass." She advanced on him. "I repeat, how could you do this?"

"Do what, wife?" He had the audacity to smile at her.

Reanna almost reeled backward. "What? Do what? Kick those children out of a home they had come to love, you bastard. Take little babies and throw them out into the dirt."

Realization flashed on Killian's features as he put his fork down and leaned back in his chair. "Really, is this display necessary?"

Reanna had to physically stop herself from attacking him. "Those children are cold, and hungry, and scared, because you've shown yourself to be the heartless monster you truly are."

"Those children are brats, nothing more," the witch across the table said. Bored hand under her chin, she looked up at Reanna with a sickening smile. She tapped her fork impatiently.

Reanna whipped around the table, stopping when she was leaning over the red-haired witch. "I should have sliced your throat the first moment I saw you, Miss Von Houten."

The threat in Reanna's voice was real, and the smile, along with the color in the woman's face, disappeared.

"I recommend that in the future, you keep your vile opinions to yourself, witch, or I will amend my earlier mistake."

Von Houten's eyes slid downward, landing on the venison on her plate. Her fork tapping stopped.

Faced with only a mass of red hair, Reanna stood straight and turned to Killian. He was not pleased. His jaw was set, twitching.

Reanna wasn't about to be intimidated. She strode back toward her husband. "And you, you are pathetic. You turn to a witch like her to keep you entertained. But of course, it should not surprise me." She threw a hand wide. "Cowards need cowards, and you have proven yourself to be nothing but one."

"Reanna—" His voice was low, near exploding.

"No, goddammit, don't you dare say a word. Only a coward would throw out children into the cold. They're orphans, Killian—did you realize that? Did you realize that I set up an orphanage?" Her hands flew up in disgust. "Not that it would matter to you—you don't want anything to do with me. But really Killian, are you that much a scum of a man to take out whatever ridiculous hatred you have for me on innocent children?"

"The children had nothing to do with you," Killian gritted out between clenched teeth.

"You are wrong, Killian. They are everything to me. And they have everything to do with me. How you hate me. What, was making love to me too much for you? Too genuine? Because I know you felt it. I don't know a damn thing about men—that much is obvious—but I know you felt what I did that night. And you're a blasted imbecile to deny it."

She took a deep breath against her body shaking, then took a few steps to the door. By the entrance, she slowly turned back to him, her voice now soft, almost pitying.

"You are not a man, Killian. You are a coward. A bloody bastard. And I am glad you have found a woman who can match your needs. Now if you will please excuse me, I need to go to the children."

CHAPTER 9

"My lady, thank the good lord." Joan hurried over to Reanna, who had just opened the door of the decrepit shack. "I just didn't know what to do. I was just waiting and praying and hoping that Thomas found you."

"He did, and he is a courageous little man for it."

Thomas smiled sheepishly from across the room at Reanna's comment. He had been mostly cleaned up and was playing with his youngest brother, Henry. The shack was so small Reanna imagined there were never any secrets in it.

Joan stepped back, looking her up and down as several of the children ran over to hug Reanna.

"Can I say, my lady, you look awful—almost worse than Thomas did."

That cracked a smile onto Reanna's face. She had come to the shack right away, but slowly, wanting to distance the scene in the dining hall from the children. But now she was drained, and she imagined she did look horrific.

"I guessed as much, Joan." She bent down to hug several of the children. "It is good to see you, my sweethearts. And apparently, it does not matter to these little ones."

"I can't imagine it would, my lady. It was really only two days, but it was a rough two days on them since his lordship kicked us out."

Reanna stood up, fury instantly flowing through her. She shook her head in disgust. "I am so sorry, Joan. I did not get a chance to tell him before I left about the children. Had I known…" Reanna really didn't want to continue her vile thought in front of the children. "Let me just say that I would have worked out a solution before I left."

"I understand, I don't fault you none, my lady," Joan said. "There was no way you could have known what was to happen. We're all just pleased you're here now."

"Thank you, Joan. Even more so, thank you for staying with the children. They could not ask for a better caretaker."

Joan blushed.

"And you have cleaned this place up nicely."

"Yes." Joan looked about her. "As much as one could, I guess. Ike and one of his lads have been by with extra boards to close up the gaps in the walls, and they brought lots of blankets and some planks for the floor. No room for beds. And cook has been sending food over. So the staff has been taking care of us as best they can in the situation. But this place is just too small."

Reanna shook her head at the mess she was quickly realizing they were all in. "Yes, Joan, I owe you an enormous debt of gratitude. I will figure out what we are going to do from here."

"That sounds good, my lady. But first, maybe you would like to freshen up? I can get some tea going for you as the children have already eaten for the evening."

Thanks to Ike, the original legless table in the shack now had legs, along with six wooden chairs around it. Reanna sat heavily into one of the chairs, and Jeannie immediately crawled up into her lap. Joan handed her a wet cloth, and Reanna started flecking off and dabbing at the mud on her face. In the tiny mirror Joan produced, Reanna could see she still looked a mess. But that was the least of her worries. She sipped her tea, her mind scampering for solutions.

Jeannie slipped off her lap, only to be replaced by Albert snuggling in. Reanna looked up at Joan. "I think the best option is for me to bring the children to London with me. I have a home there, my aunt's home, which is big, and not under the marquess's thumb. There is plenty of space, and the chances of finding suitable homes for the children are probably better there, as I cannot ask you to continue to take care of them indefinitely here."

Joan sipped her tea, nodding her head in relief. It was obvious that she cared deeply for the children, but that the current situation was too much for her.

"But I would like you to stay in the area in case any more children show up who may have heard of us. Would that be all right with you, Joan?"

"Yes, my lady, but shall I stay here?"

"No, I cannot ask you to do that." Reanna rubbed her forehead. "Are there any vacant houses in the area that are appropriate?"

"I believe the Miller's place is open—widow Miller just moved in with his daughter in town."

"Good, except for that I have no money with me." Reanna tapped her fingernail on the table.

"No money, my lady?" Joan's face crinkled in worry.

"No, can you believe that?" Reanna let out a half-hysterical chuckle.

She had been so angry at Killian that she had disregarded any thoughts of planning or foresight as to what would happen when she got here.

"It is an idiotic oversight on my part." Her finger continued to tap. "When I get back to London, I will be able to send money to rent the Miller place, but until then, do you mind slipping in as a servant at Holloton? I am sure cook would love having your help in the kitchen, mostly because she likes to talk to someone she does not have to bark orders at. And I am sure the marquess takes no note who comes and goes on his staff here."

"That will be fine for me, my lady, but what about your journey back to London with the children? How will you even get them there?"

The tapping got louder. Several silent minutes passed, and her finger stilled. Reanna picked up her tea and took a sip, not saying anything.

"What are you going to do, my lady?"

Reanna set the cup down. "The only thing I can, Joan. The marquess." She gave Albert a quick hug and slipped him off her lap. "Please excuse me, Joan, I need some fresh air."

Joan looked at her, frowning, as Reanna stood and turned to go outside.

Reanna pretended not to see the look, for she knew there was pity in it.

~ ~ ~

Reanna sat ramrod straight on the edge of a peach damask wingback chair in the partridge parlor, so named for the partridges carved into the upper moldings of the room. After staying the night on the floor of the shack with little bodies draped all over her, she had managed to flick off most of the mud on her riding habit, but she knew her hair was still a mess, even after re-pinning it this morning with no mirror. At least Joan had given her face the once-over for last splotches of dirt before she left the shack.

She glanced around the room. This was the room used for entertaining the most undesirable guests. Visually pleasing, it was nonetheless a cold room, and an astute visitor may feel welcome, but certainly not liked if they were in that room. Reanna recognized the silent message Killian was passing to her.

Her eyes focused on the portrait of two partridges across from her. One was dead, or in the throes of dying, the other perched over it, a heartbroken look in its eyes, that is, if a partridge could be heartbroken. Reanna guessed maybe, but it would have to be a pretty spectacular bird. If not the room, she had always admired that particular portrait. But it seemed foreign to her now. The room seemed foreign. Killian had managed to mar it for her. Mar the whole house. Mar what had become her home.

An hour later, Ruperton entered the room. He smiled at her. A smile that held no hope, but still showed he supported her in what she was to do. She had already talked to him when she first arrived about making sure Joan was taken care of until money could be sent.

"He will see you now, my lady."

Reanna stood. "Thank you, Ruperton." She attempted to produce a smile, but knew it didn't truly appear.

Swallowing hard, she walked into the study, not knowing what to expect.

The first thing she saw was his mistress leaning on the desk next to Killian. Maybe she should have expected the witch, but humiliation flooded Reanna nevertheless. Her feet stopped, and they almost turned on their own accord to carry her out the door.

Remember the children.

She froze, planting herself firmly in the middle of the room.

Remember the children.

That one mantra had gotten her through the ride to Holloton this morning, through the front door, and through the last hour of waiting. She needed to hold onto it.

Killian stared at her, waiting. Reanna could not see what he was thinking, but then again, she realized, it turned out she never could.

"I will be taking the children back to London," Reanna finally spat out, her voice not nearly as solid as she would have liked.

"And this concerns me how?" His voice was calm, almost pleasant.

Reanna's guard went up. Best to get to the point. "I would like a coach and several horses to travel with, and money for lodging and food."

A harsh laugh bellowed out of Killian as he leaned back in his chair behind the desk. The witch joined in. His laugh quickly ceased, but his mistress's high-pitched cackle continued on, echoing in the room. He shook his head. "Why, after your display yesterday, would I give you those things? Much less, any more of my time?"

Reanna's neck flushed in rage, but she shoved it down.

Remember the children.

Her words came out cool and detached. "I ask it not for me, but for the children. Some are too young to walk, and some, just barely. The trip cannot be made on foot with so many little ones."

"That is all well and good, but what does the misfortune of several children have to do with your embarrassing display yesterday? Was that at all appropriate behavior for a marchioness?"

So that was it. He wanted an apology. Reanna bit her tongue at what she wanted to say.

Remember the children.

Her stomach curdled as she mustered up words. "No, it was not appropriate behavior. I apologize if I ruined your dining."

The red-haired witch laughed. "You little wench, you have no idea that you did nothing but spur Killian on."

Reanna's eyes swung to his mistress, confused.

Von Houten's lips curled into a sweet snarl, and she stood from the desk, walking around the wide mahogany to place herself directly in front of Reanna. She stood a head taller than Reanna, in another flame-red concoction that matched her hair. She leaned over Reanna, the snarl deepening.

"Quite simply, twit, Killian was a tiger after you left—you got him all rankled, and that was the best sex I have had in years. Lots of scratching. Lots of torture. For my sake, you really should come around spewing your vileness more often."

Reanna took in a visible gasp of air as she stared at the woman's mouth, watching the red lips curl, sneer, around every word.

"Don't look so shocked, bitch. Or is it—" She cackled, interrupting herself. "Hilarious. You don't have the slightest notion as to how to fuck a man properly, do you? Oh, you poor little lamb. It is a wonder he managed to bed you that once."

She looked Reanna from head to boots and shook her head in pity. "It is a shame he had to. You really do not have a lot to recommend you, do you? Not looks. Not wit. Can't even clean yourself properly."

She leaned even closer, staring at Reanna's cheek. Flicking out a sharp nail, she dragged it across Reanna's skin. She held the talon up, dirt evident under her nail. "Even now you stand there, near blubbering. A double shame he had to shackle himself to a mouse like you. You're a failure, through and through. Couldn't even give him a babe."

The witch sighed, straightening. "But suddenly, I'm bored." She looked back over her shoulder at Killian, a sudden smile on her face. "Killian, maybe she should be begging you more appropriately?"

The witch blocked Reanna's view of Killian. There was no answer from him.

Spinning, his mistress walked around the desk, and moved to sit herself in Killian's lap. She rested her chin on his shoulder, her mouth next to his ear. "Really, Killian, begging would be most appropriate."

Reanna forced herself to look at Killian's face through her watery eyes. He stared at her, still saying nothing. Reanna near doubled over.

He was going to make her do it.

The depths to which this man would go. Her husband.

Stomach twisting, Reanna's right foot came up, ready to run from the room. She fought it. Fought every muscle that screamed at her to run.

Remember the children.

Reanna sank to her knees.

She opened her mouth but could make no sound come out. She did that twice, unsuccessfully.

So she closed her eyes and pictured the children she saw last night—that moment when she first walked in—beaten, scared, no hope.

She would not let them down.

She opened her mouth a third time, and forced sound out—cracked, painful. "Killian…"

She could not get past the one word.

His sudden words startled her. "You will get a grain cart and a mule." His voice was harsh, but not the mocking tone he had mastered.

He opened his desk and rummaged about. "And ten shillings. Take it and leave." He slapped the coins on the edge of the desk.

"But Killian…"

His eyebrows rose, challenging her. "Yes?"

She shook her head, not able to speak. Getting to her feet, she forced herself to step forward and pick the few coins up. She turned and stiffly walked out of the room, chin strained upwards as she tried to afford some semblance of dignity she knew she no longer possessed.

She ignored the laughter of Killian's mistress that followed her into the hall.

Reanna continued walking, head high, until she made it to the stables. The first empty stall she found, she leaned into and retched. Humiliation washed over her, waves and waves of it. She hung onto the half-door, letting spasms wreck her body.

A warm palm went gently on her shoulder. Ike pressed a wet handkerchief into her hand. It took Reanna a long moment to compose herself enough to look up at him.

He handed her a cup of water. "We all think it's been horrible what he's done to you and the children, m'lady. I wished I could have stayed out there with the children for longer to help, but that red-haired woman has us all running ragged with her demands."

"It is all right, Ike. I understand. I am just so grateful for the help everyone was able to give. Those children are my responsibility, and I was the one who failed them."

"No, m'lady, you're wrong, if I may say. Not failing. You're doing right by those children. We all knew you would. You're a mighty fine person, m'lady."

"You do not have to say such things just to cheer me up, Ike."

"I say 'em cause I mean 'em. We all feel that same way, matter of fact."

"Thank you." Reanna was truly touched by his words. Maybe the scene with Killian had been worth it.

"I got the orders from his lordship, m'lady. But I figure there be some wiggle room in the request. I got our biggest wagon, and he said mule, but we don't got a good mule right now, so I gave you a strong horse, m'lady. One that should see you all the way to London."

The two walked out of the stables. "I loaded it up as much as I could with all the food that cook had available, and lots of blankets and the like that you'll need for the journey."

He stopped and grabbed her arm. "Are you sure about this m'lady? Maybe you could stay in that shack until he left? We would all help. Or I could sneak off and come along to London."

Reanna almost broke at his kindness. "No, Ike, you have already done more than enough. I cannot have you losing your position. You have two babies to feed at home. Plus, I need you available to help Joan should any more children appear."

Ike nodded and helped her into the wagon.

"God-speed, m'lady—we all be praying for you and the children."

"Thank you again, Ike. I will send word."

She stopped the horse halfway to the Visper's shack.

One horse and one wagon to haul eleven children to London. She had no money for lodging, nor barely enough for food and the tolls. Damn.

How could she have let this happen?

Reanna gripped the leather straps as the tears began to fall. She let herself wallow for a moment, and then, just as quickly as the tears had started, she pulled her head up and demanded they stop.

The children needed someone strong, not someone who was going to cry at every turn. She needed to be that person.

With resolve, she clicked the horse forward.

~ ~ ~

The front door clicked closed and, hearing it, Killian shoved Vivienne off his lap.

She stumbled before grabbing his desk and catching her balance. "Really Killian, was that necessary?"

Her hissing voice grated the back of his neck. He pushed away from the desk, standing, and moved to the wide window, staring out at the front of the estate. "You really are a bitch beyond compare, aren't you, Vivienne?"

"Don't be mad at me, Southfork. That was damn well why you brought me along to this god-forsaken place, and you damn well know it. You brought me here to do what you don't have stomach to do." She stalked to the sideboard and poured herself a glass of brandy, throwing it back in one swallow.

She spun to him. "And after your non-performance with me last night, it was clear you didn't have it in you to do what needed to be done. I'm surprised the twit actually believed what I said, since you haven't been able to stick your cock into me for months. So don't tell me you weren't looking for this."

"You may go, Vivienne."

"Killian, this is getting tedious." Her eyes rolled. "She's finally gone, and she's taking those brats with her—be glad you're rid of them."

"Go, Vivienne."

"I'm not done."

Killian tore his eyes off the window and looked back at his mistress. "You are done. Remove yourself."

"Fine." She stomped over to the door, then paused. "I will be upstairs if you want to go for a ride or fuck."

"You misunderstand, Viv. I am done with you. I will afford you the comfort you are used to on your journey back London. But be gone by nightfall." Killian turned his attention back to the window.

"You are a fucking waste of time, Southfork."

The door slammed on her exit.

~ ~ ~

Two hours later, Killian found himself mostly drunk, teetering on his horse, and staring down at the hunting cottage that had housed Reanna's orphanage. He didn't realize his direction when he had set out, and he had let the horse decide where it wanted to go. Before he knew it, the damn horse led him here, then stopped.

He didn't move, didn't want to go in.

Silly that he hesitated at going into the place. He hadn't even seen the children in the cottage. Vivienne had discovered them while out on a ride and demanded they be removed. He had assumed they were squatters and ordered it done. And that had been the end of it.

Or so he thought.

His head started to clear. The thick spring air funneled into his mind, cleansing the sludge of brandy. He didn't want to go in, but his body was unwilling to agree with his mind, and he got off his horse, slowly approaching the tidy cottage.

Inside, neat disarray met him. Wooden toys were strewn about, as were a few chalkboards on the wide table in the middle of the room. Several colorful fabric streamers hung from the upper rafters, and Killian noticed a pile of them on the floor in a corner. Looking up, he could see a row of beds, neatly made, in the loft area in front of the bedrooms.

It was obvious that the children had left in a hurry, taking nothing but the barest of necessities.

The air in the cottage suddenly smothering, Killian stepped out the door and jumped onto his horse. Destination in mind, this time he guided the horse.

Reaching the highest ridge in Holloton, Killian could see the main road. He sat atop his horse, watching for an hour before the wagon showed, and his eyes couldn't leave it as it trailed by.

A gaggle of young children—it was hard to tell how many from this distance—squished into the back of an open-air wagon. Two sat on the driver's perch. Behind the wagon, a young boy followed on foot. The crew was led by Reanna, hand on the reins of the horse as she walked in the front.

Killian's jaw clenched.

He watched them until they crested the far hill. They moved slowly, and just as the wagon disappeared over the hill, the little boy at the back stumbled, and tripped to one knee. He got up quickly, running to catch up to the wagon.

And then they were gone.

At that moment, Killian felt the first pang of emotion he'd had since bedding Reanna, though he only acknowledged it for a second.

What the hell had he done?

CHAPTER 10

What the hell had she done?

Reanna stared at the fire, letting it die down now that the children were asleep. Thank goodness cook—or Ike—had the sense to put a tinderbox in with the food. The journey would have been miserable without fire, even though the weather had been fortunate thus far during the trip. An occasional rain, but the spring warmth had held, except in the chilly evenings. But the children seemed to sleep well enough huddled together under the wagon, as they currently were.

The last five days had been long and hard, but the children had thought it an exciting adventure, mostly, in thanks to Thomas's conjured enthusiasm. He had made it a game for his siblings and the others from the start. An adventuring game, he called it.

Reanna stretched her feet out in front of her and realized how much they hurt. Slowly, she untied the laces and eased her tall leather riding boots off. It wasn't until the second boot came off, that the agonizing throbbing started in the first foot. She inspected her feet in the low light of the fire. Both were bleeding from blisters that covered her skin. She had only walked since they left the Visper's shack, and now her feet were paying the price.

Damn her lack of foresight again—she wasn't even wearing proper walking shoes. Then again, what were proper walking shoes for an eight-day trek to London?

Realizing the pain hadn't been as harsh when the boots were on, Reanna attempted to shove her right foot back into the boot. It didn't slide in. She gripped the edges of the leather and shoved harder.

Excruciating. But the boot was on. Doubled over, she bit back against the pain as the throbbing waves began to lessen.

When she could breathe again, she eyed the left boot and braced herself, then picked it up. It was the same, even worse because she knew the torture at hand.

Head down, still trying to catch her breath from the left foot, a voice made her jump.

"Do they hurt that bad?" A small hand went on her shoulder.

She looked up to see Thomas standing by her side, his face crumpled with concern.

"What do you mean? Does what hurt?"

"Your feet. I saw them when you took the boots off. You're crying."

Surprised, Reanna touched her cheek only to find it was wet. She quickly rubbed her face with her palms. "No, no, they don't hurt at all. You should be asleep."

He shrugged.

"Here, sit down." She tugged his wrist downward until Thomas sat beside her. Reanna tucked him under her arm, his head on her chest.

"Why did he not like us?"

"Why did who not like you?" Reanna played dumb, hoping to not have to come up with an answer.

"The marquess. He doesn't like us much. Does he like you?"

Reanna stifled a bitter laugh. "No, he does not like me. Not at all."

"Why not? I like you."

Reanna frowned, staring at the fire. "I honestly do not know why he does not like me, Thomas. I wish I did know."

"Is that why he doesn't like us either?"

"Probably. I am afraid one bleeds into the other."

"Do you think he likes anyone?"

The vision of Killian's mistress, spewing cruelty, flew into Reanna's mind. She shrugged. "I guess he likes some people. People who are more like him, I suppose."

"Hmmm. That's too bad."

"Why?"

"I think if he liked you, he would like more people too. Then maybe he'd like us."

Her arm tightened around him. "Maybe, Thomas. Maybe."

They sat in silence for a few minutes. Reanna thought Thomas had fallen asleep, but when she moved to lay him back, his voice came out, thick with near-sleep. "How much longer will it take us, Lady Ana? The kids are getting tired and kind of scared that we're not there yet."

There was no use in easing the truth. "I think three days, maybe more."

"That's not too bad. They'll be happy to hear it."

"Good, now get some sleep." She grabbed the small blanket next to her and folded it, bundling it up and putting it between Thomas's head and the cold ground.

Midmorning the next day, with Thomas leading the horse, the group was working through a long stretch of the rough road in the middle of thick woods. Reanna was at the back of the wagon, walking along, singing Jeannie's favorite song for the lot of the younger ones for the fiftieth time that day.

Eyes on the youngest ones, her feet didn't stop when the wagon did, and she smacked into the low plank of wood across the back.

Hitting her stomach, it took her breath away, and it was several moments before she could swallow air. She looked up, only to see exactly why the wagon had stopped so abruptly.

Highway-men.

And one had a pistol aimed at Thomas.

Reanna ran, stumbling to the front, diving in between Thomas and the two men, high on horseback. "No. Stop." Her hands flew up, palms wide as she tried to shield not only Thomas, but the entire lot of children behind her.

"We be takin' what money ye got, ducky," the shorter one without the pistol said, jumping off his horse and approaching her.

"What?" Reanna blinked hard, not quite believing what was happening.

"Yer money, ducky. It be ours now. Hand it over." He approached her, pulling a knife from his waistband.

"No. But, what? I have no money. And the children."

"How ye be payin' the tolls without coin? Ye have some, that's sure."

He moved within swinging distance.

Reanna looked over her shoulder, praying for another traveler to show on the road. It remained empty. And now she had the wagon full of children crying behind her.

"No. Only a few shillings left." Reanna shook her head. "I swear, we have nothing."

"We be takin' yer horse, then. We can get a might bit fer it."

"What? No." Reanna stepped sideways, trying to block his path to the horse. "You cannot. How will we get to London?"

"Not me problem, ducky." He stepped around her, moving to the hitching on the horse.

"They can't take our horse, Lady Ana." Thomas poked her in the back.

The short one stopped, his hand on the horse, and looked at Reanna. "Lady, eh? Ye be lyin' 'bout the coin, then." He took a step back toward her.

"I am not lying." Reanna looked frantically at the man on the horse, then back to the one in front of her. "All you see is all I have with me."

"Horse will be fine, then, ducky." He went back to unhitching the horse.

Reanna's mind flew. Dammit. She needed that horse to get them anywhere. She had nothing to defend them. Nothing. Except…

Quietly, she turned to Thomas, putting her face in front of him. The horse's reins still in his hands, he stared at her, watching her as if she was daft, but he stayed silent. That was all she needed. After a moment, she moved her mouth to his ear, her head shaking.

"Hush. No, Thomas, I don't think they are the worst." Her loud whisper gained a notch. "I think we can do better."

The short robber in front of her turned, his eyes narrowing in suspicion. "What? What ye say?"

Reanna stood straight, setting herself in front of Thomas. "Nothing."

He stepped at her, waving the knife in her face. "Tell me what ye say."

Reanna's hand went up as she leaned away from the knife, but her feet stayed solid in front of Thomas. "Please, it was nothing. I just said I don't think you are the worst thieves we will encounter. I was hoping to hire the deadliest ones to escort us safely to London, and Thomas just suggested you two."

"We not be the deadliest? Course we be the deadliest." He looked genuinely insulted, but didn't lower the knife. "And the biggest. And where ye gonna get the coin for that, lady?"

Reanna shrugged, nonchalant, praying that her pounding heartbeat wasn't making sound outside of her own head. "In London. I can access my funds there. Just because I do not have money with me, does not mean I do not have money in town."

The knife lowered, and he crossed his arms over his chest, glaring at her. "What ye be payin?"

"No." Reanna shook her head. "You two take the horse and let us be on our way, if you please."

"How much?"

"Ten guineas. But I think we can do better."

"Ye can't, lady." He scoffed, pointing up and down the road with the tip of his knife. "We run this road from here to London. Ain't no others ye gonna hire. We be it. And we be happy to take your ten guineas."

"We would?" The tall, skinny robber still on his horse eyed his partner.

"We would. If'in you got the coin fer real."

Reanna sighed. "I do, for why else would I bother to be taking care of this many children? But it does not seem as if escorting us will fit your schedule. You seem to be in a hurry, and we move quite slowly."

"It fits our schedule just fine, lady. Ye have us, or no one."

Reanna looked around, undecided. Finally, with another sigh, she looked at the tall one. "Very well. You two will have to do. I will pay you when we arrive safely at my solicitor's establishment. But you will have to put away the pistol and knife. I will not have the children scared."

Tucking the knife back into his waistband, the short one turned to the horse, re-tightening the hitching. He pointed at Reanna. "Git those squabblers back there down fer movin, ducky. We have coin to collect."

Reanna let out an unperceivable sigh of extreme relief as she walked past him to the children, hiding a smile threatening her face.

She clapped her hands. "Sit, sit children. We are moving again."

The short man went to get on his horse, and he nudged the animal to trail Reanna at the back of the wagon. The skinny robber remained in the front and started down the road. Thomas pulled on the reins he was holding, and the wagon started forward again.

Reanna looked over her shoulder at the short one. "Thank you, good sir, for your assistance."

"We ain't good sirs, ducky. Don't go gittin thoughts on that."

Reanna smiled warmly at him. "Yes, well, you are now gainfully employed. I will speak to you with the respect you deserve."

~ ~ ~

Waiting, Reanna stood on the top step, staring at the dark red door of the house that swallowed a whole London block. Taking a deep breath, she shifted from one foot to the other in order to even the shards of pain in her feet.

After the stop at her aunt's solicitor, and her payment to "Shorty" and "Tally"—as the children had dubbed the highwaymen, since they had never shared their names—she had stopped by Killian's townhouse. She had found Miss Melby there, who had been in near hysterics over Reanna's whereabouts.

Bringing Miss Melby with her to her aunt's Brook Street home, they had spent a whirlwind week of hiring staff and nannies, and setting up the household.

The dark red door opened in front of her, and Reanna was shown into an impeccably decorated drawing room that still managed to be cozy in its elegance.

"Reanna. Wonderful. It is you. I was hoping I heard Wilford correctly. For I would certainly not see most anyone in this state. Forgive me for not standing. Come in, come in."

The voice of her friend—Reanna's only friend, truth be told—floated up. There had been plenty of acquaintances through her aunt during her stay in London, but only one person Reanna had actually felt she could sincerely call a friend, the Duchess of Dunway.

Reanna searched the room, her eyes eventually landing on the back of the long moss-colored sofa in front of her. The duchess's head popped out above the carved wood top of the furniture. Then her hand came up, waving Reanna in.

Reanna walked into the room and around to the front of the sofa, only to see the duchess half-lying on a wall of pillows, feet propped up on the sofa, and an open book resting on her huge mound of a belly.

All anxiety in the pit of Reanna's stomach dissipated when she saw the duchess's smiling face. Reanna had often wondered during the months in Holloton if their friendship had remained intact, for the duchess was married to Killian's best friend.

"You. You are pregnant."

"What? Why, yes. Of course. I thought you knew," Aggie said. "Did you not receive the letters I sent?"

"Letters?" Reanna paused, eyebrows collapsing in confusion. "I received no letters at Holloton."

"None?"

Reanna shook her head.

"None at all?"

"I am afraid not."

For a moment, Reanna thought she saw a flash of annoyed anger in Aggie's eyes, although it didn't seem to be directed at her. But then Aggie waved it off with a bright smile. "Well, no bother. You have just discovered the most important news I had with your very own eyes, and I am delighted to see you. Sit, please."

Reanna moved to the chair by her friend's head. "When is the babe due? You look…"

"Huge?"

Aggie laughed, and it was the dry, throaty laugh that had always warmed Reanna's soul. She had missed that laugh.

"Thank you for holding back the analysis, but it is true. I am huge. The midwife says the babe should be born anytime now. And I have been stuck on this sofa or in bed for weeks. Devin will not let me out of the house." Aggie shifted on the pillows so she could see Reanna more directly. "But enough about me. How long have you been back?"

"About a week."

"A week? You have been hiding yourself away from me. Why on earth did you not call or at least leave a card? I would say that I have due right to be upset at you, if I was not so happy to see you. I have been so worried about you. Up at Holloton by yourself," her nose wrinkled, "is no place to be."

Reanna relaxed on the chair. It was the first time in more than a fortnight that she had sat without a child in her lap, and the two minutes with Aggie had already lifted her spirits. "You do not know how good it is to see you, Aggie. I apologize for not calling sooner, it has been a frantic week at my aunt's home since we arrived."

"Your aunt's home?" She stopped, eyeing Reanna. "Killian did not come into London with you?"

"No."

"And you are not staying at his townhouse?"

"There is no reason for me to be." Reanna's head went down slightly.

"Is it really that bad between the two of you?"

Reanna looked back up, coldly determined. "It is, but it is of no consequence. Truly. I have put that behind me."

Aggie frowned. "I am sorry to hear that—for Killian's sake. But I will not pry."

"Thank you."

"Let us change the subject." Aggie turned bright. "First, please pour some tea for yourself. I would do it, but once I get into the wedges I have ground into this sofa, I have a hard time getting out."

Reanna laughed and leaned forward to the tea set in front of her. "Would you like a fresh spot?"

"No—yes. It is a blend that is supposed to spur the babe into making an appearance, and I have been drinking copious amounts of it. Too much so, but I am willing to keep trying."

Reanna handed her the tea, and Aggie moved the book off her round belly and set the cup and saucer in its place.

"So tell me," Aggie said. "What has been so frantic at your aunt's home?"

Reanna took a sip of her tea, wondering where to start the tale, and how much too actually share with Aggie.

"It is an odd chain of events, but up at Holloton, I met a little boy, Thomas, when I was out on a ride."

"You learned to ride? Good for you."

Reanna smiled. Holloton had been good for many things, she had to admit. "So the boy, Thomas, was poaching from Killian's land. You can imagine how horrified he was at being caught. But it turned out that his mother had died, and his father was long gone, so that left him to take care of five younger siblings. Can you imagine?"

Aggie shook her head, rubbing her belly below the saucer.

"Yes, and he is only nine years old. So I went back with him to his house, and convinced him to bring his brothers and sisters and stay on the estate. Things just evolved from there, and before

I knew it, I was running an orphanage in one of the old hunting cottages on the estate."

"How fantastic."

"Yes, it was. Until…" Reanna took another sip of her tea, hiding her eyes.

"Until what?"

Reanna took a deep breath, hedging, and placed her tea-cup and saucer on the small table.

"I do not want to know, do I?" Aggie asked. "So you better tell me right now."

"Until Killian arrived. He sent me back to London, I had left, and then the next day he had them removed from the estate."

"He what?" Aggie jerked, sending the cup and saucer to the floor, tea flying, as she clawed her way upright. "He kicked out orphans? Children?"

Aggie's face flooded bright pink as her feet hit the floor and she leveraged her hands behind her back to move her belly upward. "The bloody ass—really—orphans? I mean Killian can be a bugger—but orphans? That is beyond low. He is going to pay. I am getting Devin."

Reanna grabbed her wrist. "No, sit, sit down, Aggie. Lie back. It is over and done and we are all right. We are all here in London now, safe and settled—all the children—and I will not be uprooting them again."

Reanna could see the anger throbbing in Aggie's neck, and she immediately regretted sharing Killian's contribution to the story. "Please, sit. It is not worth your energy, and I do not plan to get into trouble with the duke if he were to see you in this state—this upset."

Aggie sank back onto the sofa. Her face still glowed pink, but the throbbing in her neck lessened. "Fine. I will deal with Southfork at another time. Bastard." She grabbed a green-tussled pillow and tucked it behind her lower back, punching it in the process. "So you are here with the children at your aunt's home?"

"Yes. My home now, actually. It was a gift from her after the wedding. The house and a monthly stipend are in a trust for me. I had thought never to need either of them, but she was very right, and I was very wrong."

"How many are there?"

"Eleven from Holloton, and I am not quite sure how it happened, but we picked up two more on our way through London to my aunt's home. And another two showed up on our doorstep yesterday."

"Incredible. Fifteen."

"Yes. I am going to start trying to place them in homes next week. Which brings me to one of the reasons I am here, aside from visiting with you, of course."

"Any way I can help, I am yours—as long as I can do it from this couch, of course."

Reanna smiled, grateful at the blanket generosity from her friend. "First, can you think of any good homes these children might go to? Maybe to a barren couple with good breeding, or to a couple where a solid trade could be learned? They are all such smart children and I have already started lessons with them. I want to be extremely careful with placing them, and I know so few people here in London."

Aggie nodded, enthusiasm replacing her earlier anger. "Yes. Yes. I can think of a few possibilities right off. I will start making a list today. And drafting out introductions for you, since I cannot make them in person. At least not right now."

Reanna exhaled. "Thank you, that is such a relief."

"It sounded like you had a second topic you wanted to talk about?"

"I did. I had hoped to ask for some help or guidance, but I did not know you were with child, and I do not want to stress you any more with my problems."

"Nonsense. My brain has been turned to mush by this pregnancy, so this is a nice diversion. I will actually be happy to be using my brain again."

Reanna nodded. She didn't want to admit it, didn't want to do it, but she had to. She had no other options. "My aunt was generous with the monthly stipend she set up for me, but the trust is tightly monitored and the money only available monthly."

"And?"

Reanna took a deep breath. "And I made such a mess. I spent it all. I had to pay the men who accompanied us to London. I sent some back up to the nanny at Holloton, and then I had no idea how much money it would take to set up a household, and feed fifteen children, and get them new clothes, and pay the nannies and the maids and the cook. I do not know what I am doing, and I am weeks away from the next installment."

"Breathe." Aggie reached out, grabbing her hand. "Come now. Breathe. We can figure this out. I am more than happy to get you whatever funds you need."

Reanna silently thanked her friend for not mentioning Killian's name when she explained about the lack of funds available to her. There was supposed to be pin money per the marriage contract, but Reanna had no idea how to access it, or if it even really existed. "Truly? You must believe I would not ask if it was not necessary. And I will be approaching some of my aunt's acquaintances to see if they would be willing to help out in some fashion."

"No."

Reanna blinked hard at Aggie's outburst. "No?"

"No. I am sorry," Aggie said. "I did not mean to yell like that. There is no need to ask anyone else for anything. Anything extra you need, please come to me first. I will take care of everything you or the children need."

"You will? Aggie, that is too generous, but I—"

"No. Just come to me, or the duke. All right?"

Reanna nodded. She had no idea what she did wrong, but it was clear by Aggie's face she had made some grievous error.

"Good. Now, did you go to anyone else with your request?"

Reanna shrugged. "I did visit with two of my aunt's friends that live nearby. They managed a bit for me."

Aggie bit her lip, shaking her head. "No. That will not do. You need to revisit them and let them know that all your needs are being met."

"I am sorry, did I do something wrong?"

"You did everything right, Reanna. Right by those children. But let us keep it between us for now, is that all right?"

"Yes. I guess that is fine. I am overwhelmed by your generosity. I will try to be very careful with the donation. I have been trying, but I am afraid I am not very good at tracking the money."

Aggie patted her hand. "Excellent. That is somewhere else I can help. When I had to take care of my family's estate when my brother was missing, I struggled through the hard documents— the investments—but keeping track of the daily finances, that part was easy. We just need to write down everything coming in and everything going out. It truly is that easy. Know what you are dealing with, and deal with it."

"Aggie, all your help, are you sure? You have already offered more than enough."

"Positive. And if I have my way, this will end up very well for all involved." Aggie smiled. "You have gotten me excited. I am going to draw up some lists right away. And you must come tomorrow. Bring what you know of your finances so we can start on that, and then we will also tackle a list of possible couples." She rubbed her belly. "Assuming, of course, the babe does not decide to make an appearance. I need to stop drinking that tea."

Reanna laughed as she stood. "Aggie, truly, a thousand times thank you." Her voice turned serious. "I was not sure that you... that you would still see me. Still want to be my friend. I know how close Killian is with the duke—"

Aggie wasted no time in interrupting her. "No, not another word. I consider you a good friend, Reanna, and would not let anything or anyone infringe upon that."

"Thank you, it means much to me. I look forward to tomorrow." Reanna started to the door of the room.

"Oh, and Reanna, if I may say so..."

She stopped and turned back to Aggie. "You may, whatever."

"Your husband has been a fool beyond compare, and I am extremely disappointed in his behavior. That is all."

She smiled, and it warmed Reanna's heart. She had a friend again.

CHAPTER 11

"This had better be good, Aggie." Killian strode into the drawing room at the duke's townhouse. "Dragging me out of the countryside edges on the extreme."

"It is." Not glancing up at him, Aggie's eyes were focused on a set of papers strewn before her on a low table. After a moment, she tore her eyes upward and leaned back on the sofa, ten fingernails scratching her protruding belly in sweeping circles. "Do you think I want to do anything right now in this state?"

Killian's eyes flashed over the mound of her belly under her shapeless blue dress. She had gotten awkwardly large in the month since he had last seen her.

"No. I do not suppose you do."

"I already caught Devin's wrath for going out the other day, which is why you are here, instead of us coming up to Holloton to talk to you."

"What is so important?"

"Your wife."

"My wife?" Killian gave her sharp look.

Closing her eyes, Aggie's palms flattened hard onto her belly, and she swallowed a few shallow breaths.

"Do I need to fetch Devin?"

Aggie shook her head, eyes still closed. After three more deep breaths, she opened her eyes.

"You actually just missed Reanna. She just left here."

Killian ran to the door.

Aggie's voice followed him out into the hall. "Her hack is parked two blocks west."

On the street, Killian immediately spied the back of Reanna's dark hair pinned up in a heavy chignon. She was walking away, a block and a half in front of him. Killian started to run, willing her to slow down. And then, remarkably she did, almost coming to a stop.

He sped up, and five steps before he reached her, she stepped forward onto the road—right into the path of a pair of horses and curricle barreling down the street.

Killian's heart stopped. Didn't she see the carriage bearing down?

The horses veered to avoid her, and Killian bolted. He lunged, catching her arm and jerking her back and off her feet just before the curricle crushed her.

Killian bent over with his hands on his knees, catching his breath as he stared down at her.

Sitting on the ground, she looked up at him from the side of the street, dazed. "Where did you come from?"

The horses reared as the man driving the curricle jerked to a stop and jumped to the street. He ran back to Reanna.

"Miss, I am so sorry." He reached down and grabbed Reanna's upper arm and pulled her to her feet. His other hand went to her shoulder, trying to steady her. "My deepest apologies—oh, Miss Halstead, it is you."

She looked up at him, eyes hazy. "What…"

"Miss Halstead, I am dutifully embarrassed. These new horses of mine are hard to keep on track and when I took the corner—are you all right?"

She looked up at the man, eyes not focusing on him as he inadvertently shook her body during his explanation. She seemed to be concentrating on his flashing front gold tooth. "I—I seem to be fine, sir. Who are…"

The man continued to try to right her, even though she was clearly back on her feet. "Jonathan Nettle. I am an associate of your father's. We met once at your father's estate in Suffolk. I did not realize your father sent you to London. He had indicated otherwise."

Reanna shook her head, eyebrows scrunched as she looked up at him between the shakes.

"I understand the shock. I really am so sorry, Miss Halstead, I knew I never should have taken the horses out in the busy streets until I had right control over them, but they just got away from me—I really do not know how I will be able to make this up to your kind self. I really am so very sorry—"

Killian jerked Reanna back out of the man's clutches. "You can start by taking your groping hands off my wife." The growl was more than evident in his voice.

"Your, your...wife?" His eyes darted to Killian, and the sudden flood of whiteness on Nettle's face contrasted against his front gold tooth.

"Do all of us a favor, leave and get those devil horses off the streets."

The man backed away. "Again, my deepest apologies, Miss Halstead."

"Go." The word from Killian was not to be denied.

The man hustled into his curricle and the horses trotted, now in control, down the street.

Killian's fingers still tight around her upper arm, he spun Reanna around, shaking her. "What the hell is going on, Reanna—you almost got yourself killed."

Head rolling at the shake, Reanna steadied herself and looked up at him, blue eyes glassy, then out to the street at the passing carriages. "Oh."

"You know that man?"

She looked over her shoulder at where the curricle had disappeared, shrugging. Her eyes closed, and after a moment, she shook herself. The blue in her eyes looked clearer when she opened them. "Thank you, my lord. I am surprised you bothered to stop that."

"Why would I not care whether you got mangled by a carriage, Reanna?"

She closed her eyes again, and Killian watched her features twitch as she took several breaths. She looked gaunt. "Please let me go." She didn't try to remove her arms from his grip.

"Reanna, look at me. You need to listen to me."

She opened her eyes again, and there was a coldness in the blue that matched her voice. "Have you not said enough to me? Have you not done enough to me? Let me go." She didn't pull her arms away, just coolly challenged him with her eyes.

Killian let his fingers loosen.

Arm free, she turned from him, looked both ways in the street, and crossed to the waiting hack. Killian watched it amble down the cobblestones.

What the hell was that? And where the hell was she going? For that matter, where the hell was she staying? He knew it wasn't at his townhouse.

He spun around, setting back to Devin's townhouse and Aggie.

"What the hell is going on around here, Aggie?" Killian started before his feet were in the drawing room. "Devin sends me an urgent message about me being in financial straits. And then my wife shows up here. What is going on?"

The duchess hadn't moved from her spot on the sofa, but the strewn papers were now neatly stacked in front of her. "Excellent. You actually want to listen to me now, instead of grumbling at me?"

"Where is Devin? He was the one that sent word that I am in financial straits?"

"He is at the shipping company's offices. But he did not send word. I mean, he did, but he did so at my request. I actually know why you are in financial straits. And Devin wanted me to explain."

Killian shook his head, trying to follow the madcap logic. "You do? And?"

"You are not in financial straits. Not really. Do not worry on that. But the gossips will be wagging soon. People are speculating you have lost your fortune."

"What? Why?"

"Killian, sit. You are making me nervous standing there agitated like that." She waved her hand at the wingback chair next to him.

The last thing he wanted to do was sit, but he also wanted to rush Aggie along. He bent to the edge of the chair.

"Thank you. First off, your fortune. It is one of the two things I need to tell you about your wife."

"My wife?"

"Yes, your wife. She called on me several days ago and mentioned she had approached several acquaintances of her aunt's for donations to support the orphan home she has set up at her aunt's residence."

Killian jumped up. "She what? She brought them here?"

"Yes. You heard me. And then asked for donations. She did it discreetly, approached only ladies, but it happened nonetheless. I know I do not have to tell you what that is doing to your reputation. And the last thing you need is people gossiping about how the Marquess of Southfork cannot afford to feed a few stray mouths."

"Bloody hell." Killian slammed a fist into his thigh.

"Yes, well, it is your own doing, so I would cap that misplaced anger you are displaying right now. I had her re-approach the ladies to tell them the finances were all worked out and that she had been mistaken. So this should fade soon enough."

Aggie paused, rubbing her forehead, and then she looked him straight on, her green eyes cutting to his soul. "Did you truly kick her out of Holloton with the children, Killian?"

Killian's jaw clamped closed. He had. And Aggie knew about it.

It was all she needed to see, and she rubbed her forehead again, hissing a disappointed sigh with the shake of her head.

"Two things. You said two things, Aggie. What is the second?"

Aggie avoided looking at him, and he could see she didn't want to continue.

"What is it, Aggie?"

"She is in pain."

"Pain? What?"

"I am not sure. But she has been here several days in a row, and when she stands, she tries to hide it, but I see it. It is physical pain. I have hidden a lot of pain in my day, so I know what it looks like. Something is not right in how she is moving. Walking."

"Hell."

"I do not want to ask this, Killian, but did you do something to her?"

Killian sighed, his eyes going to the front window of the drawing room. A clock in the corner ticked seconds by. Aggie was going to wait this one out.

Killian shook his head. "No…yes. Not what you are thinking, though. I did not touch her."

"What did you do?"

"I sent her back to London on her own."

"And?"

"With the orphans. And a cart and a mule."

"You what?" Aggie heaved herself forward, starting to move to her feet, then sat back down, eyes closed, hands on her belly once more. Her eyes clamped closed. "She didn't tell me that. Hell, Killian. Anything could have happened to her, you know."

"I am aware. I did not think she would make it far from Holloton. I thought it a lesson for her rudeness."

"*Her* rudeness? Do I even need to counter that statement?"

Killian shook his head. "I have been scouring the countryside trying to find her and the kids since she left. I never imagined she would actually make it far, much less to London."

Aggie cracked her eyes open at him. "A cart and a mule?"

"My stable master overrode me and gave her a horse instead of a mule."

"That matters?"

Killian shrugged. "But how in the hell did she get from Holloton to London with all those children?"

Aggie closed her eyes again, shaking her head. "Reanna has depths you have no idea exist, Killian. Depths you cannot even imagine."

Killian stood, silent, head bent, properly chagrinned.

"Did you see her outside?"

"Yes."

"And?"

"She hates me."

"Understandable. She has every right to that notion. Really, Killian? Booting orphans? That is the lowest thing I can even imagine. It is a wonder that I do not hate you."

The hands rubbing her belly sped up. "You are only lucky that Devin still believes in you, because without him, I would have given you up for a deep hell a long time ago. He has hope for you, and as he is not always the most optimistic type, I am going along with it for now. But you had better damn well start fixing this mess, Killian."

"Why do you think I am here?"

She took a deep breath, nodding. "Excellent. I am not up for one of our 'discussions.' You have been aimless for months, now. And I was getting worried. Devin as well. You need to make this right, Killian."

"I do not know if I can. I am pretty sure it is too late."

"No. You can." Her voice softened. "It is never too late."

"How? I have done the unforgivable. Things you know nothing of. There is no path to recover."

"Nonsense." Aggie waved a hand. "You beg forgiveness, and then you rebuild her. Moment by moment. Word by word. Make this right, Killian. Make this right."

CHAPTER 12

"Where is Lady Southfork?" Killian peered into the dim light in the entrance at Reanna's aunt's townhouse. He had just spent the last four hours talking with Devin, planning how to mitigate the rumors of his lost fortune. It would force sizable, showy investments in areas he would rather not, and the whole of it had only stoked his anger at Reanna for what she had done.

Gone begging. His wife.

"Sir, I'm afraid I can't help you. The household be asleep." The middle-aged woman stared him in the eye. A good three heads shorter than he was, she stood before him in the doorway, blocking his way with her considerable girth. A battle ram that wasn't moving.

"Good lady, I will not repeat myself again. Where is my *wife?*"

That got her. As she started sputtering, Killian slid past her and advanced onto the staircase.

"Your wife?" She reached after him, but Killian easily stepped out of her grasp. "If you mean to say you're the marquess, well, you've got a whole different problem coming your way, young sir."

Killian bolted up the stairs and hit the first landing. He stalked down the hall, opening doors and ignoring the maid that was puffing up the steps, spouting threats after him.

The first door—kids. The second door—kids. What should have been the main chamber—kids. Killian went through five doors on the floor and only found children nestled cozily in beds.

He took the steps three at a time to the next floor and repeated the process. Only children.

Patience at an endpoint, he stopped by a wall lantern and turned back toward the graying woman, who had finally caught up to him. "Where the hell is she?"

Hand on her hip, her finger flew out at him. "She is nowhere you need to know about, sir." But then the woman couldn't stop her eyes from flickering upwards.

Killian didn't miss the motion.

"What? She's hiding in the servants's quarters from me?" He stormed past the lady and went up another flight of stairs.

"Sir, please do be quiet." She rushed up after him, not ceasing her bickering as she heaved herself up the stairs. "There be children sleeping at this time of night."

"I am only interested in one child at the moment, Miss... Miss..."

"Collier."

"Miss Collier." Killian reached the next hallway of doors and began slamming them open. More kids.

"Sir, please, the children are sleeping!"

Killian whipped to the lady. "Tell me where the hell she is and I will let the children sleep."

Miss Collier shut her mouth. Not giving him anything. Stubborn wench.

Killian turned to the last two unchecked doors on this floor. The first one—children. The second, he opened, and the blackness caused him to take a moment, waiting for his eyes to adjust. He stepped into the room.

There, lying on the blankets of a tiny bed under the low-pitched ceiling, was Reanna. On her stomach, she wore only a flimsy white chemise that had fallen up to mid-thigh. A crack of moonlight filtered in through the slit of a window, landing on her hair that spread out in a dark halo above her.

Killian didn't think it was possible, but all of his anger dissipated in that one second.

His eyes searched down the lines of her body, until he reached the top of her calves. She was wearing boots. In bed.

What was going on here? She was in the smallest room in the
house, sleeping near naked, save for her thin chemise and boots.

"Sir, I must demand of you, please don't go any further."

Killian looked back at Miss Collier, who was now not
barking orders, but pleading in a whisper.

"Is she all right?"

"Please, your lordship, come back in the morning. She will
see you then, I'm sure of it." She had grasped Killian's arm, and
was tugging him back out of the room. "Just please, don't go any
farther. Don't wake her up."

The sudden change in the woman's attitude made Killian
take the few steps toward the exit. Once in the hallway, the
woman reached past him to quickly close the door.

"I repeat my question." Killian looked down at her. "Is she all
right?"

Miss Collier motioned for him to follow her to the stairs.
Killian followed.

"She is fine. As fine as a woman who's working herself to
death can be, I suppose. She don't sleep none."

"Working herself to death?"

"Ever since she set this place up and hired me. That's all I
seen." She began down the stairs. "Lady Ana has been trying
to place children, and more keep showing up. On top of her
running all the house, and the money, she spends every other
moment taking care of the poor souls. 'Specially at night. One or
two or more are usually crying. I don't think she eats. When we
finally force her to bed, she makes herself get up a few hours later.
I've not seen her sleep for more than three hours in a spell."

Killian followed her down the stairs. "How long has this
been going on?"

"It's been more than a fortnight since she came here with the
lot of the children, I understand. She hired me a couple days after
setting up. The little thing's been exhausted for too long now, but
she don't stop. None of us can get her to stop."

They reached the second story landing just as a wail came
from one of the rooms. "Excuse me, your lordship, but I'm

needed. I'm sure you can show yourself out?" The hopeful look on her face was almost laughable.

"Yes, I will."

She nodded and turned away from Killian, scurrying to a door down the hall, the origin of the young cry.

"Oh, one more thing Miss Collier."

"Yes?"

"The boots. Why was she wearing the boots?"

Miss Collier shrugged her shoulders. "I'm not rightly sure, sir. It be the oddest thing. She hasn't taken them off once, near as I can tell, since I been here. When I ask, she just mumbles some nonsense." The cry cut through the air again, and Miss Collier disappeared through the door.

Killian stared back up the stairs for several long minutes. Then he turned and went down the steps to the entryway.

"It's you, ya bloody sod."

"What?" Killian spun around, and out of the shadows in the hallway above, a little boy with fists clenched, about six, looked down at him through the dark wood balusters. It was a look of hatred.

"You're the damn bloody reason. I heard Miss Collier call you 'your lordship.'"

Killian walked across the landing to see the boy closer. "And just what, am I the 'damn bloody reason' for, young man?"

"She don't take her boots off 'cause of you."

"What?" Killian's hand ran through his hair. Had he walked into a mad house?

"They're too bloody. I saw them halfway back."

"What? Hold on." Killian came up the stairs to the boy. "Now what? The boots are bloody?"

The hatred in the boy's eyes didn't lessen, and Killian wondered if he was going to get hit. Instead, the boy answered him. "Yep. Bloody. Her feet. On our way here. She shoved 'em back on—those boots—when she thought we were asleep. But I saw by the fire. She cried. It made me cry."

Killian knelt down so he was eye level with the boy.

"Why was she crying?"

"I guess 'cause they hurt so bad. She made me ride on the horse sometimes, even though I should have walked too. Thomas walked, so I should have too, 'cause I'm the next oldest boy. So my feet are fine. But she walked and never rode. Kept saying she had to be down to lead the horse or take care of us. Just them two took care of us. Thomas 'cause he's oldest and her because she's the grown up."

His little fists were still balled at his sides. "She told me not to blame you, but I do. I know you're the bloody sod who made us leave—and made her walk the whole way."

The little boy had worked himself into such anger, Killian actually did expect that he was about to get punched.

"Well, I am sorry you had to walk to London."

Just like that, his fists un-balled and he shrugged. "It don't bother me much. Like I said, I got to ride some. It's Lady Ana the one who's hurting. We all worried about her."

"I am sure you are." Killian stood up. "Thank you, young man—"

"Albert. I'm Albert." He looked upward. "You going back up there?"

Killian could see the boy didn't like that prospect very much. "Yes."

"Lady Ana not gonna like that."

"No, I don't suppose she is." Killian pointed down the hall. "Back to your room, young man."

To Killian's surprise, the boy listened and spun to go into the room closest to them.

Killian leaned on the banister, taking a deep breath, and then exhaled it with the hope that it could take all of his idiocy with it.

What the hell had he done?

With another deep breath, he went to the stairs and up two levels.

Opening the rickety door, Killian stepped quietly into the room, and seeing a lantern on a short dresser, he went over to it, lit it, and turned up the wick for the smallest flame.

Even in the small bed, Reanna looked tiny. She had shifted in her sleep, and was now on her side, facing the wall, balled tightly, her knees to her chest.

His head wedged under a rafter, Killian watched her for minutes, watched her bare arm quiver with every uneven breath she took.

What the hell could he even say to her? What now?

Nerve finally worked up, he went across the room and put his hand on her bare shoulder. It was a light touch, but she jerked awake, turning toward him, murmuring. "What, is it? The babies?"

And then her eyes caught his face.

"Oh, god no." She shoved at his hand. "God, no. No. Not you. Don't touch me."

He tried to move his hand to her shoulder again. "Reanna, I am not going to hurt you."

His touch sent her flailing, screaming as she pushed back into the wall away from him, boots clawing on the bed to hide herself. "No. Stop. Not you. No. Don't touch me. God no. Not you."

Bent over Reanna, trying to calm her, Killian heard the whoosh of air just before a line of wood cracked him across the back.

Pain lashed his spine, and he spun, hand instantly on the wooden broom handle that had just smashed onto his back.

He ripped the stick into his hands, shoving, wood across neck, and pinned his attacker to the wall.

"Stop. Killian. No. It's Thomas." Reanna screeched. "Stop. Killian. Stop."

She scrambled off the bed.

"Stop. Killian. He's just a boy. Stop."

In the initial flurry, it took a moment for Killian to realize Reanna had fallen and was dragging herself across the floor.

She grabbed his ankle, desperately yanking on him.

"Killian, stop. Please don't hurt him. He's just a boy, Killian. Stop."

Killian's eyes flew up from Reanna and focused on his attacker. It was a boy. Probably not even ten years old.

Killian dropped the handle from his neck. "Get the hell out of here."

The boy coughed and grabbed at the stick, trying to wrestle it back. "No. You let Lady Ana go. You don't touch her."

"Thomas, no. Stop." Still on the floor, Reanna pointed at the door. "Out of the room, Thomas. Out. I am fine. I was asleep and I was just surprised at being woken. I am fine. Please, Thomas. Just step out. Please."

The boy stopped, looking back and forth from Reanna to Killian, eyeing Killian like he was the muck of the Thames.

"Please, Thomas."

He tore his eyes back down to Reanna. "Okay, Lady Ana. But I will just be outside. You just yell if you need me."

"Good. Thank you, Thomas. I promise I will be sure to yell if I need help."

Thomas shuffled to the door, eyes still wary on Killian.

"Close the door on your way." Killian's voice stretched just over his rage.

Thomas slowly closed the door behind him, but left it cracked.

"All the way."

The door clicked closed.

At the sound, Reanna collapsed face down on the floor.

Killian walked across the room to turn up the wick on the lantern. He stepped back to her, his boots near her head.

"Please. Please, Killian, just go. Leave me alone. Please." Her voice floated up to him, small and cracking.

"I cannot do that, Reanna. You are in pain. I can see it."

She didn't look up at him, didn't move. Killian watched her back rise and fall in heavy breaths.

"I am fine, Killian. I do not need your help. You can leave with a clear conscience."

"I will not leave you in a huddled mess on the floor."

"Please, just go. I am fine."

"Prove it."

Finally, she looked up at him. "What?"

Fresh tears lined the grimace contorting her face. Killian found himself hoping they were just tears of physical pain, and that his very presence wouldn't produce that look.

"Prove it. Get up. Walk over to the bed, Reanna, and I will leave. That simple."

"Damn you." Her voice was a whisper. "You cannot just come in here. Come in here and hurt one of my children and order me around. No. Not after…not after…No."

Her head fell back to the floor.

"Just leave."

Killian bent down, balancing on his heels. "If you can walk back to the bed on your own, Reanna, I will leave. I promise."

Silent minutes passed, and Killian refused to move.

With a vicious growl, Reanna pushed her upper body up and went to her knees. Heaving, she shifted her right boot under her body, and shot up.

She made it two steps before falling to her knees.

So she began to crawl.

Bile hitting his throat, Killian picked her up, and her arms flew, slamming fists at him.

"Dammit, Reanna, I am not going to watch you crawl."

He set her on the bed, and she scratched away from him, fighting to the furthest corner, and then curled up in a ball facing the wall.

"Leave. Please. Just leave."

Killian watched her shaking back. Trying to not let her shake become his.

He walked backward to the door, eyes not leaving Reanna, and opened it. Stepping into the hallway, he was greeted by both Thomas and Miss Collier. Both looked like they would be happy to murder him on the spot.

Killian tried to ignore their glares. "You. Thomas, is it? Would you please go out to my driver and tell him to fetch my doctor."

Thomas's look went from anger, to moderate suspicion. "You gonna help Lady Ana?"

"Yes."

"All right, then." He spun and ran down the stairs.

Killian looked at Miss Collier. He didn't figure she would be as easy.

"I am going back in, and I would prefer not to be interrupted."

"What you prefer doesn't sound like it agrees with what Lady Ana wants. Your doc can come and tend to her, but you need to leave her alone, sir."

Killian struggled for control. Why did everyone think they could boss him around when it came to his own wife?

"She cannot walk, Miss Collier. She needs help. Real help, and this is not the place for it."

"Says who?"

"Says her husband. Frankly, Miss Collier, I am removing her from this place one way or another. But I am thinking it would be best if a scene was not made. You said yourself children were sleeping."

Miss Collier looked over her shoulder, then down the hall at the other doors. She shook her head, exasperated. "Bollocks. Fine. But the likes of you better be kind to her. Not that you have it in you."

She turned and stalked down the hall before he could reply. And better for both of them that he didn't.

He opened the door, stepping back into the room and closing the door. Reanna hadn't moved from her balled position, if anything, she looked smaller than before, shrinking into herself.

Killian went over to her and stopped at the bed. She knew he was there, he could see through the light chemise her body tense at his approach.

Killian reached down to the top of her calf, slipping his finger under the leather at the top of the boot.

She jerked away, knocking her knee into the wall. "God, don't touch them. Don't touch me. Go, Killian, just go."

Pulling his hand back to his side, Killian sighed and sat down at the foot of the bed. He gave her as much space from his body as possible, but he wanted it evident that he wasn't about to leave. Not now.

"Reanna, I have a doctor coming to help you. But your feet. Your boots." He rubbed the back of his neck. "Hell, Reanna, you walked all the goddamn way to London in them."

A coarse laugh escaped from the curl of her body. "Of course, that is what you would concentrate on. My failures never cease with you."

"Reanna—"

She craned her neck up, fire in her eyes. "Yes, I walked all the way to London. What the bloody hell did you expect me to do? Beg you again and again? I have already been on my knees before you too many times, Killian. And it did me no good. It was quite clear you were done with me. I may have failed you, but I sure as hell was not going to fail the children."

Killian's eyes didn't leave hers, even the louder she got. He would take it. Gladly. Anything but the shell of her quivering from his touch.

"We cannot do this here. There is not enough light, nor everything the doctor might need. I am taking you back to my townhouse," Killian said, voice calm.

"No." She whipped herself upright. "I will see the doctor, but here. Only here."

"Reanna, this is not going to be comfortable. Do you want the children to hear this? From what I can tell, this is going to be painful. Extremely painful."

"It already is. I can keep my mouth closed." Her arms crossed in front of her chest. "Only here."

"And if you cannot? If we are in the thick of getting these boots off, and god knows what is under there—and you cannot hold it in? What then? You screaming. What do you think that is going to do to the children?"

She shook her head, eyes going to the ceiling. "Unfair."

"Unfair or not, we both know doing this at my place is the best option."

Eyes trained on the wooden beam in the ceiling, she heaved a sigh. "Fine."

"Good." Killian stood and looked around the room. Finding her robe, he grabbed it and started to drape it across her shoulders, but she twisted and snatched it from his hands, wrapping herself.

He moved in front of the bed. "Come. I am carrying you down."

"What? No. The children. They cannot see me being carried out of here."

"Reanna, that is silly. You cannot walk. How else do you propose making it down the stairs? Besides, the children are asleep."

"Are they? Not with this noise." She pointed to the door. "Go out there and look, Killian."

Biting back a blaspheme, Killian stepped from the room into the hall.

A gaggle of eyes peered up at him. At least eight children jockeyed for position on the nearby stairs.

Killian spun back into the room, closing the door.

"They are out there, are they not?"

"Yes."

Reanna's voice turned soft. "I need to walk down, Killian. I refuse to scare them. I refuse it."

"You cannot. You could not even walk to the bed."

She swung her legs off the bed and tied her robe closed. "I can."

With a deep breath, Reanna pushed herself to standing, gasping against the pain. She teetered for a moment, and just as Killian was going to grab her arm, she solidified and held upright.

Killian stepped in front of her. "Reanna, you do not have to do this."

"Move out of my damn way, Killian. If you are making me leave, then I am doing it by my own accord. I will not scare the children." Her glare was lethal. "I will not."

Killian stepped aside.

Reanna struggled to the door, boots shuffling on the wood planks. She stopped, grabbing the door-knob, and her head fell as she took several quick breaths. When she raised her chin, a bright smile had appeared on her face.

She opened the door and walked into the hallway, her steps even and light.

"What are all of you doing up?" She clapped her hands. "You know better than to agitate Miss Collier at this time of night. Bed." She clapped her hands again. "Back to bed for all you."

The children scrambled at her words, giggling at Reanna's light scolding. Apparently, she didn't discipline them often.

She followed them down the stairs, hand gripping the railing, knuckles white. A step behind her, Killian could see her fighting for every step. Fighting the almost imperceptible hiccup her foot would do before touching a stair. Fighting the racking pain every time her toes took on her weight.

But her smile was effortless.

She took pain better than any man he knew.

It was the longest three flights of stairs Killian had ever walked.

Miss Collier waited at the main landing.

"Will you be all right here tonight, Miss Collier?" Reanna didn't slow her smooth gait. "Miss Mildred should be here early in the morning."

"I'll be fine, my lady. Don't you worry on us none." Miss Collier opened the front door, eyes glaring at Killian as they walked past.

"Excellent. Thank you so much, Miss Collier," Reanna said over her shoulder. "I shall be back tomorrow."

Miss Collier's reply was a grunt, and then she closed the door behind them.

Killian's hand instantly went to Reanna's elbow for support, but she jerked away. The jerk caused her to fall against the railing, and her feet slipped. She stumbled down several steps before she caught the railing. By then, Killian had grabbed her shoulders to hold her upright.

She didn't cry out. Just heaved a breath and grabbed the railing with two hands, pulling herself to standing. She managed to lean away from Killian's hands in the process.

Reanna stepped down the last few stairs, walking to Killian's coach. Just as his driver let down the step, Killian saw his doctor coming down the street in a phaeton. His driver gave Reanna his hand to step up into the coach, and that, she took willingly.

"I need to talk to the doctor and will be back in a moment," Killian said, leaning into the carriage.

Reanna sat ramrod straight in the coach, hands in her lap, eyes closed. She didn't acknowledge his words.

Killian ran down the street, and after a quick conversation with his doctor, he was back to the carriage.

It was empty.

He looked at his driver, who looked inside the carriage.

Surprise at the open opposite door was on his face. "I did not hear her get out, my lord, I was watching you. She didn't go back inside."

"Bloody hell." Killian ran around the coach. "Reanna. Hell. Reanna." He couldn't exactly yell for her. Not with the entire orphanage up and probably watching out the front windows.

Moonlight was his friend in searching the dark street, for a few houses down, it gave her away, huddled deep into the shadows next to a set of stairs. She hadn't gotten far.

"Dammit, Reanna." He stepped into the darkness.

He stopped in front of her, then took a moment to collect himself.

She sat, arms tight around her drawn legs, head hiding in her knees.

Killian bent, one knee in the dirt. "God, Reanna, do you hate me that much?"

There was no answer. He didn't expect one.

He wrapped his arms around her and was surprised when there was no resistance. Picking her up, Killian was shocked at how light she was. She had to have lost a quarter of her weight since their wedding night.

Halfway back to the carriage, Reanna looked up at him, and Killian's heart stopped at the utter defeat he saw in her face.

"I…I cannot get them off." Her voice was tiny. "I have tried over and over. It just hurts so much. I think with the blood and the stickiness…"

Killian swallowed hard. "We will. We will get them off, and fix you. I swear."

CHAPTER 13

Killian had his driver's brandy in hand before the coach moved, and he forced Reanna to take five healthy swallows before they had made it two blocks. By the time they reached his townhouse, Reanna was swaying, her eyes glassy.

That was good.

She didn't fight his touch when he carried her from the carriage into the house. He even felt her lean into him in a near snuggle. The wonder of pain and brandy.

Up the stairs in his townhouse, Reanna in his arms, Killian started to turn into the chambers next to his, but a pang of guilt stopped him. His mistress's things were still inside. Hell, Vivienne had decorated the rooms to her own whims. Rooms that rightfully belonged to his wife.

One more thing that needed correction.

He moved onward to his own chambers and laid Reanna on his bed. With the slightest moan, she went to her side, curling up, her shift moving upward and exposing her legs.

Killian lit several lamps for solid light, then stood by the bed, looking down at her. The damn boots. Brown leather beat to hell, flat soles with low curved heels, and both were lined at the top with dainty tassels, three on one boot, only one left on the other. Perfectly suitable for riding in fashion. Perfectly unsuitable for walking.

His forefinger set gently onto her calf above the boot, and he flicked a chunk of dried blood off the skin. Running his hand through his hair, he sat down on the bed by her waist and looked up at her closed eyes.

"Reanna."

Her eyes flew open, lazily tracking across the room as she rolled onto her back. When her eyes met his face, her lips instantly widened into a smile. "Oh. You. It is you."

Killian froze.

She pulled her hand up from the bed, her fingers touching his jaw. "Your face is…is still beautiful. Still so handsome. Warm. Rough."

She let her fingers trail up, palm on his cheek, but as quickly as the smile had appeared, it flashed away, sadness taking root. "You. You killed my heart."

She snatched her hand away and rolled back to her side.

Killian closed his eyes, shaking his head against the pain in her eyes. Against the pain he had put there, pain that tore at his chest.

He had done that. Killed her heart.

Her left foot twitched, moving the bed, and Killian ripped his eyes open. One problem at a time.

"Reanna, I am going to untie the boots."

She didn't answer him, but she did give a slight nod without looking at him. That would have to do.

As gently as he could, Killian untied the laces that ran up the front middle of her left boot, then loosened and pulled the laces free from the leather. He repeated the action on the right leg. Bits of dried blood edging the top of the boots flaked off.

"God, Reanna, how the hell did you get to London?" Killian muttered under his breath.

"I walked."

He looked up at her face. Eyes still closed, her head was half buried into the coverlet. "That was not the best plan."

"I did not have a choice, Killian. You took that away from me. Just so easy for you. Just like that. You took it away." Her voice lilted up and down, words thick.

Killian bit his tongue. He wanted to blame her. Wanted to rail at her for being so stupid as to walk all the way to London. She should have stayed close to Holloton. She shouldn't have left the area.

He didn't want this whole damn thing to be his fault.

But it was.

He cleared his throat. "I am going to try to pull the left boot off."

She went silent again. Her bottom lip slipped under her teeth as she nodded, and her fingers dug into the coverlet, gripping.

Killian took a deep breath, grabbing the short rounded heel and the toe of the left foot, and began to pull.

A scream was his instant reward. Agonized. Terrified. Reanna jerked her foot away and scrambled back on the bed, panicked by the pain. It cut through her drunken haze, and her eyes found focus on Killian.

"Goddamn you. What the hell are you doing?" Her back flat against the headboard, she pulled her feet up under her chemise.

"Reanna, I'm trying to help you," Killian said more softly than he imagined he could.

"Help? But the pain…they can stay on…" She closed her eyes, head bobbing. "Have you not done enough to me?"

Killian moved closer to her, but didn't dare touch her. "Reanna, we have to get your boots off. You are going to maim yourself if you do not let me help. We have to get them off now."

"But why? Why now? Maybe they will get better."

"You know they will not, Reanna. How long has it been since they have been off? Weeks? They need to come off."

"Why would I ever believe what you have to say?"

Killian sighed. Valid question, he had to admit. "Because I am your husband."

She gave a half laugh, brimmed with bitterness. "Yes, and I am your wife. And that has not turned out quite so well for me."

A knock on the door interrupted Killian before he could reply, not that he had anything to say. He stood up from the bed, grateful for the interruption. "Come in."

Fifteen minutes later, Killian's doctor had examined Reanna's boot-clad feet, and after conferring with Killian, both men eyed Reanna warily from across the room.

Killian walked over to her, then sat again on the bed. "Reanna, Doctor Leiars thinks the best way to remove them is to soak your legs to loosen the scabbed blood from the leather. And then we hope we can cut the leather off in sections. He thinks this should cause the least amount of pain, but the scissors may end up slicing already bloodied areas. It might get painful."

Arms hugging herself, Reanna nodded acceptance.

"I can give you more brandy, but I think you have already had too much. The doctor has laudanum—"

"Yes."

"Good." He turned toward Leiars. "The tub is full. Shall we get started?"

It started off simple enough. Soaking the feet was fine. Reanna sat on the teak deck surrounding the copper tub, legs dangling in the warm water as the laudanum took effect.

But the second the doctor pulled her left leg from the water and started cutting the leather away, the agony started.

The soaking had not done enough to loosen the leather molded to her skin, and chunks of scabs ripped from her body with every swatch of leather.

Reanna tried to bear it, head curled into her chest, silent sobs racking her body, until halfway down her calf, the scissors sliced deep into her skin.

Pain overwhelming, she tried to escape, her silent scream cut off as she slipped down into the tub. Head almost going under, Killian grabbed her before she swallowed any water. He pulled her up, and she immediately twisted away, head over the edge of the copper tub, and threw up, her body revolting against the pain and drug and alcohol.

Spasms tore through her body, and all Killian could do was hold one hand on her shoulder, and the other flat on her back so she didn't slip deeper into the water.

When the spasms subsided, Killian got onto the teak ledge, and lifted Reanna out of the tub. He settled her in-between his legs, arms wrapped around her, her wet body on his chest.

The doctor pulled her left leg back out of the water, and restarted his removal of the boot. She didn't fight the doctor. Didn't kick at him, even though Killian could feel the agony racking her body. Feel her gasps for breath.

It was only after the first boot was fully removed, that Killian recognized the severity of what had happened.

Both men stared at Reanna's left foot in horror. Free from the binds of the leather boot, her foot pulsated in a mutated mass of blood and puss. Toes were barely recognizable.

And they still had the other boot to get off.

Killian was the first to pull out of the shock at the grotesque sight. The sharp pain momentarily ceased, Reanna silently cried in his lap. He picked her up and moved to the other side of the tub so the doctor could get her right leg up on the ledge.

He nodded at Doctor Leiars to get on with the other foot.

Killian's hand went on her wet forehead, smoothing back the hair. "You did well, Reanna. There is just one more foot to go."

The scissors slipped at that moment, and new waves of agony washed over Reanna's face, her body arching.

"Oh god, why?" Her eyes found focus on Killian above her. "Why? What did I ever do to you, Killian? What did I ever do to you?"

Her head went down as she tried to curl into a ball, her body only burrowing deeper into Killian's hold, her voice pleading. "What did I ever do to you? What did I ever do to you?" Sobs convulsed her body. "Why? What did I do?"

The sobs overtook the words.

Halfway through the second foot, she passed out.

Holding full force the pain he had created, Killian had never been more grateful for anything in his life.

~ ~ ~

Killian's forehead went hard into the palm of his hand. Elbow propped on the walnut desk in his study, he let his arm take the weight of his head as he stared at the piece of vellum in front of him. It was the last from the tall stack of papers he had pushed to the edge of the desk.

The first letters from Reanna were tear stained, ink smudged to the point half the words could not be read. The dotted intensity of the splotches on the vellum got less and less the deeper into the stack he got.

Until they disappeared altogether.

It took him hours to go through the letters.

He had never read them. Never bothered to even look at them.

And now he was staring at it.

...I can no longer afford the tears that come daily, nor the way my heart aches every morning and every evening...

He looked up, bleary eyed, and reached for the last of the brandy he had too much of since getting Reanna settled in his bed.

Taking the last swallow, he set the thick cut glass down and grabbed the last sheet. He gently laid it on top of the neat stack.

The reality of what he had done over the past year was beginning to set in, the words that were spoken, the actions that were taken. Killian was quickly beginning to hate himself for it. He had tried to ignore it. Then deny it. But it was time to accept the ruin that he had caused. Bitter though it was.

He leaned back in his chair, staring at the empty glass. His current stupor did nothing to lessen the guilt. Lessen the doom he had created.

Killian eyed the elaborately cut design on the thick glass before him. The opulent motif fit perfectly into the world he had needed to create.

But he didn't care for it. He never had.

Why had he kept something he hated for so long in his life?

He grabbed the glass, flipping it, and smashed it down, shattering it, shards cutting into his palm.

CHAPTER 14

Staring up at the dark grey canopy above, Reanna concentrated on the waves of throbbing pain in her feet, following them as they vibrated up her body, into her head, filling her ears.

At least it was steady, even. Not the unpredictable, searing, breath-stealing agony she had been hiding from the children for the last week. This pain she could deal with. This pain she had already figured out, and she welcomed it.

Between the brandy and the laudanum mangling her mind last night, Reanna hadn't known where she was. But now, in the calmness of the morning when she opened her eyes, it was obvious this was Killian's room. She had always wondered about it during their courtship. Wondered what it would be like to be immersed in the scent of him. They essence of him.

Flat on her back, her feet heavily swaddled in white linen and elevated by pillows, her eyes took in Killian's sanctum. Enormous bed, the softest silk linens surrounding her, and the room was large, with very little in it except the bed, a short desk, one chair by the fireplace, a chess set on an ottoman, and a bureau. Lots of space and air. But the oddity of the room was that it was almost completely void of color. Blacks and greys. Only the dark walnut furniture gave a hint of color, if one could count the darkest brown grain a color.

Without even moving, the first thing she knew was that her stomach was still uneven. She had never taken laudanum before, much less mixed with straight brandy. The second thing she discovered was that she was naked, only the silk coverlet keeping her warm. No wonder. From the snippets of memories she managed to grasp onto of the previous night, anything she was wearing had either been ruined by blood or the contents of her stomach.

She wondered how many times she had thrown up. She distinctly remembered retching two times. Hell, maybe it was three or four times. She cringed as dry heaving on Killian's shoulder flashed through her mind.

She pulled her hand from under the cover, touching her face and hair, loose, and still damp at the roots behind her head. There wasn't a trace of any rogue substance on her head or hair. Somehow, someone had cleaned the mess of her up.

"How is the pain?" Killian's voice cut into the open air in the room, slightly echoing.

She turned her head to the sound, only to see him walking in from the adjoining room. That was where his tub was, if she remembered correctly. He walked toward her, casually devoid of most clothes, only a loose, open white linen shirt and pants on his tall frame. His bare feet moved silently across the dark wood floors.

"The pain?" he asked again.

"Vicious."

"Should I fetch Doctor Leiars?"

His eyebrow cocked at her, and Reanna thought she recognized actual concern on his face. She closed her eyes against it. She had to remember who she was facing. She knew full-well Killian wasn't capable of real concern for her well-being.

She shook her head. "No. No laudanum. No brandy. My stomach does not agree with either." She took a deep breath, fingers rubbing her collarbone. "I can stand the pain. It is not as bad as it had been during the last week."

He eyed her, uncertain, seeming to waver between going out the door to get the doctor, and coming closer to her. He chose closer.

He stepped lightly, almost as if approaching a timid kitten, and came to the side of the bed. Stopping, he stared down at her, and Reanna braced herself. His face was a mask, the same mask of indifference that was there each and every time he had crushed her.

She closed her eyes and turned her head away from him. She couldn't take him right now. Not right now. Not as raw as she was.

The bed moved as he sat down on the edge, and Reanna found herself pleading with God. Please no. Not right now. Whatever he had to say, couldn't it wait just a few hours? Even one? Just enough time to gather her wits back about her.

"Your feet, Reanna. They were…they were grotesque. When we first saw them, Leiars didn't think you would ever be able to walk on them again. He wanted to amputate some toes."

Reanna's eyes flew open. "What? My toes? No. No. Did he…" Her voice choked off. She only felt pain radiating from her feet, so much so that when she wiggled them, she couldn't even tell if all her toes were still in place.

He reached for her hand above the covers, but instinct sent Reanna's hand jerking away. She tucked her exposed arm back under the covers.

Killian drew his hand onto his thigh. "No. I did not let him. And once we got through the scabs and blood and puss, he agreed. He thinks they will heal. Some toes may go slightly crooked, though."

Relief hitting her, she sighed, closing her eyes again. "If I am going to be fine, why are you telling me this?"

"You need to know what you did to yourself, Reanna. What you almost lost. So you never make a decision like it again."

She kept her eyes closed against his words, shaking her head, disbelief lining her lips. "So you are scolding me? Truly?"

No answer came from Killian, and Reanna refused to open her eyes to him. He could scold her all he wanted. Maybe she could try to go back to sleep while he did so.

The silence edged on. The bed didn't move, didn't twitch. She guessed he was staring at her, and his heat next to her hip was starting to cross the silk barrier and warm her skin.

Damn. She just wanted him to leave. And instead, he was going to hover. Hover silently. Silently and staring.

He must be concocting how he was going to kick her out of his life this time.

Well, there was no need. She wanted out of here just as much as he wanted her out of here. Her right hand moved out from under the covers and went to her forehead, rubbing it.

Still silence.

Blast it. She was going to break. He wasn't leaving. Fine. If he wasn't going start his latest crushing of her, she was going to prod him along. She wasn't going to lie there, heart thundering in her chest, stomach twisting, waiting. Not on top of her current pain.

She rubbed her head again, eyes not opening, and the words hurt against her throat. "What do you want from me, Killian? What?"

No answer.

She opened her eyelids, forcing herself to meet his brown eyes. She had once thought those were the warmest eyes she had ever seen. But now she knew differently. Whatever she saw in them, she was wrong. She always had been. She had no idea what she was looking at in that moment.

"What? What do you want?"

His eyes didn't break from hers, but several of Reanna's painful heartbeats passed before he opened his mouth. He looked as though he was actually considering an answer.

"I want you to heal. I want you to not kill yourself with work and worry. I want you to smile. I want to hear your voice light, not weighed down by pain. I want you not to flinch away when I touch you." His hand went to rub the back of his neck as his voice lowered a notch. "I want to erase time, Reanna. I...I want you to look at me like you once did."

Reanna blinked. Blinked hard. What the hell was he saying?

Her mouth opened and closed several times before words escaped. "How I looked at you?" She shook her head, trying to right his words in her head. "How I looked at you? I don't know who you are, Killian. I never knew. And I am not that person anymore. I don't want to be that person. That person was naïve in the worse possible way—she was naïve in love. It was not real. That cannot be me again. My heart could not survive it. And I cannot do it to ease whatever new conscience you have apparently developed."

"What if it was real?"

"Killian, no."

"What if it was real, Reanna? Not what we had. What we could have. You loved—"

"No. No. Don't you dare speak about love to me. You don't know the meaning of the word, Killian. And you sure as hell don't deserve to utter the sound of it."

His eyes narrowed at her. "There are things you do not understand, Reanna."

"Yes." She chuckled. "You are right. I do not understand a damn thing you have done to me, Killian. But here is what I do understand. I gave you everything. Every little piece of me. You didn't want it. You. Did. Not. Want. It. And I lost everything. Everything. Who I was. Hopes. Dreams…Love."

Her voice cracked. "I lost it all because I gave it to the wrong person. You were the wrong person. I lost it because you just threw it all away. You threw me away." Her words stopped, choked off.

Killian stood from the bed without word, took a step away, and Reanna almost took a breath. But then he turned, moving back to the side of the bed, staring down on her again. His fingers traced little circles on the coverlet.

She yanked her hand up from the under the covers, palm going across the bridge of her nose and pressing hard against the tears that had already started to escape.

She had been done with the tears. Months ago they had dried up. And the well that had just replenished to overflowing wasn't fair.

Not now. Not like this. Not in front of him. Not when she couldn't move from the bed and run away.

"What if, Reanna? What if we started, from today onward? What if it was real? What if I was real?"

"No. Do not ask me, Killian. Please do not ask me."

"You were right that night at Holloton, Reanna." He sat again, this time, his weight hitting the bed heavy. "Our wedding night. I did feel it. I didn't want to. I tried to convince myself it was not real. But I felt every second of that night. And I haven't felt anything in a long time. Not before. Not since. Not until last night."

Her hand flew from her eyes. "Last night? Watching me in torture? Watching me in pain? That made you feel?"

"No. God, no." He grabbed her hand, snatching it before she could move it away. "It was not just your feet. Those had to be fixed, one way or another. And that was hell for me, to know I did that to you." He sighed, running his free hand through his hair.

"It was your hand. The moment you put it on my cheek before we started on your feet. Even in pain. Even hating me. Even with all that, your hand was gentle. Your hand on my face, it felt...it felt like that was where it should be, where it belonged. Like it had been missing for my whole life, and it found its way home."

He took a deep breath, shaking his head as his eyes closed. "And then you moved it along my face, and I could feel callouses on your hand."

She tried to pull from his grip, but he held tight, turning her hand palm up. The pad of his thumb traced the raised red welts that had dotted her skin for weeks.

"The depths you would go to for those children. The depths I made you go. These are mine. I put them there. Your feet. I did that to you." He looked up at her. "What I did is unforgivable, and I will not ask you for forgiveness I do not deserve. But you must know how sorry I am."

He moved her hand, letting it slip from his fingers to a gentle rest on her belly.

"I have much to atone for, Reanna. All I ask is the chance to do so."

Without another breath, he stood and walked out the door.

Reanna started to flip onto her side, but the movement sent fresh waves of pain radiating from her feet. She fell onto her back, and settled for turning her head on the pillow to stare at the closed door.

The tears started to fall, soaking the pillow within a minute.

Even after all this time, she still was not all right. He still had the damn power to crush the air from her lungs. To shred her heart.

It wasn't fair, and she hated herself for it.

Hated herself for not being able to hate him.

~ ~ ~

After two quick unanswered knocks, the door to his study opened, and Killian jumped up from behind his desk.

"Aggie, good God, what are you doing here?" He ran around the desk, grabbing her hand and elbow as she waddled, and led her over to the settee. "You cannot even move. Why in the hell did Devin let you leave the house?" He clasped both of her hands to help ease her down into a sitting position.

Leaning back on the vine-patterned silk, she took a deep breath, looking at her belly. "He did not. He was gone when I left."

"He does not know you are here?"

"No. I sent him to the offices. I have not had one minute alone in days. I normally love it when Devin is nearby, but right now he has no control. I make the smallest twitch or an extra breath of air, and he jumps up, hawk eyes on me, pacing, worried the baby is going to just slip on out and bounce onto the floor." Her hand swept in exaggeration as she settled into the cushions.

"He is convinced I should be doing nothing but sitting still and breathing. I know he just wants to make sure I am all right, but the smothering has reached new heights."

"So you snuck out?"

"I did not sneak. Miss Collier called on me about fifteen minutes after Devin left. She told me what happened last night, and I was worried about Reanna, so I came over. Devin was not at home, so there was no sneaking." She waved her hand. "I know I should be hidden away from the world right now, but I could not let this rest."

"Aggie, you need to be at home. That baby is going to come out at any second. Is your carriage still out front?" He walked to the window facing the street and looked down. "Good. Home for you."

"No, wait. Just five minutes, please? A few minutes, and I will go home, I promise. I have already visited with Reanna."

"You walked upstairs? Ludwig didn't announce you. Hell, Devin is going to kill me."

"I wanted to visit with Reanna without you hovering. So I asked him not to let you know I was here quite yet. Please, sit. I cannot stand to have another man pacing in front of me. Days of watching Devin do it has made me dizzy."

Killian crossed his arms in front of his chest, looking down on her. "I will stand in one spot, then, for your sensibilities. So Reanna was awake when you went up there?"

"Yes."

"How do you think she is?"

"Honestly, she is confused."

"Confused? About what?"

"About you. She does not know what to think. All of a sudden you want her? Why? You want to move on? For what purpose? Of course she is confused. That, and she thinks you are going to close down the orphanage. Or at the very least, not let her go back there."

"She hates me."

"I would not go that far, only because I do not think she is capable of hate. But if so, yes, you well deserve it."

Sighing, Killian turned and sat next to Aggie, elbows balancing on his knees, hands clasped in front of his mouth.

Aggie lifted a hand from her belly and placed it gently on his shoulder. "Killian, you know you are one of the dearest people to me. Sometimes I may dislike you, but I always love you. You are family. But you also know I never approved of what you have done to Reanna in order to achieve your revenge. You have been a complete bastard to her, and now you are going to have to deal with the consequences your own idiocy created."

He turned to glare at her. "That is harsh."

"I only say it because I want you to understand the magnitude of what you have done, so you can try and fix it."

"I do not think it can be fixed."

"Rubbish. Your idiocy is in the past. There is nothing for it, now. So how do you get her to think about the present, and not the atrocities you set upon her?" She bit her lip. "That is a tough one. Does she really know anything about you? About your past? About your childhood?"

"No. And she said I killed her heart. Killed her heart, Aggie. How do I come back from that? How do I make amends?"

"Maybe you start by acknowledging that you have had all the power, and with it, you have taken away everything in her life. Now you need to give it all back to her."

"How would I even begin that? She does not trust me. She does not like me."

"I do not have an answer for how to do it, but I can tell you how you don't do it. You don't take away from her what her world has become."

"The orphans?"

"Precisely. She has built something very admirable on her own, and you cannot just ban her from that. Those children are her life, her world. They are what she trusts. And you are right, she does not trust you right now."

"But she is killing herself over them. You saw the pain—how frail she is."

"You cannot underestimate how much they mean to her. You took away her innocence, Killian. You did that, and it crushed her. Do you not understand that these children—their innocence—are everything to her? That she will do anything and everything to see that they remain innocent for as long as possible? You cannot take her away from them, Killian."

"So I need to send her back to her aunt's home?"

Aggie smiled, her sparkling eyes plotting. "That is where fortune has smiled upon you, my friend. Even she knows she is stuck here until her feet heal. There is already too much mayhem at her aunt's home. So you have been granted time. Use it wisely. I think she can learn to trust you. And I think if you want it, she may even find a way to love you again."

Aggie's face tightened into a wince, and the rubbing on the top of her belly sped, but after a moment, her smile reappeared. "Reanna has an incredible soul, Killian. Of all the women to be an ass to, you picked the right one. She loved you once. You did not want her love, and you tossed it aside. But she did love you. Now you just need to decide how far you are willing to go."

Killian rubbed his forehead. "She is different now, Aggie. Aside from not believing a word I say, she questions everything. I don't intimidate her like I once did, and she is not afraid to challenge me. And she cares so deeply. So many in her place would have turned bitter, mean, but she didn't. She moved on, making a life for herself. I found that out at Holloton from the staff. She learned to ride, and then once she found those children, she put all her energy into them. She found purpose. Purpose without me."

A wide smile cracked Aggie's face as her eyes brightened at him. "Killian, you want your wife, don't you? You have actually decided that you want her. For her and her alone."

"Maybe." Killian's eyes went down, shaking his head with a sad chuckle.

"There is no maybe in this, Killian. There is only yes or no. You cannot break her heart again. You cannot take this lightly."

Killian took in Aggie's words. She was right. He had to be sure. Hell. He was sure. He looked up at Aggie. "Yes. Yes I want her. I did not know what I had, much less what I lost. Since the day we were married, I have seen nothing when I close my eyes except for her face. No matter what I did to erase it. And now, what she has done. Who she is. You were right about her depths, Aggie. Last night. What she did for those children, it—"

"Oh, hell." Aggie's face froze in shock.

Killian snapped to his feet. "What is it?"

The liquid running down along the front of the settee and dripping to the floor told him all he needed to know.

Gripping her belly, Aggie looked up at him, her face petrified white. "My water…"

Killian grabbed her wrists, pulling her to her feet. "Bloody hell."

Aggie's breath sped up into quick, shallow bursts. "Killian. Get Devin. I need him. Now, dammit."

"No. I am getting you home. Devin would kill me if he knew you were out of the house and I didn't immediately send you home."

"I don't care if you get killed or not, Killian, I need my damn husband."

Killian dropped her arms, and took a step to the door.

"No, Killian. Stop. Don't leave me." Her hand flung out to him.

"I am just going to get Ludwig."

"No. Don't leave me."

Killian grabbed her hand while leaning toward the hallway, his voice bellowing, "Ludwig." He turned back to Aggie and wrapped an arm around her back, walking her forward. "Out to the carriage."

Ludwig appeared just as Killian opened the front door.

"The duke needs to be found immediately," Killian said over his shoulder. "He is most likely at the shipping offices. Have him found and sent to his townhouse as quickly as possible. And the duchess's midwife. She must be brought to their house as well."

Ludwig nodded and disappeared while Killian half-carried Aggie down the front steps to her carriage.

Her first hard contraction hit in the coach.

In pain, Killian now knew Reanna was a silent screamer, taking in the pain and holding it tight within. Aggie was the exact opposite. Aggie was a screamer, not shy about letting the entirety of London know her body was being ripped apart. She also had a vicious grip on Killian's hand.

Her townhouse was only ten minutes away, but that gave plenty of time for the bones in Killian's hand to come near to cracking during the two contractions Aggie had during the ride.

Her screams in front of her house brought several staff outside, so Killian had help in getting her up to her bedroom. Once she was flat in bed, Killian tried to stand up, but Aggie's death grip on his hand refused to yield.

"No. Don't leave me, Killian. Please. I cannot do this alone and Devin is not here."

He sat down on the bed, trying to fake a smile against watching the pain rack her body. "I am here."

His hand went to her forehead, smoothing the hair away as another set of screams tore from her throat. At their silence, Killian brought his hand down, wrapping his fingers around their clamped hands. "I am here as long as you need me. You do not even need to ask."

She nodded, relief evident as a slight smile cracked her lips. "Thank you. I am sorry about your settee."

Killian smiled. "It is all right. I was planning on getting rid of it anyway. I was planning on getting rid of a lot of things."

Her eyes turned serious. "Killian. If anything should happen—"

"Nothing is going to happen, Aggie. You are wicked strong, and you are going to birth this baby by your sheer damn willpower. And the baby will be healthy. And you will be healthy. Nothing is going to happen."

She closed her eyes, and tears squeezed past the outer edges of her eyelids. "But if something happens…you need to get Devin through it. Whatever it takes. I don't know what he would do. Promise me." She opened her eyes. "Promise me you will take care of him."

"You know you don't need to ask."

"I need to hear the words, Killian. Promise me."

"I promise. Whatever it takes."

Her other hand came up to go over his. "You are a good man, Killian. You just have to remember that. No matter what has happened, what you have done. You are good. I know it. Devin knows it. You need to make your life right. You need—"

She doubled over as a scream ripped away the rest of her words.

"Bloody fucking hell, Killian, what the hell are you doing with my wife?" The words boomed over Aggie's scream.

Killian stood from the bed, but Aggie's grip didn't let him escape. Killian was trapped between a seething, out-of-breath Devin who was two steps away from killing him, and a screaming Aggie, who refused to release his hand.

He got one hand up to ward off his friend. "She's in pain, Devin. Did you really want her to be alone?"

Devin stepped past him, wedging himself between Killian and Aggie. He tore Aggie's hand from Killian's, and she clamped onto him, screams still suffocating the chamber.

Killian stepped out of the room.

~ ~ ~

Fourteen hours later, Killian heard a new scream tumble down the stairs of Devin's home. A baby's wail.

Killian sat up on the sofa in Devin's study. He hadn't slept— only a deaf man could with Aggie's constant screams. An hour after the baby's cries quieted, Killian saw the midwife leave. But no Devin, no staff came into the study.

Pacing for the next hour, Killian's heart began to sink when Devin's valet, face drawn, came into the study and requested his presence upstairs.

Heart slowing to crawl, Killian walked upstairs, stopping at the door to harden himself against whatever was inside the bedroom.

He knocked.

Footsteps thudded across the floor, and the door opened. Devin stood, eyes sunken, exhausted darkness shadowing his face.

But even through that, he beamed.

"It is a boy," Devin said, his voice only a crack above a whisper.

Killian didn't want to ask. "Aggie?"

"I do not think she will be able to talk for weeks. Beyond that, she is as fine as fine can be after childbirth."

Killian let his held breath escape.

Devin opened the door wide. "Come in and meet my son."

Killian stepped into the room, following Devin into the dim light of a few lamps. Aggie was propped up on the bed, back against a wall of pillows, baby in her arms. She looked exhausted. Exhausted and beautiful.

Devin went over to her and she handed the bundle of swaddling into Devin's arms. He turned to Killian.

"I told her it could wait, but Aggie wanted to ask you right away. And I was not about to argue with her after what I just witnessed."

He held out the bundle to Killian, and after a second of trepidation, Killian took the baby from Devin. Fast asleep, the baby had thumb solidly in his mouth, cheeks flexing in and out with sucking.

Killian looked up at Devin, then to Aggie. "He is splendid."

She smiled at him and then leaned forward, face grimacing at the movement, to poke Devin in the back.

He looked over to her, smiling as he rolled his eyes. "Yes. What my wife has no voice for right now, and would like to ask you, is if you will be his godfather, and, God forbid, his guardian should the need ever arise?"

Killian looked up from the baby at the two of them, shocked. His eyes landed on Aggie. "I…that you trust…"

Aggie's scratchy voice, near silent, interrupted him. "Of course we trust you, Killian. We still have faith in you, the good in you, even if you have lost it in yourself."

"We do believe in you, Killian," Devin said, grabbing his wife's hand. "There is no one we trust more, and we would be more than honored if you said yes."

Killian looked down at the babe's semi-round face, watching the tiny eyes scrunch, and was more humbled than he had ever been in his life. "Yes. Then yes. I am the one that is honored."

At the sound, the baby yanked his thumb from his mouth and bellowed. Aggie motioned for him, and Killian cradled the baby to Devin, who passed him to Aggie.

"Excellent." Devin slapped him on the shoulder as they walked out of the room and clicked the door closed behind them. "Oh, and I apologize for my thoughts of killing you."

Killian eyed him. "I did not know you were considering it."

"I was. But it was only because my wife was screaming and you were in the closest proximity to her. If it had been anyone else, they would be dead right now."

Killian smirked. "Good thing it was me, then. I hope she is not in too much trouble for visiting my house. She was just trying to help with the mess I made with Reanna."

"I would rightfully be livid. But how can I be after what she just did? She just gave me the most precious thing in the world. It has made me whole in a way I never knew possible. I cannot even describe the ridiculous amount of pride I have in that little being upstairs."

Killian smiled at his friend, nodding as he opened the front door to the first morning light. "I did not even ask. Does he have a name yet?"

"Does 'Boy' count?"

Killian cocked his head in question.

Devin smiled, waving the comment away. "No. Not yet. I will keep you posted. Thank you. You took good care of Aggie when she needed it most. You were there. You know how to do that, be there, without fail. It is a unique skill of yours."

"It is?" Surprised humility, genuine, lined Killian's face.

"Yes. You show up for those you love without fear or hesitation. It is your greatest strength. And it is why we believe in you." Devin pointed to Killian's carriage. "Now go fix your mess."

CHAPTER 15

Reanna stared at the black chess piece on the board, tapping the white piece in her hand on her chin. She had slept most of yesterday, but in the evening, after several lonely hours awake, she had requested the chess set by the fire be moved onto the bed within reach.

She was used to constant noise and movement with the children, and couldn't settle her mind until she had something other than the grey silk canopy above the bed to look at.

Sitting upright, propped against the headboard, she had already worked through two practice matches against herself since last night, and had just started a third, when, without a knock, the door to Killian's room opened.

Her heart immediately started thudding. She hadn't seen Killian since yesterday morning. And the things he had said to her—the things he left her with, had done nothing to quiet her rambling mind. Then he disappeared. And now he was walking toward her, his jaw set, determined, and Reanna braced herself, wondering if this was it.

This was when he would kick her out of his life again.

He looked like he hadn't slept in days, wearing only a rumpled white shirt and buckskin breeches. His sandy blond hair was mussed, run through what looked like a thousand times.

She cleared her throat. Best that she just got right to it. "I will be leaving now? You disappeared yesterday and I was not sure what to tell the staff about where to move me. I tried, but I still cannot walk. So I was not sure what room to move into, or if you would allow me to go back to my aunt's home."

He didn't stop his movement at her words; instead, he continued forth and sat down on the bed by her heavily bandaged, propped-up feet. He fiddled with the bandages, then looked up to her.

"Has the doctor been by?"

"Twice yesterday. Once this morning. He is not concerned. He said they are healing fine."

Killian nodded. "You will stay in this bed until you are healed."

Reanna's forehead wrinkled as her breath caught.

His eyebrow arched. "Is it not comfortable here?"

"No. It is fine. Your staff has been very kind to me."

"They are your staff as well."

She tilted her head, staring at him until it hit her. There was only one reason he would let her stay in place. "So you will be leaving London, then?"

He gave her an odd look, not answering. "Aggie had her baby. It is a boy. Healthy."

"What? When did that happen? I just talked to her yesterday. Is she all right?"

"She is fine. That was where I was yesterday."

Reanna nodded, twisting the white chess piece in her hands. Why was he staring at her like that, his brown eyes cutting into her? He wasn't here to kick her out. So what was it?

The awkwardness of his silent proximity intensified. Reanna broke. "I imagine you are in here for a reason?"

He slid forward along the bed, his hip brushing her thigh. "I made a decision last night."

"You did?" Reanna braced herself.

"Yes. A decision—from hence forward—to be completely honest with myself, with you, with everything in and about my life."

"All right...so what does that mean?" Her fingers tapped on the coverlet. "I am not sure what you want out of me, Killian."

"This is my first chance at honesty with you, Reanna. Of not holding back. I do not know how to do this. I have always had a plan. Always known how to move forward. But with you. I do not know how to move forward. Not after the things I have done to you."

He shook his head slowly, and then his hand went under her chin. She couldn't stop her head from slightly jerking away, and her crown hit the headboard. His fingers remained in place, lightly caressing her skin.

"Give me a chance to prove myself. That is what I want out of you. Just a chance. A chance for me to at least prove the possibility of us."

She took a deep breath, her chest rising at his words, the air sinking deep into her lungs. It did nothing to steady herself against his words. Against the trap he was surely laying. She couldn't forget she had been through this before. She couldn't forget the pain.

Even if in this moment, she thought she saw raw honesty in his brown eyes. She couldn't trust her own sight. Her heart pounded. She had to listen to her head. To the reality of the past. She was not going to repeat her mistakes.

Putting the chess piece down in her lap, she exhaled the deep breath. She would have to return his honesty with her own. "I do not think I can."

"Why not?"

"Why not?" She closed her eyes, shaking her head, then opened them, eyes trained upwards at the grey canopy. "I once thought...Killian, I once thought you were the world. My whole world. But now...now I do not see anything in you. I cannot allow myself to see anything in you. Since the day after we were married you have given me nothing but pain. I do not know how to get beyond that. And I hate you for asking me to do it."

His hand dropped from her. Turning on the bed, he looked out the window that faced the courtyard. His hand went to the back of his neck, rubbing it. "I understand."

He let a few seconds slide before looking at her. "What if promised you no pressure? Just asked for your time? While you are here, healing. Just your time."

Reanna picked up the chess piece again, staring at it, twisting it in her hand. How could she even answer that? She was stuck here, regardless, at least until she could walk again. All of her time was his if he demanded it, and he damn well knew that.

He pointed at the chess set sitting on the other side of the bed. "I did not think you played."

"I learned at Holloton. Both Ruperton and Evans took turns teaching me."

"You got embroiled in their chess?" Disbelief sent his face into a half smile. "Their matches are legendary."

"Yes, and I did not know what I was getting into. They both taught me how to beat the other—never surmising that what they were actually doing, was teaching me how to beat their very selves. So you can imagine their surprise when that actually happened."

"You beat both of them?"

"Yes. And I felt dreadful after all the time they had invested in me." She smiled. "But then they started to conspire against me, so they lost my sympathy. But they are the dearest."

"Would you play with me?"

Reanna's eyes swung to the chessboard, then to Killian, then back to the board. She was going out of her skin lying in this bed by herself, so it would be delightful to have someone real to play with. But it was with Killian. She would have to remember that. The damage he could do.

She nodded.

"Excellent." He stood. "I would like to clean up, and I have a few items to tend to, and then we shall play?"

Reanna nodded once more.

Killian walked to the door, but then stopped, turning back to her. "Reanna, I promised no pressure, and I will abide by that. But make no mistake, I have intentions of doing everything in my power to get you to see me again. Me. Who I am. Who I can be."

He closed the door behind him, and Reanna sank against the headboard.

Had she had just invited the devil to a game of chess?

~ ~ ~

Two hours later, Killian had a tall side table with a wide overhang brought into the room, so it would hover over the bed and Reanna's legs, affording her a straight view of the chessboard. She said silent thanks, for her neck was already beginning to crimp for the awkward angle she had sat too long in earlier.

He pulled up a chair, settling it next to the bed and facing her over the table.

In silence, they both busied themselves with setting up the board. Again, as when she had first seen the set, Reanna wondered at the origin of the unique figures. The pieces were wooden, crudely carved, and at first, Reanna had a hard time discerning which piece was which. After studying them closely for some time, she could make out the intention of the carver. Several of the pieces had clearly been thoroughly worn by fingertips, the black and white paint giving way to the wood grain beneath. At one time in the past, it had been a well-used set.

"I apologize that I had them move the set to the bed. I needed something to occupy my mind, but I did not mean to impose on its use, if you intended it not to be touched," Reanna said as she set her queen in place. "I did not realize until I saw it up close how old it must be. And because it is in your room, it must be important to you."

Killian's hand paused for just a moment, and then he continued setting pieces, not looking up at her. "It is. It is actually a good thing it is being played with. It has been much too long since it was last used. My maternal great-grandfather carved the pieces, since he couldn't afford to pay for a set. I never knew him. But my grandfather taught me to play using this set when I was very young."

"Your mother did not come from money?"

"She did, actually. My grandfather was very poor as a child, but he made a fortune in shipping. Even with that, I still remember him telling me this was his most prized possession. He died, fortune lost, by the time I was five."

"Then I do apologize. I did not mean to impose on something so valuable to you. Perhaps you have another set in the house?"

Killian shook his head. "No. I am glad you wanted to use it. I doubt my great-grandfather spent the time carving it to have it sit, gathering dust." He looked at her directly, catching her gaze, his brown eyes flickering heat. "Your hands on it please me."

Reanna dropped her head at his words, heart speeding and throat instantly thick. This was a mistake.

She fidgeted with her pieces, lining them to perfection in their boxes. She had completely underestimated what he could do to her with one look. With a few words.

Remember the pain. Remember. She needed to not do this. Not be near him. Not now. Just as she opened her mouth to tell him, he interrupted her thoughts.

"I am sorry I disappeared again for a few hours earlier. It took longer than I had intended. I wanted to settle some things with the orphans."

Reanna's head snapped up. "What have you done?"

He blinked hard, head cracking back at her accusing tone. "Everything I hope you would approve of. I had sent word to have Miss Melby and Miss Collier hire four more staff yesterday. I wanted to check on their progress. Along with giving them both a healthy increase in pay. Miss Melby is handling the household staff, and after my run-in with Miss Collier, she seemed like the likely person to be in charge of the children while you are away."

Reanna immediately regretted her snap. "Oh. Thank you. Miss Collier is the perfect person. I do not even like to tangle with her. But I am not sure if...I am trying to be very careful with the money allotted to me from the trust."

"I did not want you to worry about what was happening at the Brook Street home while you are here. Nor do I want you to ever have to worry about money for those children again. Whatever you need. Whatever they need, it will be made available. Without question."

Reanna eyed him. He truly did look like he was telling the truth. Maybe she could believe him about this one thing. She nodded, letting a slight smile break. "I did not intend on needing your assistance with them, but thank you. That does ease my mind."

"Good. Your move."

Sixteen moves in, Reanna set her bishop down. She looked up to see Killian eyeing her.

"Tell me of your mother. I know she died young."

"She did. I was four." Reanna shifted awkwardly. "I have very little recollection of her."

"Do you know anything about her? Do you look like her? Have her temperament?"

"I only know what my aunt has told me. I understand my mother and aunt were great beauties in their day. So I am not sure how much I actually look like her."

Killian's hand paused, rook in mid-air. He looked up at her sharply. "You are beautiful, Reanna. How do you not know that?"

"No. I..." A blush crept up her neck as she shrugged. "I apologize for my lack of grace at the compliment. You are the first person to ever speak those words to me."

"I find that hard to believe. You never had a suitor in the country? Never a rogue stable hand trying to catch your eye?"

Her head shook. "No. Father requested I mostly stay indoors. I never knew many people in Suffolk. A nanny. Then a governess and a tutor, and a few elderly neighbors, that was all."

"No one your own age?"

"No. Even our staff was older." A frown creased her face. "Was that odd? I never gave thought to it."

Killian's eyebrows settled from their arches. "No odder than anything else, I suppose."

She nodded, her eyes falling. "Now I think...I know...I was just alone."

"I know the feeling." He set his rook in place. "Your turn."

Reanna eyed the board. She had already worked five moves ahead, and as long as Killian kept playing to her strategy, she didn't need to think. But she did need to stall. Best to make your opponent think you're struggling, when possible, per Evans advice.

She fingered a pawn she wasn't about to move. "My aunt would never discuss it directly, but I gathered that although the Vestilun sisters were beautiful, there was very little money in the family to back their looks. My aunt alluded more than once to trading her beauty for money. She married an elderly viscount that died within two years. But I do not know about my mother's circumstances when she married my father. Father never discussed my mother with me, and Aunt Maureen's least favorite subject was my father."

"She does not care for him?"

"An understatement. She hates him. Still, to this very day. Hates him with a passion. She looks like she wants to spit every time he is mentioned. But I do not know why. Just one more thing I do not understand."

"What else do you not understand?"

Reanna moved her fingers from the pawn and picked up a knight, rubbing her thumb over the nub where a nose had existed long ago. She set it in place, then looked up at Killian, eyes slightly narrowing. "Sometimes, I honestly feel as there is a whole world around me that is happening, spinning around me, and I know nothing about it, much less how to navigate it."

Killian coughed, looking down and hastily grabbing a pawn. He plopped it down in the nearest square.

"Before I came to London, I thought my life normal. I could not imagine much more. But then I got here, and all of this." Her hand swept wide. "There is so much. And then Holloton, and then the Visper children, and then the castaway London children. All worlds I had never known existed. So much of it is cruel. I am stumbling through all of it, and it makes me wonder what else I cannot imagine."

"If you are stumbling, you are the most graceful stumbler I have every witnessed," Killian said, his brown eyes sincere. "Your lack of knowledge is a gift. It lets you see things for what they are. You see things that are not right, and you want to fix them, Ree. No hesitation."

The blush returned to her cheeks.

"It is actually quite remarkable. You are quite remarkable."

She looked down, avoiding his eyes. She had no idea how to accept Killian's words. Looking at the board, she realized he had just made an oddball move with his pawn. She reworked her next moves.

"What about your father? What is he like?"

Reanna didn't look up, concentrating on the board. "He did not spend much time at the country estate in Suffolk. He prescribed what I should learn, what I could read. He fed and sheltered me. We never spoke of much past my studies."

"Do you like him?"

She paused, tilting her head up as she gave the thought serious consideration. "I guess. My life was lonely. I did not know it then, but I do now. He was never mean to me. But at the same time, he never regarded me that much. It is probably why I did not recognize—"

She cut off her own words when she realized what she was about to say.

"What did you not recognize?"

She shook her head, eyes dropping from him.

He sighed. "It is why you did not recognize that I did not regard you. We were together, but I did not regard you. Is that what you were going to say, Reanna?"

She looked up, meeting his eyes. "It was rude, I should have held my tongue better."

"No. No you should not have. Your tongue is fine, Reanna. You were only speaking the truth, and I do not need to be protected from the truth. I did that to you. It was my rudeness, not yours."

~ ~ ~

Reanna lifted the silk shawl from her shoulders, letting her arms feel the warmth of the sun's rays as she scanned the gardens surrounding her. Perfectly tended high evergreen hedges lined the walk, dropping every few steps for views into rectangular beds of roses, hollyhocks, and peonies, many just starting to bloom.

In a break from their usual daily schedule of chess in the afternoon, Killian had suggested she sit outside in his gardens. He had even promised to bring the chess set outside, so they could play in the fresh air.

Her feet had been healing well, and she was down to a layer of thin gauze over the scabs after the last week and two days. Every one of those days, Killian had come to his room in the afternoon and played chess with her until darkness settled.

Killian was good—just as good as Ruperton and Evans—and they had, thus far, split their matches evenly. After losing the first two matches to him, she had been surprised when she had finally beaten him. He seemed to take it as just a matter of course. He played very differently than Ruperton and Evans, and she was enjoying the challenge of learning his thought process and then applying it against him.

He never demanded conversation from her. He happily answered questions and would entertain her with stories. And he would slip in questions about what she liked, what she thought, but only after Reanna initiated the conversations.

But he never put any pressure on her for anything more. Never, except for the three words he left her with every night.

"I want you."

Every night. Even on those nights that their games went into the wee hours, he would set the table aside, and move to sit next to her, his face close enough she could feel his breath on her skin. He would never touch her. Never ask for more.

Just those three words.

"I want you."

And then he would stand and leave. No pressure, just as he promised. He would tell her what he wanted her to know—and then leave.

Every one of those nights, Reanna had to close her eyes to him, head down. Fighting with herself to not look at him. To not crack open the well deep inside where she knew she had hidden all her love for him. For who she thought he was.

Her mind ruled her life now. Not her heart. She continually had to remind herself of that.

Reanna leaned back on the bench, tilting her face to the early summer sun, as sweet honeysuckle danced along the light breeze to her nose. She hoped the kids were outside at the park by her aunt's home on a beautiful day like this. A day where everything seemed right, even though much of it was wrong—and only because the sun was shining, brightening the soul.

Killian was right about getting her out of the house. He had helped her hobble down the stairs and out to the wrought iron bench in the middle of the gardens, then had disappeared, leaving her to her thoughts. Within an hour outside, she felt like a new person.

Mind thankfully blank for a change, she watched a snail make a slow trail across the cobblestones that lined the garden path. A familiar voice startled her, a voice she had missed terribly, and it came from around the corner of the evergreen hedge.

"Lady Ana. Lady Ana."

"Thomas?" She started to stand, then sat back down. Her feet were still too tender for real steps. So she settled for sitting on the edge of the bench. "Thomas is that you?"

He rounded the corner, full run, and spied her. Without hesitation or warning, he jumped into her lap. She didn't even note the pang of pain the jolt sent through her feet. Thomas was worth any pain.

She clasped her arms around him, squeezing him hard. "Thomas, my dearest, how I have missed you. Are you alone?"

He pulled back from her grasp to look up at her face. "Just me, today, Lady Ana. We all miss you terribly, but Lord Southfork said only me today. Maybe others tomorrow. Not too much at once he says."

Killian rounded the corner at the last of Thomas's words, and he stopped at the evergreen border, arms crossed along his chest, watching the scene.

She looked over Thomas's head to Killian, tears brimming on her lower lashes. "Thank you." She said the words, but knew no sound made it past her choked throat.

He gave one nod, smile on his face, then took a step back and disappeared around the corner of the hedge.

Her eyes swung back to Thomas, and she couldn't resist clamping him hard in her arms again. He took it for few seconds, hugging her back, and then wiggled free, settling himself on his knees next to her. He kept a hand on her arm, though, and Reanna squeezed it, not letting it go.

"How are you? What have you been up to? How are your brothers and sisters and the others?"

"Good. Learnin'. And the others have been learnin' too—the old-enough ones, that is."

"Learning? Who is instructing you?"

"Lord Southfork got us a tutor. Said we had some catchin' up to do. He didn't like the first one he got though, said that one went out-of-place with us, so he got us a new one. Which is good, 'cause that first one sure liked how his ruler snapped."

Worry sank into Reanna's stomach. "But the second tutor—is he all right? Is he being gentle with all of you?"

"No 'he.' His lordship got us a lady instead. She's nice."

"So Lord Southfork has met her and approved of her?"

"Sure. He's been watching. He's been coming 'round every day."

"He has? What does he do over there?"

Thomas shrugged. "Talks to us, mostly."

"Do you mean to Miss Collier and the staff he hired?"

"No. To us. Talks to them a bit, but mostly talks to us. Those that are old 'nough. He says I would make a good captain."

"A captain?"

"Yep. He says I'm a good leader. So I would make a good captain. Or solicitor. He said I would be good at that too, 'cause I take care of the others so well and I'm smart. I like captain better, though. Sounds like more fun, being on a ship and all. He said I could choose what I wanted. But schoolin' first, he said, either way."

Reanna nodded, mouth slightly ajar in wonder. "I think he is right. You would be wonderful doing either of those things. How has the learning been coming along?"

"We have lots of ladies there now to help us, so I don't have to do as much. His lordship said that should give me lots of time to get to the learning. I like the numbers so far, but not the writing so much."

Reanna smiled at Thomas. He looked ecstatic at getting the chance to properly learn. Hiring a tutor had been on her list to get done, but in all honesty, it would have been another month or two before she could have found one she could afford. Killian had already gone through two in a matter of days to find a proper fit.

She took a deep breath, letting a good portion of her worry dissipate.

"Tell me, what are all the children doing today?"

"They went to the park. But I wanted to come here. You are much better than the park, Lady Ana."

Reanna couldn't resist snatching him and giving him another hug. He exaggerated a sigh, then giggled—not seeming to mind too much.

"All right, then. You must tell me everything that has been going on. I miss all of you so much. So I want every detail."

~ ~ ~

Killian rounded the corner of the evergreen hedge after sending Thomas in the carriage back to join his brothers and sisters. Reanna and Thomas had chattered for hours, their laughter floating up from the gardens and in through the open window in the study.

Eyes seeking her out, Killian took a deep breath, hoping to not be greeted by disappointment. He had hated to interrupt them, but he also knew Thomas's younger siblings were somewhat lost without him around. Especially with Reanna not in residence.

She turned to him just as he started down the path to her, the light in her eyes not waning when she saw him.

She beamed. He would do this every day if it meant she would look at him like that.

"Thank you. Thank you." Her hand went over her chest. "I needed that. I miss them so much."

"Good. I was afraid it might just make you sad."

"Oh no, that made me happy—stop. Don't step on the snail."

Killian looked at his feet. A hair in front of his right boot, a thumb-sized snail slugged a trail across the cobblestones to low mounded grass. Killian looked up at Reanna, smirk raising his cheek.

"Thomas and I have been watching him. He has been working on crossing the chasm for some time. I do not wish him squashed. I want him to make it, as I rather hope he will succeed."

Killian stepped past the snail and sat next to Reanna on the bench, smirk still in place. "God-speed, then, little snail."

Reanna laughed and swatted his arm. It was just flicker of a movement, but it was her, voluntarily touching him without reservation. He would take it.

"I would have brought Thomas by earlier, but I did not want him to see you hostage in bed, feet under the bandages." Killian leaned back on the bench, his elbow resting along the top line of it. "He is the oldest little boy I have ever met, but he is still little, and I did not want him to be scared if he saw you unable to walk. I imagine he did not even notice your feet today."

Reanna shifted on the bench to look at him, head tilting, errant dark curls from her upsweep touching her shoulders. "No. You are right. He is unusually brave, but he can still get scared. I never would have made it to London without him."

Killian's head shifted down, eyes trained on the snail.

"I am sorry, I did not mean to mention—"

"No, Reanna." His eyes swung to her. "I never want to hear you apologize again for the fact of what I made you do. It happened. I did it. I set you on that path, and by the grace of God, you survived it. But I will never try to pretend it did not happen. Nor will I wish you to forget it. If mentioning it, if talking about it is what you would like, then I will gladly do so. I will listen to anything, as long as you are talking to me."

Her blue eyes went downward, watching her fingers twist together. She nodded and then raised her chin. The light was back in the aquamarine of her eyes. "What I would like to talk about is the children. Is that what you have been doing daily in the morning? Thomas said you have been there every day since I have been gone."

Killian shrugged, half in honest modesty, and half in relief that Reanna chose not to speak of her journey. That could only go badly for him. "I wanted to get to know the children. I wanted to know why they are so important to you."

Reanna nodded, and Killian could see she held her breath. "And?"

"And I see it. Every single one of them is special. Unique. Each one wants so much to belong—to be part of the rather large family you have created. What you have done for them is beyond compare." He grabbed one of her hands from her lap, encapsulating it in his. "You are beyond compare."

She let her hand sit in his without the slightest tug to remove it. "But I had not thought past the next week with the children, nowhere into the future. But you, you already have Thomas a profession. Or two."

"He told you?"

"He did. I am impressed you discerned so much about him in only a few days. He is very excited."

"Anything he wants to do, anything any of them wants to do, I will find a way to make it happen. The girls will all have dowries worthy of any man, and the boys will attend the best schools and apprentice with only the most intelligent. Unless they decide they want commissions, like I think Thomas is leaning."

She smiled at him. A smile he had never thought to see from her again. A smile of shy adoration. It flashed long enough for him to see it, to read it perfectly, but then it disappeared.

"No. Do not look at me like that." She pulled her hand from his. "This is not fair."

"What is not fair?"

"I am no match for this, Killian. What you have done this past week. What you are doing for the children. And then you produce Thomas for me—Thomas, with the rest of his life secure. It is not fair."

Killian's lips curled up at her words. "I said I was going to be honest, Reanna. I never promised fairness."

He snatched her hand back into his. There was no letting it go. "I want you, Reanna. How your fingertips curl around chess pieces. How your tongue slips ever so slightly past your lips when you are concentrating on the board. How you light up every time I mention the children. That light is there for them, and it makes me jealous. Ground shakingly jealousy. But also desperate to put that light in your eyes—and do whatever it takes to keep it there."

He shifted closer to her on the bench. "You believe the good in everyone, Reanna. Everyone except me. God knows I deserve that. But I want—I need to change that."

"Killian…"

He lifted his fingers, brushing a dark lock from her cheek. "Just try and remember how it was when we first met. How everything was possible with us. It can be like that again."

She closed her eyes to the touch of his knuckles on her cheek. "I do not think it can, Killian. What I believed, what I hoped for when we first met, none of it was reality. The only thing that was real was my naivety."

"Out of all of it, all our time together, remember our wedding night." He trailed his hand down her neck, watching her smooth skin prickle behind his touch. "That night alone. That was real. That was me. That was who I am. Who I am with you."

She turned her face from him, eyes closed to his words. A breeze floated past them, freeing the scent of honeysuckle caught in her upsweep, the light scent juxtaposed to the rich darkness of her hair.

Killian leaned over, his lips soft on Reanna's neck. "Do you remember this?"

Her skin tensed under his mouth. "I remember waiting for you when you never came."

He brushed strands of hair backward, giving access to trail his tongue along the delicate skin behind her ear. "Do you remember this?"

"I remember your mistress laughing at me."

His hand slid down from her neck, to the roundness of her breast. His lips followed, teasing every inch of the way. "Do you remember this?"

"I remember the long walk to London."

Killian worked his way up her skin, reveling in the smooth morsels. As much as her words spoke to deter him, her body arched to his touch, her lips slightly parted. He pulled back when he got to her jawline, catching her juicy bottom lip with his thumb.

She didn't open her eyes to him, but neither did she put up any resistance. He kissed her then. Hard. Soft.

His tongue made its way to hers, and she responded to the invasion, even though he could tell she fought how her body betrayed her mind. His hand went deep into the thick hair at the nape of her neck, and he tilted her head for deeper access.

She went soft. His. No resistance to the kiss, only complete submission. Killian took advantage, exploring, teasing, biting.

God, he wanted her.

He edged from her mouth, forehead resting on hers as he opened his eyes, searching her face. A tear slid from the corner of her eye.

"Killian," she whispered, opening her eyes to his, "why are you doing this to me?"

"Is it so bad?"

She shook her head and the tear tumbled down her cheek. "But do you know what you are asking me to forget?"

He didn't answer, could only turn his head, avoiding her. Then his eyes swung back to hers, intensity burning. "Yes. But God, Reanna, do you know what I'm asking myself to forget?"

She jerked away from him, stung, grabbing his wrist and pulling his hand from her neck. "No. No I do not. You said before there were things I do not understand, Killian. And now you say that."

Killian stood from the bench, turning from her. Damn. He had never intended to breathe a word of her father to her.

"Was there a reason? A reason for what you did, Killian?" She wiped the tear from her cheek. "The smallest part of me has begun to hope that this was all a misunderstanding. That there was a reason you were forced to do those things to me. That it was not really you. Because how you have been to me this past week is who I always thought you were. The good in you. I can see it like I never did before."

Out of the corner of his eye, Killian watched her move to the edge of the bench, hands gripping the iron as if she was going to try and stand. He turned back to her, if only to stop the motion. He wasn't going to watch her put herself in pain.

She stayed seated. "Killian, if there was a reason...then maybe...maybe it would all make sense and I could move on. I do not want to believe that what you did to me is who you really are. I want to believe the good. The good I see in you right now."

Killian crossed his arms over his chest, jaw flexing as he stared at her. "There is a reason."

"Tell me."

"It is a reason that will make you want to leave. I cannot have that. Your feet are not healed yet."

"Honesty. What about that?"

He shook his head. "I will not tell you until your feet are healed. Then. Then I will tell you."

CHAPTER 16

"I miss your lap, Lady Ana. Miss Mildred's lap is bony, not soft like yours." Reanna looked down at the big brown doe eyes of Jeannie, curls hanging past her eyebrows to catch her lashes. The little girl rubbed her bottom on Reanna's thighs, snuggling in.

"I would think any lap that is open is a good lap to sit in."

Jeannie shrugged. "Yours is just better. That's all. When you comin' home?"

Reanna glanced up at Killian down the walk. He went down to his knees, bending over and holding several evergreen branches up off the ground so Albert could poke his hand in the dirt under the needles. Albert was giggling uncontrollably as Killian pretended to snap the branches down onto Albert's hand, again and again. Reanna couldn't hear what they were saying, but the laughter easily reached her ears.

Killian was an expert at continuing this unfair assault. After Thomas yesterday, today he produced Albert and Jeannie, and Reanna's heart instantly re-melted after the stalemate she and Killian had found themselves in the previous day.

And now he had been laughing with Albert for the past two hours. Albert, the one who rarely strung three words together, was now spitting out words, jibber-jabbering with glee to Killian.

Unfair. Completely unfair.

She looked down at Jeannie, tucking a curl from her forehead behind her ear. "Soon, I think. As soon as my feet are all healed."

Reanna had no idea. She couldn't wait to get back to the children, but yesterday when Killian kissed her, there was a large sliver in time that she actually considered him. Considered him wanting her. Considered letting him have her—and whatever that meant, whatever he wanted of her.

It was a guttural instinct that spurred that thought into her head, and just as quickly, it disappeared when he mentioned a reason. A reason for everything.

Could it possibly be that easy? And whatever it was, could it possibly overtake what she had begun to think of this new Killian? This new one that made her laugh, produced the children, listened to her, challenged her, and saved her from her own damn self.

If she had fallen so completely in love with him before—and that was when he barely regarded her—how was she ever going to withstand him when he gave her his full attentions?

She had resisted at first—spending the time with him, yet refusing to actually see the man in front of her. She told herself he was merely a diversion to keep her mind off of worrying about the children. How they were getting on. Did they have enough food? Were they driving Miss Collier to bedlam?

Killian played chess with her, and she could concentrate on something other than the children. She welcomed the distraction, since she hated herself when she worried about something she had no control over. The first six months in Holloton had taught her that.

But minute by minute, hour by hour, Killian sat in front of her and managed to etch himself into her thoughts, into her subconscious, until she was seeing him again. Truly seeing him.

She hated it at first. Hated that he could still command her attention at the slightest movement, the slightest flick of his wrist. Hated that his voice could hold so much concern for her. Hated that his smile made her chest constrict, taking her air.

But she saw him again, and there was nothing for it.

Her heart was the first to betray her, with its insistent thudding that sped when he walked into the room every afternoon. And then her body followed suit.

Their hands would brush over a chess piece, and her arm would tingle at the sudden heat. He would help her out of bed, arm wrapped around her back, fingertips brushing her ribs just under her breasts. She loved the sensations that it sent through her body, pooling deep within her. Yet hated that it was forcing her to acknowledge him. Acknowledge what he could do to her with one touch.

One touch, and all she wanted was him. His arms around her. His body on top of her. His mouth on her neck. Her body's memory of their wedding night was still too ingrained, still too poignant to forget. And much, much too easy to remember.

How he watched her, looked at her, was so different from before. If his brown eyes weren't smoldering, threatening to take her breath away, they were intent, truly watching her, listening to her in a way she had never experienced with him. He actually seemed genuine in wanting to know her.

That was, of course, when his eyes weren't heated. She read very clearly in those moments what he wanted to do to her body. With her body.

Whatever the reason for his actions when he tossed her aside, Reanna was beginning to wonder if she really wanted to know. If it was possible for her to maybe move forth without knowing.

Jeannie twirled the purple primrose she had plucked from the flower bed across the cobblestone path, looking down on the white linen cloth wrapping Reanna's feet. "Do they hurt?"

Squealing, Albert jumped up and ran full speed down the path from Killian, jumping onto Reanna's lap, and ramming his sister in the process. He collapsed in a fit of giggles, dirty hands smearing Reanna's peach muslin dress.

The pain vibrating from Reanna's feet was not as intense as she guessed it would be, so she had a chance to lock Albert in her arms, tickling him. His giggles turned into yelping laughs as he tried to wiggle free. Reanna didn't let it happen.

"There, not so smart to run from me, young sir, when that is your reward from your savior." Killian strolled down the path, smacking dirt off his hands, smile on his lips.

Jeannie hopped off the bench and went to his side, grabbing his hand and dragging him along the path. He was completely at ease with the children, and they with him. It discombobulated Reanna. She knew he had been visiting them, but there were no reservations on their parts. That could have only come from actual time spent together.

"Lord Southfork, I apologize for interrupting." Head down, Miss Mildred, one of the nannies, stepped in from the opposite path. "But if Jeannie and Albert are to make the evening meal, we should be on our way."

"Miss Collier will have your hide, if you are not back?"

Miss Mildred's eyes darted around, until she looked at the ground, nodding. "The other children were already jealous of Albert and Jeannie."

Killian looked down at the two sets of matching eyes staring up at him hopefully. "Time is up, little ones."

Their faces fell.

"Not to worry, Lady Ana will be healed and back in your clutches in a short time. Off you go. I do not want to cause tears of unfairness at the house."

Both children hugged Reanna, then grabbed Killian's hands and trudged out of the garden.

Within minutes, Killian reappeared, smile on his face. A smile directed at her, enticing her into things she knew she needed to avoid.

Even with all that had happened, there were moments she saw him, and her breath caught at the raw masculinity he exuded. Dark blond hair tussled—probably from the children—his white linen shirt was open partway down his chest and had splotches of dirt on it, matching the splotches on his buckskin breeches. His ease with the art of play was as strong as his ease in a formal drawing room.

He sat down comfortably beside Reanna, his spicy scent filling the air around her.

"There is such beauty in those children," he said, picking up the purple primrose Jeannie had left on the bench.

"They adore you. I wondered if Thomas was an anomaly, but you were all they could talk about to me."

He leaned forward, forearms resting on his thighs. "It very much surprised me that I would adore them as much as I do, as well. I had no inclination that would happen."

Reanna's heart sped, thudding hard in her chest. Extremely unfair. "Neither did I."

He turned his head to her. "You adoring them or me adoring them?"

"Both. But you...you have surprised me. I would not have thought it of you."

"Because you only knew one thing of me, Reanna. It was all I let you see. The part that hurt you. But I am so much more. I never myself knew how much more."

He sat up straight, turning fully toward her. "I have a proposal for you, but first, I have to tell you something."

"Go on."

"The children. I know that you will do anything for them—have done anything and everything for them. So I want to make very clear that what I want to do for the children—school, commissions, dowries, whatever they need, is a very separate thing from the two of us. I want to do all of those things for the children, regardless of what happens with us. I never want you to feel pressured by me, or anyone else, into doing something you would rather not for the good of them. So I had trusts drawn up for each of them that will ensure their respective futures."

Reanna's eyebrows arched. "You did? Truly?"

"Yes. It is already done. I want you, but I also want you choosing me for me, not because you are protecting the children, or trading yourself on their futures. Nor do I want you to worry about them, should you decide you cannot move on with me."

"Killian, that is...that is beyond generous. Thank you. So your proposal—what is it?"

"The rest of your time here. What if you did not live in the past? Did not live in the future? And I did not either. What if it was just us, the two of us, for this time? Just us. Who we are in this moment. When you are healed, I will tell you everything. Complete honesty. But not before you are healed."

"You want to pretend?"

"If you would like to call it that. I prefer to think of it as concentrating on this moment in time. The time we are in. For the few days we have left until I tell you everything. We live in this moment. Who you are. Who I am. Give yourself that freedom."

Freedom. That would mean unlocking her head. Unlocking her heart. Could she really do that?

"God knows you are different than before, Reanna. However that has happened, it took the past to make it so. It took the past to make you who you became. You are a woman with a rock-hard spine, but still with all the gentleness of a butterfly. That is the woman sitting in front of me. That is the woman I now know. The woman I want. You."

He grabbed her hand, running his fingers up her arm as he moved in, his face close to hers. "But it blows both ways, Ree. I can do anything you want me to. I can be who you need me to be. But you need to give yourself permission to see that in me. Who I am now. The man right in front of you. Not the man from the past."

Reanna closed her eyes, drawing vibrating air into her lungs as her head shook. "It is the fear in my gut."

"Tell me."

She opened her eyes, only to see dark flecks of intensity in the brown of his eyes. Intensity in trying to understand her. In trying to make her see him.

She took a deep breath. "Since we married, my heart has failed me, my mind has failed me. Again and again. The only thing that has not failed me is that visceral fear deep in my stomach."

"Fear?"

She gave the slightest nod. "Every time that I have felt it, the fear building up, telling me that maybe I should not be doing something—that I should be inside, safe from the world, safe from something new, safe from a challenge, choosing easy—I ignored it. And every time I had ignored my twisting stomach, done the thing I least wanted, it has turned out to be better than I imagined. It has made me whole when I was nothing.

"Learning to ride, even though I was deathly afraid of breaking my neck. Learning chess from Ruperton and Evans, even though each time I sat down with them, I thought my lack of intelligence would be glaring. Following Thomas home, when I really just wanted to ride away and pretend that I never saw him. Travelling to London with the children. Every one of those moves was the wrong one, according to my stomach. But every move was the right one. I would not be where I am right now, if not for all those times my gut curdled against me, and it would annoy me so, that I would ignore it."

"And what is the fear telling you right now?"

"It is telling me to run. That you will only cause me more pain. Pain that I would not survive."

Killian dropped his gaze from her, and after a moment, he stood, his hand slipping from hers. Then he held out his fingers to her. "Are you going to listen to your fear, or are you going to ignore it?"

Reanna shook her head, eyebrows raised. She truly could not manifest an answer.

With a deep breath, but no words, she put her hands in his and went gently to her feet.

Killian slid his right arm under her shoulder and around her waist for full support. His left hand went across her front to her far hip.

Reanna froze. This hold was nothing like earlier when he had helped her hobble down to the garden. This was him, all over her, his shoulder muscles tense under her fingertips, breath mingling with hers.

"What are you feeling, Ree? Right now, in this one moment in time?"

She turned into him, letting her forehead fall forward and rest on his chest. His heartbeat thudded on her skin, steady, patient. What did she feel? What did she truly want? And could she honestly admit to it?

"This is hard. Too hard. You turn parts of me inside out, Killian. Raw. Aching for your touch." She kept her head down.

Killian didn't reply, but she could feel his muscles tense, coil, at her words. He stayed silent.

Minutes passed, and she couldn't move. Couldn't breathe.

As long as her eyes were open. As long as she saw that today was today, and tomorrow he could be gone or send her away again. As long as she protected that part of her heart, the place where hoped live, she could do it.

If only for a few days. Her body begged for it.

Besides, she could leave. He promised it. So what was the harm? What was the harm in quenching her constantly pulsating body? Quelling her imaginations, her dreams of him. What was the harm, as long as she controlled her heart?

Breath exhaling, she pulled back, eyes travelling up his chest, his neck, to meet his brown eyes.

"I want you." The words slipped out, breathless, before she could control them, before she was even sure she wanted to utter them.

But once they were in the air, a wicked flush invaded her— her body betraying everything she held fast against. The pit in her stomach morphed into a burn. A burn she could not ignore. Could not deny. Whatever the future, whatever the past. She wanted him in this moment.

Her hands went around his neck, fingernails curling against his skin. "I want you. And damn the past. Damn the future. I want you now."

Body uncoiling, he was on her in an instant, his mouth capturing hers. His tongue, his breath hot, matching the fire she felt under her skin.

His arm around the small of her back, he took her weight, even as his free hand came up, diving into the thick of her hair, slanting her head for deeper access.

Reanna groaned, and he pulled up slightly, not allowing her air away from his breath. "If I don't carry you upstairs right now, I will be taking you on the bench, world be dammed."

"Take me wherever you want, Killian, I don't care."

He picked her up, mouth on hers, and brushed past the evergreen hedge before her words finished.

Kicking the door closed in his room, Killian was to the bed in three strides, landing on top of her, hands working her dress.

She didn't note the fabric ripping as she was busy tearing away his linen shirt and buckskin breeches.

His naked body, in all its glorious weight, covered her, and she gasped, half in exploding desire, half in pain.

Killian jerked up. "Shit, your feet."

She grabbed his shoulders, pulling him down onto her. "No, they are fine, I just forgot. It is only my heels. I will be careful."

He held fast against her hands straining him downward, staring at her. "No."

His eyes flipped up, looking around. He grabbed her wrists, removing her hands from his neck, and straightened on his knees.

"No." Her breath sped, "Killian, don't leave."

"Not a chance, Ree." His mouth met hers, kissing her sudden alarm into submission. "Just better positioning."

He slipped his hands under her waist and flipped her onto her stomach, taking care that her feet didn't hit the bed hard.

His mouth went behind her ear as his left hand slipped down to her breasts, cupping it, teasing the nipple. "On your knees."

She pushed up, but was not quick enough for Killian, and he lifted and moved her, setting her upright on her knees, her belly flat against the top of the wide mahogany footboard.

"The top of your feet, do they hurt?"

"No."

Groaning, his chest covered her back as his left hand recaptured her breast. His right fingers slid down between her belly and the footboard, landing between her legs, parting and invading her folds at the same time.

Gasping at the touch, shockwaves riveted her body, and Reanna reached back, nails digging into his neck.

"The pain—is this all right, Ree?"

All Reanna could do was nod through a purring moan as her body rode the rhythm his hand set. Both of his legs slid forward between her calves, parting her thighs even further as his heat mingled with hers. The tip of him rested, nudged into her while his mouth attacked her neck, teeth running along the curves of her neck.

"I will hold out until you come, Ree, again and again, but hell, I want to be in you, driving deep into your body. But not until you tell me to. I will wait until—"

"Now, Killian, now. I want you filling me. No more waiting. Now."

He slammed up into her, months of pent-up desire unleashed in the thrust.

Gasping, her hands left him to grip the smooth, carved wood of the footboard, leveraging herself against his onslaught. But he would let her gain no space from him, both of his hands on her breasts, then moving down to her hips as took her from below.

She leaned forward, doubling over the footboard as his thrusts sent her to the edge, screaming. And then his fingers went deep, propelling her into a chasm of blinding light, her body arching. She could feel him expanding deep within her, and she held hard against his final throes, meeting him thrust for thrust until he exploded.

For harsh moments they panted, Killian covering her and the both of them draped over the edge of the footboard. Killian managed to move, still deep within her, and lifted Reanna, laying them down on their sides.

Arms wrapping her, his face deep in her hair, Reanna fell asleep in his sticky hot cocoon.

This moment was hers.

And it came with no regrets.

~ ~ ~

Reanna woke the next morning, alone. She knew it before she opened her eyes. Knew it before the shadow of dreams left her.

She stayed still, eyes closed for long minutes, willing it to be different. Willing there to be Killian's warm body behind her. But it wasn't.

He had left her again.

The tears started immediately once she acknowledged the cruel fact that Killian was gone. She glanced around the room to confirm, and it was true.

She had been stupid.

She had thought she could protect her heart, but it wasn't possible. Not with Killian. Not since the moment he kissed her last night. Not since his hands touched her skin. She had thought she could control herself. She couldn't. She had gone whole heart—she wasn't capable of any other way with him.

Curling into a ball, she dragged the silk coverlet to her face, soaking it within seconds with silent tears.

"Ree, Ree, good God, are you hurt?" Killian's voice rushed across the room to her.

She turned in the bed to his voice.

He landed on the bed, his hand on her shoulder. "Ree, what is going on?"

She looked up at him, blinking away the tears, the emotion. "I thought…I thought…You were not here when I woke up. So I thought…"

"You thought I left you again?"

She nodded. She couldn't get words past the lump of fear in her throat.

"I was just downstairs arranging for the children to visit today."

"Oh." She sat up, wiping her cheeks with the palms of her hands as she shook her head, her eyes trained on her lap. "I cannot do it, Killian. I am too vulnerable with you. I cannot. Waiting for you to…"

She took a deep breath, then looked up, meeting his brown eyes, not able to keep her voice from cracking. "I want you— God, I want you, Killian. But I cannot handle being destroyed again. I cannot."

He moved forward on the bed until she could feel his breath on her skin. Hand gentle on her cheek, he traced a wet line with his thumb. "Reanna, I promise you, right here, right now. You will never open your eyes alone again. If that is what you need to believe in me, believe in us, I will be here. No matter what. I will be here. Give me a chance to prove it."

She looked into the depths of his eyes, searching for truth. She wanted this so badly, it hurt, aching, deep in her chest. And then she saw it. The flicker, the raw honesty in his words, in his intentions.

She would need to learn to trust this.

She nodded, her cheek brushing his hand.

His other hand went to her face, capturing her before she could look away. Killian did his own searching, his eyes following the contours of her face, reading her eyes.

Satisfied with what he saw, he drew her close for a slow kiss, then pulled back, smiling. "It is raining, so it is the perfect day—I have some things I want to show you. I would like your opinions."

"My opinions—on what?"

"You will see. Food and dressed first."

An hour later, Killian helped her down the stairs from his room. His hand wrapped around her ribcage, planting solidly above the high waist on her violet muslin dress. His fingers slid up as they walked, taking full ownership of the bottom of her breast. It wasn't the polite hold he had offered in the past few days, it instead, bordered on mauling. But, she had to admit, if he chose to maul her like this from here through eternity, she wouldn't mind.

They passed by several rooms before he steered her into his study. Or what she assumed was the study. It held a wall of bookcases, full, a desk and one chair behind it. That was all. No other furniture.

She realized that was the exact thing that she had thought strange in the other rooms they passed, but did not think to comment on it.

He moved her behind the desk, setting her onto the lone chair.

She looked up at him as he half-sat on the desk, facing her. "Where did all your furniture go? I could have sworn I saw things in the rooms when you brought me outside."

"Actually, I was waiting for you," Killian said, excited gleam in his eye. "I realized that I had never cared for much of my furniture or décor in this house. All of it was for show, for the fashion, but that did not mean I liked any of it. I have gotten a few pieces that I am confident I like and will suit me. But the rest. The rest I thought I would leave to you. You and your tastes."

"You just removed everything?"

"Much of it went to your aunt's home. It did look like the children were wearing through your aunt's silk furniture rather quickly. So if you would like to help, I would appreciate your choices. I want this home to reflect you. To be for you."

"But Killian—"

"There is no pressure attached. Whatever will happen in the future, will happen. But I have to believe, have to remain optimistic that someday...someday this will be your home. Your true home, with me. Please?"

Slowly, Reanna nodded, both awestruck and unnerved that her opinion would mean so much to him.

No pressure, indeed.

CHAPTER 17

Her feet had actually been fine for three days. She wasn't limping, and they caused almost no discomfort. But she had held off from admitting it. Even limped a little in front of Killian, so he wouldn't question her progress.

But there they were, two feet, ten toes, smooth and scab free. The new skin pink and shiny.

She didn't want this to end. She wanted to stay in this bubble where Killian adored her, listened to her, twisted her body into the most imaginative contortions. She didn't want to know whatever it was that Killian had to tell her. Even though she knew she needed to hear the truth. Needed it to fully move on with him. And it hurt how much she needed to move on with him.

"You have them uncovered." Killian walked into the room, interrupting her thoughts. "Let me see."

Before she could rewrap them, Killian sat on the bed and picked up her leg, fingers slipping into the crook behind her knee where he knew she was ticklish.

She laughed as she jerked her leg away, but he caught her ankle and set her left foot on his lap, silently looking over the skin. He ran his fingers over the new skin, leaving no crook untouched. Satisfied with the first, he silently grabbed her right foot and gave it the same examination.

Done, he set both of her feet onto the bed, and looked up at her. Solemnness had replaced the playfulness in his eyes. "They are healed, are they not?"

Reanna nodded, unable to force the one word past her tight throat.

"How long have they been like this?"

Reanna swallowed hard. "Three days."

His head went down, eyes avoiding her. Then he slowly stood from the bed. It took long moments before his eyes met hers. "We do not have to do this, Reanna. We can go on, never speak of a day before you came here. Let it be past. Untouched. Unexamined."

"Killian…"

He gave one curt nod, straightening. "It is nice out today. Will you meet me in the garden in an hour?"

Breath deserting her, Reanna gave the slightest tilt of her chin.

Killian backed out of the room, disappearing behind the closed door.

~ ~ ~

He waited on the bench for her, words flying through his mind. What he would say—what he could say. How could he tell her this, the truth, and still convince her to stay?

His gaze shifted down to his weathered chess set on a low table in front of him. The staff brought it out here on the nice days, and he knew Reanna was comforted by its very presence. Something tangible, the first bridge between them. Hours spent staring at the board had been his way in. His way into her mind, her heart. It was the only reason she had learned to listen to him again. But little black and white pieces couldn't fix this.

Damn himself for promising the truth.

But he wasn't about to lie to her.

If she needed this, he would give it to her. He would give her the whole damn bloody world if it meant she would stay with him.

He heard her light footsteps crunching on the gravel granite path deep in the gardens behind him. She had chosen the long winding path to the bench, not the straight, cobblestoned path. Her footsteps were even, not hiccupped or jerking. She was healed. As healed as he could make her.

The crunching slowed, and Reanna appeared through the opening in the evergreen hedge, the trepidation lining her face doing nothing to mar her beauty—the glowing beauty that he had seen come alive over the past weeks. No, the trepidation only gave a haunting quality to her blue eyes.

Was it possible she didn't want to do this as much as he didn't want to do this?

Silently, she approached him, then stopped a step away, looking at him and then to the bench, not sure what to do with herself.

Killian held his hand up to her. "Please, sit."

She took it and sat, but kept a swath of distance between the two of them.

"I am not sure how to start this, Reanna. How to explain what happened. Why I did what I did to you."

Her hand slipped from his, landing in her lap, and her eyes followed. "Was it something I did?"

"What? No. God no. You are what's right, Ree. I was what was wrong for a long time. But no more." His hand went to her cheek, fingers settling on her neck just below her upsweep, thumb tilting her head up. "The whole of it, it didn't have anything to do with you, Reanna. You just got caught. Caught in my hate."

"Hate?"

"It is not an excuse, but I have been living in hate for so long, Reanna. I was mired so deep in it, there was no escape. And I did not even recognize what I had become. My hate became habit. Became who I was without even realizing it."

His hand dropped from her cheek to grab her hand. "But you were—you are—the light banishing all that hate surrounding me. For the longest time, I turned my back to it, to you. But your light. It is too bright. It brought me out of all that."

Her eyes were full of confusion, yet didn't waver from his. "I do not understand this, Killian. Who do you hate? Why? And how did I get caught in whatever you are talking about?"

"Your father."

A sharp intake of breath, and she jerked her hand from his. "My father? What? I did not think you even knew him."

"I do. I know him well."

Reanna rubbed her forehead, and then her head snapped up. "You. You ruined him, didn't you?"

"Yes." Killian was surprised she put it together so quickly.

"What did you do to him? Why? I have never heard how or why he was ruined, only that it happened."

"This started long before I was born." Killian ran his fingers through his hair. "My father had vices. Vices that brought him down to hell. He was a good man, a good father, a good husband. But he was addicted to gambling. Gambling on investments. Gambling at the tables. He tried time and again to stop, but he was addicted, and there are those that prey on men like him. Offer them riches. Cheat them. His desperation was taken advantage of. Debt after debt piled upon each other, and eventually, every tangible piece of the estate was lost to one man. Your father."

"But that is money, Killian. You now have all the money you could ever need, and yet you did all you did to me because of money?" Her voice had grown weak.

Killian turned from her, eyes locked onto the rectangular patch of primroses across from them. "Had it only been a lost fortune, things would be different today. But it was not. Your father suggested to mine that death would be the most honorable way to clear the debts, to save the family. With complete ruin imminent, my father killed himself to avoid scandal—to avoid marring the family line."

Her gasp was not a surprise. Killian could not bring himself to look at her. He did not want to see the pity he knew was in her eyes. Beyond himself, only two living people knew of his father's suicide, Devin and Aggie. And now Reanna.

He stood from the bench, back to her. "It was then I started dreaming of my revenge against your father. I went into the military early, too early, was promoted from the ranks, met

Devin, and eventually rebuilt a fortune, much to Devin's credit and support."

"So how did you ruin my father?"

Killian turned to her, crossing his arms over his chest, voice, factual. "It took years, but piece by piece, we ruined all of your father's investments. Sometimes by proxy. Sometimes through acquaintances. Until all your father had left was his sizable investment in one of Devin's shipping companies. And then we sank a ship, bankrupting the company."

"You sank a ship?"

"We did. No one died. But it ruined the company. Your father was penniless, and he blamed, very publicly, Devin for it. Questioned his honor, which of course, Devin would not stand for."

Killian paused, not sure if he should continue. Reanna was quickly turning pale, mouth slightly askew. But he promised her honesty.

He took a steadying breath, and continued.

"They were to duel, and I was to stand in for Devin. It had been the plan all along. But your father never arrived for the duel. Left town a coward. Ruined. And then six months later, you appeared in London."

There was very little reaction in Reanna's posture, and Killian wasn't sure what that meant. He moved to sit next to her on the bench.

"You, I had not planned on, Reanna. I thought we had taken everything from him, every chance he had to ever live a comfortable life again. I did not think he would whore out his own daughter."

She recoiled. "Whore me out? No, he would not."

"He did. You came to London as his last hope. He had one thing left to sell. You."

"No. He wanted me to have a season." Her breath visibly sped, her hand gripping the edge of the bench as she leaned forward, curling against his words.

"Reanna, you came into town with a list in hand of eligible bachelors."

"You knew that?"

"Of course we did. The list—did it consist of young, virile men?"

"No."

"Did they all have money, lots of it?"

"Yes."

"Were they, to a one, old, lecherous creatures?"

Eyes wide, she nodded.

"He whored you out, Reanna. I know it is hard to hear, but you were his last chance. The money you would have given him access to was his last desperate grab against becoming a pauper."

She stood as her hand went to her chest, pressing back against the rapid rise and fall of her lungs. "And then you…"

"Yes. I have more money than all of those fools combined, and your father got greedy. He did not think twice about agreeing to our marriage. The solicitor I sent to him said he near drooled when he was told I was hoping for your hand in marriage."

She staggered backward from him. "Oh, God. You never. You truly never even…liked me. Never even looked at me."

Killian shot to his feet. "Reanna—"

"I was a pawn?"

There was no use in dishonesty. "Yes."

"A tool used merely for revenge? The last pawn?"

"Yes, but—"

"No. Stop. I fell all the damn way in love with you, Killian. And you never even liked me." Her hand flicked up, finger pointing. "You never once even saw me. All you saw was your revenge."

She whipped away, taking a few steps, then spun, stalking back toward Killian. She stopped a step away from him, heaving, and kicked the table under the chess set hard, sending pieces flying and clattering to the cobblestone.

Her face cringed in pain, but it only stoked her fury. "I have spent half of a year trying to understand why you would hate me so. I changed everything—every damn thing—about myself, trying to please you. Trying to become interesting, the type of woman you could love. And you damn well never even saw me."

"No, Reanna," Killian interrupted her, voice low, hands clenching and unclenching. "I did see you. Our wedding night. Our wedding night, I saw you. And hell. It shook me to my very being. All my hate. Gone. Just like that. That one night threatened to take every intention of revenge I had and shred it."

He swallowed the step between them. "I lived for more than twenty-five years in hatred. In planning revenge. And one night with you, and I forgot about it." His arm flew up. "Considered giving up every thought I ever had on revenge. But I could not let that happen. I was too damn scared. Revenge was the only thing I breathed. Revenge was the only thing I was. I could not let that go."

She took a step backward, spinning away from him. "Hell, Killian…I thought…I mean, I knew you must have had your reasons, but…" Her head angled to the sky, and Killian could see tears starting to fall. "I was nothing to you—ever. I am such an idiot. How could I have not seen that in you? How could I have loved you so much and never once seen the reality of what was before me?"

He stepped in front of her. "You are not an idiot, Reanna. I built a life where even I didn't know what reality was. You were the first real thing I recognized in…in forever. You don't understand—"

"I don't understand what?" Her wet eyes narrowed on him. "That you could possibly be an even lower person than I thought you were? That your own self-righteous vengeance would allow you to—without a second thought—destroy me?"

"No, that was never the case."

"That was exactly what happened. You destroyed me. And do not try to tell me you did not know what you were doing. I begged you. Begged you. I was on my god-damn knees in front of you, Killian."

His eyes closed, her words slicing through his chest.

"You did all of this without any regard to who got hurt in the process." Her head shook. "It makes me sick to think I was blind enough to love you. Stupid enough to marry you."

"Reanna—"

"It is time for me to leave this place, Killian. I want nothing more to do with you."

Before he could reply, she spun away from him.

Head high, she walked out of the garden.

CHAPTER 18

Killian staggered into Devin's study, squinting in the low light and fighting the bleariness in his eyes. He was greeted by the sight of Devin's long legs straight out in front of him, back arched on the sofa, the baby sleeping soundly on his chest. Devin's hand covered the full length of the baby's back.

Killian turned to escape the room. Even in his current inebriation, he was not willing to disturb the tranquil scene.

"Stop. Don't make me speak above a whisper."

Killian's foot stopped mid-air, and he looked over his shoulder at Devin.

Devin waved him over with his free hand, pointing to a wingback chair across from the sofa. Killian shuffled silently into the room, slumping into the chair.

Devin eyed him for a moment. "I know that look. I assume your driver must still be under strict orders to deliver you here when you ask to hit a gaming hall?"

Killian nodded, not meeting his eyes.

"So what would have driven you to your current depths?" Devin's voice remained a whisper.

"I told her."

Devin's eyebrows arched, but he didn't say a word. After a minute, he shifted his feet close to the sofa, and stood, leaning back so his solid hold on the baby didn't waver. He walked over to Killian. "Here, hold him." Devin tilted the boy backward on his hands, holding him out to Killian.

Killian held his hand up in refusal.

"Hold him. It will sober you."

"He will not wake?"

"Doubtful. He has kept both Aggie and the nanny up for the past twenty hours. But he has been fast asleep for an hour.

I doubt the ringing of Bow Bells could awaken him—but keep your voice low for good measure."

Killian held his hands out, taking the baby, and mimicked Devin's earlier posture, leaning back in the chair and settling the baby on his chest. The smallest sigh and twitch, and the baby settled, cheek on Killian's heart.

Devin was right—the baby's tiny sweet puffs of breath were completely sobering.

Devin walked over to the sideboard and pulled two glasses, setting them in front of the decanter of brandy. He poured the first glass, then glanced quickly over his shoulder at Killian. He set the second glass back to its proper place, empty, then picked up his own, taking a healthy swallow as he turned and walked back to sit across from Killian.

"He is a wonder," Killian said.

"He has a name now. Andrew Theodore Stephenson."

"For your great-grandfather. Well done."

Devin took another sip. "What did you tell her? Everything?"

"Most of it."

Devin's head tilted. "Your mother?"

Killian shook his head. "No."

"And her reaction?"

"She hates me."

"Did you expect anything less?"

Killian paused, mulling that question. "No, I suppose not."

"So what will you do now?"

"Nothing. She wants nothing more to do with me."

"And you are just going to accept that?"

Even with the baby on his chest, Killian managed a shrug. "What else can I do?"

"I think it is time to review." Devin leaned back, tossing an arm along the top of the sofa. "You spent the last fourteen years of your life plotting the downfall of one man, not to mention the years of dreaming about it before that. You never once reversed course, never gave up, never contemplated defeat. And you succeeded. Now, in this moment, you are facing a wife with a heart the size of the ocean, and one little setback, and you are done? I must say, a tad weak, my friend."

Killian's eyes narrowed on Devin. "I destroyed her. Time and again. Do not underestimate the damage I have done. I am nothing in her eyes."

A smirk fell onto Devin's face. "You may have destroyed her, but you also fell in love with her, didn't you?"

Killian let his head fall backward, looking at the coffered ceiling. "It does not matter. I am not worthy of her."

"Debatable."

"I do not know what convoluted mind would debate that."

Devin shrugged as he stood and poured himself another glass. "My convoluted mind, for one. Aggie's convoluted mind, for two." He turned back to Killian. "Anyone that knows the whole story—your whole story. Which, when truly told, includes your mother, as well."

Killian's eyes went down to the dark fuzz on the top of the baby's head. He moved his free hand to caress the tiny hairs sticking up, surprised by the soft smoothness of babe's head.

"I went too far with her. Her anger runs deep."

"I have found that anger is a good thing sometimes, at least when it comes to my wife. It means she is paying attention. Those moments Aggie is the angriest with me, always precede the moments she loves me the most. Anger means Reanna is still engaged with you. It is something to work with."

"Aggie is stubborn—how do you even begin to erase her anger?"

Devin smirked. "I am not at liberty to explain, but I do have my ways. You know me to be charmless, but Aggie apparently thinks differently."

Devin swallowed the last of his brandy. "As for you, my friend, stay in front of Reanna and accept her anger. You cannot change what you avoid. You talk of stubbornness? My wife would tell you that you have the ability to wear down anyone. So show up. Be there—wherever she is. You are a hard one to deny."

Killian's eyes went back down to the baby.

He had to get sober.

~ ~ ~

Reanna looked out the front parlor window of the small, but cozy townhouse as she stood from the chair. She hated to rush the meeting along, but she wanted to get back to the Brook Street townhouse as quickly as possible to check on the mother and baby that had joined the household this morning.

Pounding on the front door had woken the household at daybreak. By the time Reanna had a robe on and had made it to the foyer, Miss Collier had already answered the door. A bloodied, sobbing woman, baby in arms, was pleading with Miss Collier to take her baby.

It took some time to actually understand the woman, but once Reanna had ushered her into the front parlor and had her seated, the woman calmed enough to get coherent words out. Fresh blood still trickled down her face, as words tumbled. "He will kill me, and the baby, when 'e finds me. Kill me, 'e will. 'E already tried. Ye need to take me boy. I'll leave 'em here with ye. This place keep comin' to lips of folk. No matter me own life. Ye keep 'im safe. Please. Please. I beg ye."

It only took Reanna a second to decide what to do. "Nonsense. I refuse to separate you two. You will both stay here and be safe from your husband."

"No ma'am. Just me boy. 'E's all that matters."

"I am going to round the doctor to come and tend to your face, and then you will stay here until we can find a suitable, safe life away from your man," Reanna said. "You will be safe here. I promise."

The woman, Pertie, had relented, but Reanna had to leave for this appointment just as the doctor had arrived.

Yes. She needed to get back quickly.

Reanna turned to the Jacobsons, a childless couple who were hoping to take in four-year-old Cynthia. This was Reanna's fourth and final interview with them. "I see the rain has not stopped, but I must take my leave."

The couple walked her out of the parlor to the door.

"Thank you again, so much, Lady Southfork. You do not know how much this means to my wife and myself. Rain or no, this is truly a blessed day." They both beamed at the prospect of Cynthia becoming theirs. Mr. Jacobson put his arm around his wife, squeezing her shoulder.

The small gesture concurrently warmed Reanna's heart, and stung it with jealousy. So simple. So loving. So honest.

She took a deep breath and produced a bright smile. Cynthia would be very happy with these two, who clearly adored each other. Mr. Jacobson owned a large blacksmith shop, a solid trade, and their household was simple and loving, perfect for the little girl. Cynthia was one of the children that had been abandoned at the townhouse during the time she had been healing at Killian's home. Killian had given orders to the staff that any child showing up at her aunt's home would be taken in.

"It is indeed, Mr. Jacobson. I know Cynthia will be very happy with you. She has spoken of little other than you two since she met you. She is very excited, and I appreciate your patience with my sometimes probing questions. I meant to cause no discomfort in asking them."

"No, we understand. You want the best for Cynthia, and we have no secrets. I am impressed you would go to such lengths to ensure the happiness of the child." Mr. Jacobson opened the door.

"Thank you for understanding. Will you be ready for her tomorrow, possibly at two?"

"Two would be fine. Do tell her we are most excited."

"I will. We will be by at two tomorrow."

Her new driver, Filbert, stepped quickly up the stairs, umbrella open and ready to shield her on the stairs down to the carriage. It had only been a few days, and she was still getting used to his enthusiastic assistance at every turn.

Filbert, the large carriage, and the matching horses had appeared three days earlier. After a weeklong besiege of gifts to the home from Killian—all of them attached with some purpose to the children—Reanna quickly discovered how hard it was to refuse gifts that the children immediately latched onto. And then they would inevitably ask about Killian visiting. It was hard to deny them both his presence and his gifts. So the gifts had stayed.

But Reanna had reached her breaking point with the carriage and was about to send Filbert on his way, when the children began crawling all over the carriage, glee on their faces.

The carriage was long, with an extra middle bench, for transporting the lot of the older ones together. But before Reanna could open her mouth, she knew she was going to give in. It was easier than watching eighteen little faces fall to disappointment. And for what—her own pride?

"Did it go well today, my lady?" Filbert asked, water from the umbrella streaming over half his hat as they went down the stairs.

Ignoring his appalled look, Reanna shifted the pole of the wide umbrella so it covered both of their heads. "It was wonderful, Filbert, they are a delightful couple, and this last visit convinces me that Cynthia will find a lovely home with them."

"It is good to hear, my lady."

Filbert stepped out from under the umbrella to open the carriage door. He assisted her onto the carriage step, and Reanna froze, half in, half out of the carriage.

The bastard was sitting there.

"Reanna, please, come in. You will catch a chill out there." Killian was sitting in the back corner, ankle resting on his knee, relaxed as though he owned the very air around him.

"I will, if you would be so kind as to exit immediately." Her voice was ice.

"I am afraid I cannot do that. The chill out there is even worse than the one in here."

Reanna lifted her foot already in the carriage to back down to the street, but Killian shot forward, grabbing her arm and pulling her into the coach.

She landed awkwardly on the backward facing bench.

Stunned, Filbert stood outside the door with gaping mouth.

Killian didn't look at him, his eyes were trained on Reanna trying to right herself. "Filbert, if you please, drive. Drive anywhere. Just close the door and drive."

Indecision clear with his stutter, he looked back and forth between Killian and Reanna. "My lady?"

She tossed a hostile glance at Killian, who still held her arm firmly, before she turned to Filbert. "It is fine, Filbert. Do as he says. My home shall be fine. I will let you know if I need assistance."

With a quick nod, Filbert closed the door and collapsed the carriage steps.

Reanna jerked her arm away from Killian's grip.

"Their loyalty so quickly wanes," Killian muttered.

"You question his loyalty to me?"

"I did hire him."

"Is the choice between us that hard?" she said, not hiding the venom in her voice.

Killian cocked an eyebrow at her remark, but said nothing. He moved back, sitting on the middle bench, brown eyes running over her body, head to toe.

"What is it that you want, Killian? I thought we both understood that I want nothing more to do with you."

"We do. But that does not preclude the fact that I still want things to do with you."

Reanna's hand went to her forehead—she could feel it starting to pound. "Killian, please, what do you want? I do not have time for this."

"I wanted to tell you a few things I did not get a chance to the other day."

Reanna eyed him warily. "If I listen, will you leave me alone?"

"Honestly, no. I do not intend to ever leave you alone. But what I say may make my presence in your life a bit more acceptable."

Reanna shook her head, crossing her arms over her waist. "I doubt it will." She sighed, waving a white-gloved hand. "Fine. Speak what you need to speak."

For a moment, Killian looked unsure. Reanna wondered if he had expected her to put up more resistance. She just wanted him gone, out of sight. And if listening to him was the fastest way to that end, then he could speak all he wanted to.

"Reanna, when you said I had no conscience, gave no thought to who I might hurt in my quest for revenge, you were right. Completely right. I did not think. I did not consider for one second what my actions might do to an innocent such as yourself."

"I am no innocent."

Killian's mouth tightened as he stared at her. Then he shook his head, voice raw. "No. No, you are not. But you were, and I ruined that."

Her eyes darted to the lower corner of the carriage. Hearing him say those words, even though they were true, made her heart heavy. He had done this to her. She had to remember that.

A thick silence enveloped them until she raised her eyes to his, waiting for him to continue.

"It happened a long time ago, and I cannot even tell you when, but my life, what I did in it, it did not matter if what I was doing was right or wrong, it only mattered that I achieve my goal. Reaching my goal, having my revenge, was the only thing that mattered, because it was the only thing I knew how to do. It was who I was. And you were just a tool in that, just a pawn."

Reanna drew a shaky breath. She did not want to hear this again. "You are not telling me anything new, Killian. And I would prefer to not have to, once more, listen to how you used me."

"No, Reanna," Killian snapped forward, voice hard, "you will listen to this, because I am most assured you did not hear this the first time."

He paused and took a deep breath, regaining his control, but didn't lean away from her. "You were a pawn. You were the completion of my revenge. You were all of that. All of that until our wedding night."

"Our wedding night?" Reanna's mind raced. What had he said about their wedding night? She had been so angry a fortnight ago, she didn't even remember much of their conversation. Just red in her mind. Her limbs shaking. Snippets of words.

Killian grabbed her knees, one in each hand. "When we made love, Reanna, when I touched you. You, naked in front of me. Under me. I saw you for the first time. Hell, I actually saw everything for the first time in years. Everything outside of my revenge. A whole world. You got to something deep within me that I cannot describe. Something I did not know existed. But it was something that did not align with my goals. With what I thought I needed."

"And that was?"

"The revenge against your father. I was not ready for you. I was not ready to give up what I had quested after for almost my whole life. To give up my whole reason for being. All because when I touched you, I actually felt something. To give up everything after only one night with you? Madness."

"So instead you banished me? Even though I loved you?" She forced the flat words out.

"It was all I could think to do. It was what I thought I wanted, needed. I did not understand you, your love, or what I was feeling."

"How hard was it to understand I loved you? Adored you? Would have done anything for you?"

He shook his head. "I was terrified, and my fear blinded me. I needed to get rid of you. Of every memory. Of every touch. And I did it more cruelly than I intended. You will never know how much I would give to erase my words from the day after our wedding. From the days at Holloton."

Reanna took a deep breath, hoping to gain balance, but instead, only the spice of his scent filled her, spinning her head. "So what do you want from me now?"

"I know I should let you go. Let you live in peace. You deserve it." His hands tightened on her legs. "But dammit, Ree, I am going to be selfish. I openly admit to it. As much as you deserve to be let go, I cannot do it. I want you. I need my wife. I need you in my life, your light. You are my whole damn purpose. That I even dare to ask is ludicrous, but I want a second chance from you. Even if I don't deserve it."

"Killian…" Her eyes closed, fighting what she saw in his face. Honesty. Remorse. Desire.

Even with her eyes shut, the raw, guttural longing that threatened her very soul invaded the air around her.

"We proved it, Reanna. We proved the truth while you were healing. How much I want you." His voice went low, slow, as his hands moved up her legs, thumbs brushing the inside of her thighs through her blue muslin dress. "How much you want me. How our bodies need to be together."

She cracked her eyes open to him.

"Your body. Your heart. They know you are mine. It is only your head." His right hand moved upward, fingers going into the hair at her temple, his thumb moving across her forehead. "This beautiful mind of yours that denies me. That refuses me. That holds you steadfast against me."

He moved forward, his forehead touching hers as his hand moved to her neck. "But I know, Ree. I know your heart, your body, are stronger than your mind. I do not accept the thought that there is no room in your heart for me. I know you can love me again."

Her eyes slid closed again at his words, both fighting and willing him onward at the same time. They sat, breath melding, his fingers on her skin, unmoving, while drops of rain pattered on the coach roof.

The carriage stopped.

Against her pounding heart, against her body that Killian recognized was aching for him, Reanna's mind surged, and she leaned to her side, breaking the touch.

"No, Killian, this is too much. This…this time is worse than before. I want this—you—so badly. In a way I never knew possible. In a real way. The week we had together. I truly believe it was real. That you were real. You made me want this. But if I am wrong…the pain…" She shook her head, holding her breath as she slid along the bench. "This is too much for me to take in. I need to go inside. I need to think. Please, just leave. Take the carriage."

Silently, Killian nodded, and moved back, tapping the carriage ceiling. But then he grabbed her wrist before she could escape.

"Take as much time as you need, Reanna. But I am not disappearing. You are my wife, and I intend to make you so in every sense of the word." He loosened his hold on her wrist. "And if you need anything—anything—for yourself or for the children, please tell the secretary I hired for you. He meets with my man every other day."

Reanna nodded silently. She barely saw his face before her, for his words had clouded her mind, clouded the orderly existence she had created for herself since she had left his townhouse a fortnight ago.

The carriage door opened, and she got out of the coach, sheltered by Filbert's umbrella.

CHAPTER 19

Reanna leaned against the closed front door of the Brook Street townhouse. She had surprised herself by making it all the way in, instead of turning and running back into Killian's arms.

He was right.

Damn her own heart. Her body. She was his, and he knew it. Hell. She knew it.

Even after everything. After the truth of his revenge. After what he did to her father. She still wanted him.

And it was undeniable when he was right in front of her.

She sighed, clunking her head against the door. As she looked up the flights of stairs and the balconies on each level, the silence hit her. She had honestly hoped to get lost in the bustle of the children, but it was silent.

Miss Collier crossed the balcony above her and was a step into one of the rooms, when Reanna stepped forward, head craned to her. "Miss Collier, why is it so quiet?"

A finger went to her lips as Miss Collier stepped to the railing, whispering down to Reanna. "It be a near miracle. The little ones are all napping at once. Thomas and the older ones are with the tutor lady on the top floor. They made some sort of science machine to capture rain and figure out how fast it be falling. Who wants to know that? It's heavy, it's heavy, I say. No need to know how fast. But Thomas in particular was mighty excited by it. So you have the main level to yourself, mi' lady."

Reanna nodded, amazed. The household was in perfect order since Killian had hired more nannies and had Miss Collier take over the running of the place.

"Miss Collier, wait," Reanna whispered. "The mother, Pertie, and her baby boy. How are they?"

"Mother and baby are sleeping in the end room, third floor. The doc tended to her, said her nose is broken, but will heal fine. The baby is well."

"Good. Thank you." Reanna nodded. She regretted having to leave for the appointment with Cynthia's future parents after the drama with Pertie this morning. But if the woman was resting, Reanna was not about to wake her.

Reanna turned and walked into the study across from the front parlor. If she couldn't get lost in the bustle of the children, perhaps numbing her brain with numbers would take her mind off of Killian. Besides, she had been putting off much of the financials since the secretary Killian had hired had deftly taken over managing the household's payments.

Ten minutes after diving into the numbers, a loud banging on the door jerked her head upright. She stood from the desk, rushing into the foyer, annoyed that Killian was interrupting her so soon after she asked to be alone. And now he threatened to wake up the whole household and disturb the fleeting peace.

But it wasn't Killian at the door.

It was a heaving, fisted, filthy drunk brute of a man.

Instant fear enveloped Reanna, and she yanked at the door handle, trying to close the door, but she was too slow. Fury shook his body as he rushed her, ripping her hand from the door, pushing her back into the foyer.

His hand wrapped around her throat, shoving her against the wall.

"Where be me woman, bitch?" The man yelled into her face, his breath full of green teeth and alcohol, stinging Reanna's senses.

He banged Reanna's head against the wall, hitting a mirror and sending it crashing to the floor. Breath choked off, Reanna clawed at his arm, fingernails digging into hairy flesh. The arm didn't move.

"Where the fuck? The boy? Where be the boy?"

Reanna knew immediately who he was demanding. Pertie and her baby.

She would die before she let this bastard near them.

He loosened his grip on her throat. "Talk, woman."

"I don't know who—"

The grip collapsed on her neck, and he shoved her up the wall, jerking her toes off the floor.

"Stop ya lyin' ya little bitch. Oi know she came here. Where the 'ell is she?"

A fist flew in front of Reanna's face.

But it missed her completely, crashing into the jaw of the man.

His hand ripped off her throat, and Reanna dropped, falling to the floor. It took her a second to open her eyes and realize the man was now in a crumbled heap on the floor, a boot kicking him mercilessly, pulverizing.

Killian.

She pushed herself up, back supported by the wall, hands on her crushed throat, just as Killian wedged the man's neck under his boot.

"Are you all right, Ree?" Killian glanced at her, brown eyes furious.

She nodded.

Killian turned his attention back to the man pinned on the shiny hardwood floor. His bloodied eyes were wide as he stared up at Killian.

"I would kill you now," Killian seethed, "but I don't think my wife should have to witness the grotesqueness that is a man dying of breath. A man grasping to the last shreds of life. Shall I ask her to leave the room?"

The man managed to shake his head, converging panic and lack of air turning his face purple. One of his arms looked broken, limp on the floor, but the other managed to go weakly to Killian's ankle, trying to push him off.

Killian bent over the man, letting his boot dig into the man's windpipe. "It appears we have a situation. I can either kill you now, or if you would rather, I can have my driver deliver you to the docks, and throw you in a ship hold, never to be seen in England again. If you are lucky, you will live. If not, your injuries will bless you with a slow, painful death. Either way it develops, it is agreeable to me, as it will remove you from this land. Would you like to die now, or be delivered to the docks?"

Killian eased his boot up, allowing the man to gasp for air and sputter, "Docks."

The boot went solidly back down.

"Fine. But if you are ever seen in this city again, you will be killed on sight. That is a guarantee from me." Killian leaned down even further, death in his voice. "Do we have an understanding?"

The man nodded as vigorously as Killian's boot allowed, and Killian eased up his foot.

Filbert appeared next to Killian, rope in hand. He quickly yanked up the man's broken arm, sending the man writhing into pain.

"Well done, Filbert."

"Thank you, my lord."

Filbert quickly tied the man's hands behind his back, and yanked him to his knees, then feet. He started to drag him out into the rain.

"You heard what to do with him, Filbert?"

"I did, my lord."

"Stop by my main shipping office to find out what would be the best ship to toss him on."

"As you wish, my lord."

Killian followed them and closed the door as Filbert dragged the man down the stairs.

Fighting for breath, Reanna went to her knees and started picking up the pieces of glass from the mirror, fingers shaking uncontrollably.

Killian's sudden hand on her shoulder made her jump, and she dropped the few pieces she had managed to gather onto his Hessians.

"Oh, Killian, I am...I am sorry." The words were scratchy coming out of her raw throat. She began to brush the shards off his boots.

He came down to her level, balancing on his heels, and grabbed her wrists, turning her hands palm up.

"Stop. You are bleeding." He stood and pulled her to her feet.

"But the children. I have to clean it."

"And you are shaking. Miss Collier will handle it." He looked up the staircase, and Reanna's eyes followed, only to see Miss Collier already hurrying down the steps, broom in hand.

Killian pulled her into him, enveloping her entire body into his arms, his chest. He walked her backward, guiding them into the study, closing the door behind them. Reanna could hear him flip the lock on the door.

Her eyes stayed closed, her forehead buried on his hard chest. She couldn't control her tremors, no matter how many breaths she took.

But Killian had her. One arm around her back, one deep in her hair. He had her. Safe.

She swallowed hard through her throat that felt half its normal width. It took long minutes, but Killian didn't break the hold, didn't speak, until her shaking subsided.

With a deep breath, she lifted her head.

He looked down at her. "Are you all right?"

"Yes. I don't know…I don't know what I would have done…"

"Do not think on that." Killian stroked her hair. "He is gone. What—who—did he want?"

"A mother, Pertie, came here this morning. She was beaten, broken nose, and she had a baby she wanted to leave with us. She was sure he was going to kill the two of them. So I insisted she stay as well. They are upstairs."

"Bloody hell."

She pulled away. "I should check on her."

Killian didn't loosen his hold. "Miss Collier will do so. You need to sit."

He moved her over to the small sofa in front of the window, setting her down. Rain continued to beat and drip down on the glass behind her.

Killian remained standing in front of her, arms folded across his chest. "I am going to be hiring guards. This cannot happen again."

She looked up at him sharply, words painful as they scraped through her throat. "What? No. Guards will scare the children. And they will scare off any child in need coming to this house."

"This is not a negotiation, Reanna." He ran his hand through his hair. "Guards will be hired. I will tell them to be discrete. But this place will have guards."

He turned from her, pacing away, and then back to her. "Bloody hell, Ree, if I had not still been outside…your neck…" His hand went under her chin, tilting her head up, and he looked closely at her throat.

A flash of rage, completely uncontrolled, coiled his body. Growling, he spun away from her, punching the nearest wall. Plaster went flying.

Shocked into cringing silence, it took Reanna a moment to understand what had just happened. Whatever it was, it was not normal. She looked from the hole in the wall, to Killian's back, staring at his heaving shoulders near to splitting his dark jacket. He did not turn back to her.

She stood up and slowly approached him. Fingers light on his shoulder, he twitched at the touch, but didn't pull from her. "Killian, what just happened to you?"

The heaving slowed. But it still took long moments for him to speak. "The marks on your neck. You are beginning to bruise."

Reanna's eyebrows pulled together, confused as she rounded him. Her hand went to her throat, fingers covering the throbbing points in her skin. "I imagine they are, but what was that? The wall? Why?"

He closed his eyes, shaking his head. "The marks on your neck. I never thought…I never believed I would see anything like that again. Feel anything like that."

"Killian, you are scaring me." Her throat hurt with each and every word, but she kept on. "What you are talking about?"

She grabbed his upper arms and pushed him. At first
he remained rooted in spot, until he took the tiniest shuffle
backward. Reanna kept pushing until she had him sitting on the
sofa.

She bent, resting on her heels in front of him, arms light on
his thighs. She looked up at him, hoping she was covering the
bruising from his sight. His knuckles were already bloodied, and
she didn't want him punching another wall. "Tell me what is
going on. Tell me what that was."

His eyes glazed slightly as he looked at her. Reanna watched
as he disappeared into himself. Disappeared from her. And then
he took a deep breath, shaking his head as his face turned grey,
melding into the grey of the rain behind him.

He wasn't going to tell her.

"No. Unacceptable. You are telling me what that was, right
now." Reanna grabbed his forearm, squeezing it. "Right now,
Killian. Honesty."

Another deep breath, head still shaking, and his eyes went
to the ceiling. Moments passed, and then words started to
trickle out. "Do you remember when I told you my father killed
himself?"

Reanna nodded, a rock sinking into her stomach. "Yes."

"He hung himself in the stables at Holloton. We had no staff
then, because he had lost everything. Empty stables. So it was just
me. I found him. I was six. His body was still jerking to a slow
death. I could barely reach his feet, but I pushed up on his toes.
He only had one shoe on. I tried for an hour to lift him. He was
dead for most of it. My mother found us."

His eyes moved across the ceiling, eventually dropping to
Reanna. "She covered it up, his suicide, in order to keep the title
safe. But I still remember the burns around his neck after she cut
him down and sliced away the rope."

Reanna's hand went in front of her mouth, trying to push
back the bile that her heart pounded into her mouth. She had no
breath, not even enough to speak his name. All she could do was
tighten her hold on his leg.

"After that, with no money, she sold everything not entailed, but still there was not enough money to pay the debts. And your father kept visiting, kept demanding what he was owed. She thought she hid it, his visits from me. But I watched. I knew. Months went by and every day he would visit, harass her, demand the money. Until one day, he proposed she whore herself out to him to erase the debts."

Reanna's frozen breath escaped in an outward gasp. "No…"

"It was what he was after all along. My mother refused, at first. But as she ran out of the last things to sell in the home, the things that would at least buy us food, she had to watch me go hungry every other day. So she eventually agreed. She convinced him to send me to school. And then she left for one of your father's estates. I only saw her once after that, alive. In six years, only once. She looked like an old lady. Gaunt, lifeless, and she had marks like this on her neck."

Killian's fingers, light as air, ran across Reanna's neck, pausing at each distinct bruise. His hand pulled back as he stared at the marks.

"The next time I saw her, it was when her body was delivered back to Holloton for burial. The day after I left for the military. The rest of the story, you know."

Reanna forced down the lump in her throat, eyes not leaving his face. Watching the pain etch his eyes.

This was what she had been fighting all along, and never known it.

The pain of a six-year-old boy. The pain of a boy losing his mother. His father. It had truly never been about her. It was her father. "Killian, I am so sorry."

"What are you sorry for?"

"My father—"

"Stop." He leaned forward, eyes pinning her, voice vehement. "You are not your father, Reanna. You do not own anything he did. This is not your fault. Do you understand? You do not apologize for his actions. You are the innocent in all of this."

She nodded, silent.

He straightened, closing his eyes.

"Is this all of it? The whole story?"

His head tilted in a slight nod as he exhaled. "There is nothing more to tell."

Chest aching, Reanna went to her knees, slipping herself between his legs as her arms lifted. Slowly, her hands slid along both sides of his jawbone, moving upward to fully cup his face.

Killian's eyes closed as he drew in air. His hands went over hers. "This. This is all I want. Your hands holding me. A home. I am at your mercy, Ree. Whatever. Whenever."

Her fingers curled on his skin, voice cracking. "I am yours, Killian. I will deny it no longer. If you tell me I can trust this, I will. All of me. You have all of me, mind included."

His arms were around her in an instant, dragging her body upward, even as he crashed down into her, his mouth attacking hers. His tongue found the depths of her mouth, desperate, searching to feel the words she had just uttered.

She met his demand, teeth on his tongue, as her knees came up, wrapping herself around his waist, pressing her body into him, soft against hard.

"Trust it, Ree. Trust me." One of his hands went deep in her hair, and he shifted her head, gaining access to pull back and trail the heat of his mouth down her neck.

She needed her body next to his and fought him, arching inward, but he refused, leaning back so he had full reign on her chest, fingers finding their way under the top lace of her muslin dress and pulling the fabric down.

His mouth captured her nipple before the cool air could shock the free bud. She curled around his head, fingers deep into the thick of his dark blond hair. Already, her core was alive, begging for release, begging for Killian deep within her.

He pulled back at her shudder, looking up at her face, his eyes reflecting the same unsatisfied smoldering reverberating through her body.

His hand went up to her face, gripping her jaw. "God help me, Ree, I want you. I need to be inside you right now. But not here."

"You are not a man who denies himself what he wants, Killian."

His eyebrows arched. "Do not look at me like that, Reanna. This moment is taking every shred of will I possess to not rip this dress apart to get to your skin."

The tip of her tongue escaped, licking her lips. "And I am not about to deny you. Never again. You locked the door. And the street…" She looked over his shoulder through the window, and then went up on her knees, thrusting her breasts in his face while she leaned over him, grabbing the drape and pulling it across the glass, blocking the street view.

She moved back, making sure her nipple teased his cheek, sliding across his lips. He couldn't resist taking it in his mouth with a growl, rolling the nub between his teeth, owning it.

Her head tilted up, eyes closed as the shards of pleasure shot down her body. After a moment, she pulled away, looking down on him. "Are you about to deny me?"

Sliding a hand down his chest, she reached between them, grabbing his hardness, fingers enveloping through the fabric, tugging. Her mouth went down to his ear, hot breath wrapping the back of his neck. "I need you deep, Killian. Right now. Making me yours. Complete. Honest. All of you."

"Damn, Reanna." He turned his head, capturing her mouth again.

His hand was diving under her skirts before she caught a breath from the kiss. His fingers plunged deep into her folds, and she curled at the touch, her head landing on his shoulder as her body both arched for more and fought bursting. She didn't want it. Not without him buried inside her.

She lifted herself on her knees, edging from his hand, and she ripped at his buckskin breeches, freeing him. Fingers engulfing him, she bent down, invading his mouth as his pushed her skirt up, bunching it at her waist.

"You are not going to let me strip you, are you?"

"No," she said, breathless. "No time for that. We have everything we need right now." She positioned herself above him, letting the wet tip of him play along her folds. She hovered for an instant, playing, enticing, driving herself into agony until she could take it no more.

Killian's guttural moan pushed her into movement, and she lowered herself slowly, trembling, as every line, every ridge of him filled her.

When she had taken every bit of him in, she arched back, beginning slow gyrations that only served to pitch her body into a frenzy. Near screaming, she bit her lip, trying to hold back.

Killian would have none of it. He wrapped his hands around her hips, lifting her up and down, plunging ever deeper into her. Deeper than Reanna imagined he could go.

An instant before her scream, her body writhing, he reached up and grabbed her neck, dragging her down to him. He swallowed the scream that broke free as her body convulsed hard in orgasm.

It was minutes before sound or sight made their way into Reanna's consciousness, and she found herself draped over Killian's shoulder, gasping for breath, the aftershocks still sending tremors through her body. Eyes going wide, she popped up, looking down at him. "You are not done."

His hand went up to her cheek, slipping under dark errant tendrils of hair. "Yours was too beautiful to miss. Your body giving over completely to me."

Her hips started to swivel before she could reply. "I can still feel you throbbing deep within me. Do not deny me." Her right hand went to her breast, cupping it as she lifted it to his mouth.

He didn't take a breath before he attacked it, tongue circling, teeth pulling. She lifted herself until he was almost out of her, plunging down repeatedly, controlling every quake of his body. She taunted him, rewarded him, and when he could take it no more and strained for release, rasping growls escaping, she quickened her pace to match his groans.

His eyes were on hers when he came, deep in her, every muscle vibrating under her hands. Eyes that were honest, grateful, and open.

Promising the future. Promising a home.

CHAPTER 20

His breath hot on her naked chest, Killian fought to gain control of his muscles. His arms vises around her body, he knew he had her crushed into him hard. Too hard. But he didn't care.

She was his.

There was nothing left to tell. She knew everything, and she still wanted him. A miracle. By some good grace of an angel above, she still wanted him. He was never going to let her go again. Never.

But he also knew his footholds were tenuous. He wasn't about to make demands. Wasn't about to scare her.

Despising his own arms for allowing her even a breath of air away from him, he loosened his hold and looked up at her. "Come home with me, Ree. For real. For forever. It is your home. It needs you in it. Or, hell, if you want to stay here, I will crawl into that cramped room of yours upstairs, and live with you there, even if my head hits the rafters. Either way, my home is with you."

She smiled and her lips brushed against his forehead. "I must say, what you have done here—you have set this place up to run so smoothly, I almost felt unneeded when I came back."

"I doubt that. You are a goddess to these children."

"But you have made it very easy for me to say yes. To come home with you. And I think you knew exactly what you were doing in that regard."

Killian shrugged, smirking. His wife had become rather canny. "I do like to plan things. And I could do nothing but remain most optimistic that you would eventually forgive me. It really was the only option I was willing to accept."

She laughed. "Who said I forgave you?"

A dagger sliced through his chest, and Killian's eyes turned hard. "You have not?"

Her hands went to his jaw, her blue eyes holding his gaze, twinkling. "I forgive you—no, I forgave you a long time ago. But that does not mean I wanted to tell you. To admit to it. To trust it. But I imagine I could not have done half the things we have been doing the past weeks, were that not the truth. Or, I am a trollop. That is also a possibility."

"I will take the side of forgiveness over the trollop possibility." He craned up and nibbled her earlobe. "I rather like you as an enthusiastic wife. Inspired imaginations and all."

The madcap thudding of several children running down stairs echoed into the room.

Killian's hands went to Reanna's skirts, pulling them down behind her. "I imagine they will be trying to get in here within moments. I have to complement myself for my restraint."

"That was restraint?"

Killian shrugged as he pulled up the bodice of her dress. "I did not rip your dress in two. Does that not qualify as restraint?"

"I could say the same about myself and your breeches." Smile turning into a grimace, Reanna moved up on her knees, groaning as her legs slid off the sofa, feet meeting wood floor. "This place does have its drawbacks. I deserve the opportunity to rest my legs in peace after such strain."

Killian stood up next to her, righting his breeches and shirt. Heart pounding in his chest, he looked down at Reanna, watching her smooth her dress and tuck rogue hair back into her chignon.

"Because I will not get two words in with you after we open that door, I need to know. It is honestly your decision to make, Reanna. I will be where you are." He caught a lock of hair, twisting the silk of it around his finger before tucking it into her upsweep. "So are we to live here, or where we have the comfort of a bed in which I don't have to silence your screams? And where there is plenty of time to rub your legs back into working?"

"Those are important points to consider." She laughed, wrapping her arms around his waist and settling her chin on his chest as she looked up at him. "It is really my decision?"

"Yes. But I do prefer you make the one I am hoping you will."

"Well, at least you admit to it." Her fingers slipped around him to pointedly poke him in the ribs. "But as long as I can be over here daily, I think, above all, I like you best in your element. Big bed. Plucking flowers from the garden for me. Besides, if we bring the chess set over here, the children are bound to steal and lose all the pieces before we even set up to play."

"Not that we would ever actually get the opportunity to play."

"True."

"Are you sure? I want you happy, Reanna. Willing. Not performing a duty. After all I did—"

Her forefinger went over his lips, cutting his words. "Make no mistake, Killian, I love you. And I love that that you want me happy, but truly, I only want to look to the future. Truly."

Killian nodded, silenced by this beautiful woman who had forgiven him in every sense of the word. He did not deserve her. Or maybe he did. Maybe this was fate showing him that he was— could be a better man.

And now it was up to him not to let fate—or Reanna— down.

"Oh. I almost forgot." His hands went on her arms, stepping away from her hold but keeping contact. "I wanted to show you something earlier. But we have no carriage at the moment." He stepped to the window and pulled open the drape. "The rain seems to have stopped and I see a few stray rays of sun. Will you walk with me? Although it may rain again."

"I will walk anywhere with you. Through anything with you." She slid her hand into the crook of his arm. "But I will choose my footwear accordingly."

Killian laughed, true and easy. Comfortable. Comfortable with his wife.

After navigating the gaggle of children all vying for their attention, especially the boys with Killian, since they hadn't seen him in weeks, Killian and Reanna managed to escape only by promising to return in a few hours.

They set out, passing under streaks of sunlight in the air thick with humidity from the rain. Six blocks passed in comfortable silence before Reanna looked up at him, eyes twinkling.

"I have been curious about something for the past year."

"You have? A whole year you sat on curiosity? Do tell."

"What is your favorite color? I have always wanted to know."

His favorite color? Killian didn't break stride as he contemplated the answer. He knew from whence the question arose—she had asked Aggie that very question before their wedding. And at this moment, he was going to actually consider a real answer. A novel concept.

"I did not think it a hard question?"

He looked down at her, easy smile lining his lips. "I just want to give you a true answer. A considered answer."

"Good. I like that."

They continued on another block before Killian stopped suddenly, clasping Reanna's hand nestled in his arm to halt her. He stepped around to fully face her. "I will be honest. I do not know if I could have ever answered this question before this. But I have run though the possibilities, and now, now I know. It was very simple, and in front of me for some time. Your eyes. Your eyes hold the lightest, gentlest blue. It is that exact color that is my favorite."

Her mouth pulled back in a warm smile. "You being fully aware of your wife does create delightful charm."

His hand came up to brush her cheek. "I do not say it to charm. I say it as the truth. And we are here."

Reanna's eyes left his hesitantly, looking around, perplexed, first at the row of homes, and then at the block-long park across the street. "The park? The street?"

"This home, in particular." Killian pointed at a large brick townhouse, taking up half the width of the block.

Her eyes swept over it. "Does someone I know live here?"

"Hopefully. I bought it."

"Why?"

"For the children. They need more space than at the Brook Street townhouse. They need a park across the street. And it is a block away from our home."

"What?" Reanna spun in circle, orientating herself. "I had not even noticed we were walking this direction."

"I did plan on bringing the lot of them back up to Holloton for the summer. They deserve to be running free in the woods, learning to ride, not cramped in London. But I hope this will serve them better when we are in town."

"Killian, this…this is beyond…"

"All with your approval, of course." He grabbed her hand, stepping toward the front door. "I want you to see the inside."

Reanna let him guide her up the stairs, face craned up at the three stories of symmetrical windows. "You did have a lot of confidence you would wear me down, didn't you?"

He stopped in front of the door and leaned into her ear, lips grazing her neck. "I had confidence in how your body arches to my touch. Confidence in the capacity of your heart."

Her hips leaned into him as her breath caught. Hand up to his head, her fingers curled into the hair whisking his neck. "How do you do that to me?"

"What?" he said, lips caressing the slope behind her ear.

"Make me wish I was instantly naked, stripping your clothes off, wrapping my legs around your waist."

He chuckled into her skin. Today was not the day good fortune was going to desert him. "I truly am at your command, my lady. And this house is currently completely—and absolutely—empty. Shall we go in?"

She nodded, hands already working his breeches.

CHAPTER 21

The single sheet of vellum fluttered into her world, shattering the month of utter happiness she was immersed in.

A letter from her father.

A letter requesting a meeting.

Delivered to the door at the Charles Street townhouse Killian had just bought for the children, it was short. No explanation. No accusations. Just a simple request that she meet with him that afternoon.

Reanna immediately halted the workers bringing in furniture to the Charles Street house. Weeks of converting the spaces into many bedrooms were over, and all the house needed now was proper furniture. But Reanna needed stillness. Quiet. So she sent the workers home.

After an hour of sitting silently in an empty room to compose herself and work through the myriad of implications the letter set forth, Reanna managed to make her feet move and she walked to Killian's—hers now as well—townhouse.

Killian's study door open, Reanna stepped into the room, silently assessing him behind his massive walnut desk. Papers were strewn across the surface, and Killian's eyes were immersed in a short stack before him. His eyebrows pulled together, she had seen that look on his face often, usually directed at her. The look of intense concentration.

She tempted herself for a moment with the thought of slipping out to see her father without telling Killian. She could go and come back and Killian would never know.

But if he found out…betrayal would be all he would see.

She wasn't about to do that to him. He had finally and completely enveloped her into his life, and she wasn't about to throw it away because of what she knew was going to be a difficult conversation.

With a slight shake, she stepped further into the near-empty room. "I see your new settee was delivered." She sat down on the edge of the wine-red velvet cushions, palms testing the comfort.

Killian looked up, bright smile crossing his face as his eyes swept over her. "And this exact picture is what I was waiting to see. You sitting on it, the color a perfect contrast to set off your hair, your eyes." His look turned ravenous. "You should know that aside from you sitting there, I do have other activities planned for that particular piece of furniture. Shake the armrest."

Reanna reached out and grabbed the rounded wooden armrest, pulling on it. She looked up at him. "Sturdy."

An indecent smile overtook his face.

Heat instantly flooded Reanna's core, but she clamped down on it. Killian would be in no mood after he heard what she had to say. "I would think you would still be worn out from this morning."

His eyebrow crooked. "Have you ever known me to be worn out?"

"No." She tried to force a smile, but knew it didn't reach her lips.

His eyes narrowed at her. "What is it? Something is upsetting you."

She stood, pulling the note from her father from the apron at her waist. She walked to Killian's desk, silently setting the vellum lightly in front of him.

It only took seconds for him to scan the letter. And in those seconds, she saw her whole world crumble with every twitch of Killian's face. Disgust. Anger. Betrayal.

He looked up at her, brown eyes hard. "You are showing me this for a reason. Do you wish to meet with him?"

Not able to force words, she nodded.

Killian shot up, moving around the desk to her. "You do not know what he could do to you, Ree. You do not know the man he is."

The lump in her throat broke free. "And you do not know the man I know him to be, Killian."

He grabbed her upper arm, fingers digging into muscle. "Do not make me forbid it, Ree. Do not. I will not chance your safety."

"Truly, Killian? Forbid? Are you going to lock me in a room as well? What sort of a man are you?"

"I am a man trying like hell to be worthy of you and—"

Her forefinger went over his lips, cutting his words. "I never wanted you to be a better man, Killian. I just wanted you to be a man that I could love. That could love me."

His mouth clamped shut, his jaw twitching.

Reanna wedged her fingers under his grip on her arm, loosening his hold until she could pull his hand from her. But she kept her fingers entwined in his, trying to control her own fury that had exploded.

"Killian, you have given me more freedom than a wife dare ask of her husband. And what has happened, even with all that freedom? I am yours, Killian. Yours. I chose you above everything. In spite of everything. I chose to trust you. So I am asking you now. Trust me. He will not hurt me."

"You do not know what he is capable of, Ree."

She stepped in, closing the distance between them, her hand going along his jaw. "And seeing my father does not threaten anything between us."

He dropped her hand, spinning from her, heaving as he walked over to the window, staring at the street below.

Reanna closed her eyes, bracing herself where she stood. "I have never asked you this, Killian, but I am now. The duel. Would you have killed my father?"

Minutes ticked by as she stared at Killian's wide shoulders, breath held. He didn't turn back to her.

"Yes."

Reanna exhaled. "And today? If he were before you right now, and you had a pistol in your hand. What would you do?"

He looked over his shoulder at her. "Ree...no. Do not ask me..."

"I need to know, Killian. What would you do?"

"I would kill him." His fingers rubbed his neck as he turned fully to her. "It is the truth, and I cannot deny it, nor apologize for it. My mother, my father—their deaths demand it. I can give no quarter to your father. I must honor what happened to my parents, Ree. Right—wrong—it is the only way I know how."

Her breath cut into her lungs. The sharpness of it burned before she took an additional breath, steadying herself against his words. She gave a single, crisp nod. "I love you Killian, all of you. And if that comes with you...I hate it. I hate it...but I accept it. I have to."

He closed his eyes, head to the coffered ceiling.

"But how can you wish me to accept you as you are, and not allow me to give the same margin to my own father? Am I to not accept him as he is? He has never done me harm, Killian. I have to trust in that."

His eyes came down from the ceiling, pinning her. "Don't go...please...stay."

Her arms crossed over her stomach as she turned from him. She couldn't be steadfast looking into his eyes. "I have to go, Killian. I know you do not understand, but he is my father, and regardless of what he has done, I love him."

"I love you."

Her head snapped to him. "What?"

"I love you."

He had never spoken those words to her.

"Killian...no...please, not like this. That is unfair...don't make me..."

"Stay. Stay, Ree."

"Killian, my heart, my soul, you have them. Do not lose faith in that. But I have to go. I have to think."

"So you will not see him?"

She bit her lip, the raw honesty making her voice rough. "I do not know. I am sorry, Killian. I have to go." She turned, taking a heavy step to the door.

"Wait." He walked over to the desk, pulling open the top drawer and grasping a sheet of vellum. He held it up to her.

Reanna recognized it immediately. The monogram at the top. Her handwriting. It was the last letter she wrote him from Holloton.

"You have to know, Ree, it was not you that lost faith. It was that I never allowed it. I never had it. I have kept this letter by me—all of them—since the night of your feet."

He stepped around the desk to stand in front of her. "You did believe in our love—even if you convinced yourself you didn't. You always have. If you see him—if you go—whatever he says to you. Believe in us. Come home to me."

Reanna looked up at him, his face etched in pain, pleading. She wanted to reach out. To touch him. To promise the world to him. But she couldn't move her arm. Couldn't overcome the war going on in her heart.

Only her feet would move, and when they did, she closed her eyes to him, and walked out the door.

He made no motion to stop her.

~ ~ ~

She sat on the window seat in a second level room at the still empty Charles Street house, staring down at the street below. Carriages, carts, horses, and people streamed by in the sunlight, but her eyes saw very little of it.

She had sat in indecision for hours. And with that indecision, she had decidedly made a decision.

Two o'clock, the meeting time her father had requested, came and went, and Reanna sat on the window seat in the Charles Street house, not moving.

She sat, attempting to come to terms with the fact that Killian so had her, she wasn't about to disappoint him. Wasn't about to make him worry. Wasn't about to make him question her loyalty. For that was what meeting with her father would mean to Killian. A betrayal. There was no way around it.

And she refused to have Killian think she would betray him. Not choose him. So she had to come to terms with the fact she would never see her father again.

Now she just had to go home and tell him.

A bustling form below moved to the front steps, catching Reanna's eye. She recognized Miss Collier coming up to the door before she could knock.

Reanna stood and flew down the stairs. Miss Collier coming here could only mean something was wrong at the Brook Street house. She opened the door before Miss Collier could rap the knocker a second time.

"Miss Collier, what is wrong?"

The distress on Miss Collier's face was obvious.

"Thank the heavens, you are here. I have looked everywhere for you. It be little Eddie, Lady Ana. He slid down the banister and crashed hard. The doc is there, but the boy keeps crying for you. I got this hack." She pointed over her shoulder with her thumb.

"Quickly, then." Reanna grabbed Miss Collier's arm and hurried down the stairs to the waiting coach.

Reanna was in the hack, landing on the backward facing cushions before she realized she faced a dark figure shrunken into the back corner of the hack. She blinked hard at the sight, her eyes flying from the figure to Miss Collier, and back again.

"Father?" Her head swiveled to Miss Collier, who now stood on the coach step in front of the carriage door. "Miss Collier, I do not understand...what?"

Miss Collier shrugged her wide shoulders, and the distressed look on her face vanished. "I be doing the job I was hired to do, m'lady. With this, I be done with you and your brats."

Reanna shook her head, trying to track what was happening. "Brats? But..."

Miss Collier stepped down from the carriage and closed the door.

The opposite carriage door opened, and another man jumped into the coach. Before Reanna could react, the carriage started to move.

"Father, what is this?" Reanna leaned forward, staring into the shadow at her father. His aging startled her. The deep lines in his face showed him to be much older than the last time she had seen him more than a year ago. Much of his hair was now gone, with a few white tufts still sprouting at the crown of his head.

She looked at the man next to him. He looked vaguely familiar.

The man driving the curricle. The one that had almost run her over. The gold tooth. "Mr. Nettle?"

"Pleased that you remember my name, Miss Halstead."

"It is Lady Southfork."

He shrugged, smirk on his face.

Her eyes shifted to her father. "Father, what is going on? Why?" She pointed at Nettle. "And you know Miss Collier?"

"I do, child. I did need to see you, and she was my guarantee in making that so."

A chill ran down Reanna's spine. Her brain had finally caught up with her discombobulation, and a sudden fear set into her chest. "Your guarantee? Father, please, tell me what is going on."

"I need you to come with me, Reanna. I cannot have your refusal in doing so."

"No. Not like this." She grabbed the handle on the door. Damn the moving carriage, she was getting out of here.

A vise grip clamped onto her wrist, twisting it away from the handle.

"I did not want to do this the difficult way, child, but I will."

"The difficult way?" Her eyes went wide.

"Yes." Her father reached back and punched her.

~ ~ ~

Reanna slumped into the corner cushions of the coach, black to the world.

Halstead looked over at Nettle as he settled back on the bench. "The other issue. Is it taken care of?"

"Yes. He is down."

Halstead settled his hands on his lap. "Good." He turned and opened the curtain on the carriage, staring out at the passing townhouses, ignoring his other passenger.

"I don't think I need to remind you, Halstead, but I want her broken," Nettle said. "I have invested much in your plan, and I want her worth it. If she even utters his name, I don't need to tell you what I would do to you. You are a dead man."

Without a glance at Nettle, Halstead let the curtain drop into place, and sat back, staring across the carriage at his inert daughter.

"I recall."

~ ~ ~

He had been there for hours, watching the Charles Street house from the park across the street. The metal bench was hard, digging into his thighs. Killian shifted, waking his legs back up.

He wasn't about to let Reanna out of his sight. Not when it came to her father. He had followed her, and had been ecstatic when she chose to disappear into the Charles Street house.

That had been hours ago. And she hadn't left. He could see her silhouette in a second story window. He had forced himself to clamp down on his agitation near the two o'clock hour. But now, at four, his relief that Reanna had chosen not to see her father was palpable. It even shocked him that this one choice of hers could mean so very much to him.

But there it was. He did love her. And it wasn't just a ploy to get her to stay, to do what he wanted. Down to his soul, every part of him. He loved her.

Although Killian perked up when he saw the hack stop in front of the house, he calmed once he saw Miss Collier get out. Something had to be amiss at the Brook Street house.

He stood, starting across the park and wondering if he could approach Reanna just yet. She wanted space to think, but if something was wrong, he wanted to be there. And at this time of the day, he could certainly claim to have just stopped by the house to check on the progress of moving the furniture in. Then he could help out with whatever was happening with the children.

Killian's suspicions were confirmed when Reanna emerged, a worried look clear on her face. She hurried Miss Collier down the steps to the hack and stepped up into the carriage.

He was halfway down the street to the hack when his heart sped. Miss Collier wasn't getting into the carriage. She was, in fact, sneering.

Just as Miss Collier's heavy form moved down from the carriage step and she slammed the door of the hack shut, Killian heard a coach approaching him from behind. He did not think to turn and look at it, as he was so focused on the hack Reanna had disappeared into.

The boot to Killian's skull from behind was simple, discrete for the busy street, and effective.

It knocked him flat to the ground, blackness overriding his last flailing steps toward the carriage.

CHAPTER 22

Filth was the first thing she tasted in her mouth. And then something crawling on her neck. Reanna flicked her hand toward her head and jerked upright, only to find cold metal holding her wrist far from her neck.

Eyes cracking, dizziness instantly set in. She fought to stay upright, fought against the sway her head was determined to force.

"Ye up, dove. Good thing, that. Ye cin feed yerself, then."

Reanna's head swiveled in the general direction of where the voice came from, searching the shadows. A sliver of light through an arrow slit cast a ray across dirty hay, and behind the pile, deep in the dark corner of the room, movement.

Reanna squinted. And then the smell of the room hit her senses. Putrescence filled her nostrils—rotten food, bodily fluids, mildew—her stomach churned at the invasion.

She craned her neck around, taking in the room, trying to place where she was. Dank, grey bricks on four sides, a planked wooden door full of scratches, cold stone floor chilling her legs.

Reanna looked back to the shadow. She didn't see anyone. "Hello?"

"What of, dove?"

So there was someone in the corner. "Where am I?"

Hay moved, and a tiny old lady creaked forward, leaning into the sliver of light. Grey hair wild and matted, her eyes crinkled as she looked hard at Reanna. "Violent? Ye be a violent one?"

"Violent?" Reanna shook her head. "Me? No. What—where am I?"

"Ahhh. Ye be a crazy one like me, then. They chained ye, so it be either or. Last one be violent." She moved forward on her hands and knees, then flung her feet around and sat on the hay. "Or not crazy, and just put in here by a bastard son, like me."

Reanna shook her head, looking down at the shackle on her wrist. Feeling more cold iron, she flipped her foot out from under her skirt, and found her ankle had a shackle on it as well. She looked up, trying to make sense of the woman's words. "Am I in prison?"

The old lady cackled. "No, dove. Ye be in the 'sylum."

~ ~ ~

Hands gripping the outside of the windowsill, Killian leaned forward, staring down at the filth covering his boots.

"You know we have to keep moving." Devin leaned in, voice low. "Even in these ratty clothes, we are targets in St. Giles."

"Bloody hell." Killian slammed his palm against the rough wood of the outside of the bar, making the rag-patched window shake. "I cannot believe the bitch just disappeared like that."

"Killian, we have searched the rookeries through and through. And had twenty men on that same task." Devin grabbed his arm, pulling him from what constituted a drinking establishment in this area. "Collier is gone. Not in London. There has to be some other link in this. Reanna could not just disappear."

Killian looked sharply up at Devin in the moonlight. "Yes. Her father. You know that. But he is more of a phantom than Collier. He is not in any of his old haunts, not at his country home. It was all he had left. He has disappeared as completely as Reanna has. How he has done it, I do not know. I left him with nothing. Nothing."

With a nod, Devin started walking down the tight street. Swearing with every step, Killian followed.

Devin slowed his gait so Killian could catch up. When they were in step, Devin spoke softly. "Killian, it has been a month. We have found no trace of Reanna. No trace of her father. No trace of Collier. You cannot continue this."

"Continue what?"

"No sleep. No food. Constant searching."

Killian's feet stopped. "I am finding her, Devin. Do not question that. I will find her."

Devin paused, turning to his friend. "And what then?"

"What do you mean?"

"What if she left on her own accord, Killian?"

"Do not—"

"What if, Killian? You have to consider the possibility. With her father—"

"Stop. Right. There." Killian's fist clenched. "Do not dare insinuate what you are, Devin. Reanna is not her father. She would never."

"Are you sure?"

Killian spun away from him, then stomped down the street, muttering at the trailing Devin. "Were it not for your baby at home, you ass, I would have already knocked you bloody flat out and left you to the cutthroats, Dunway. Do not continue to push this."

They walked on in silence, Devin a step behind Killian, mouth clamped tight. Killian stepped over the torso of an inebriated man strewn across the street, face-down in muck. Devin nudged the drunk's head with his foot as he passed, positioning the man's nose above the mud so he would be able to breathe.

A few quick steps, and Devin was in line with Killian once more. "I apologize. I did not mean to question her integrity. I thought I had objectivity on my side. But upon further reflection, I do not think objectivity is going to get Reanna back. I do not know her like you do."

"Damn right you don't. Just ask your wife what Reanna would or would not do."

"I have. And not to worry. Aggie is steadfast in her defense of Reanna as well."

They stepped onto the main thoroughfare and Devin stopped a hack. They both got into the carriage in silence.

Killian's eyes stayed fixed out the window of the coach, searching. Searching as they had done every minute in the past thirty days. Even in sleep, his dreams searched for clues.

"She is waiting, Devin. Waiting somewhere for me. I know it as I know my own breath. I just need to find her."

Devin leaned forward, his forearms on his knees. His eyes shifted out the window, searching the dark alleys. "We will, my friend. We will find her."

~ ~ ~

Reanna looked in the far corner of the cell for the twentieth time.

"Ye see 'im now? He be jumpin up and down fer ye."

Reanna looked from the corner to her friend. "No, Gertie. I am afraid I do not. You know I believe you when you say you are seeing the spirits, but I do not have your...gift. Just because you are determined for me to see them, does not mean they are determined to be seen by me."

"Posh. Ye just need to be tryin' harder."

Reanna sighed. Putting aside Gertie's ability to see and chat with ghosts, she was the dearest person in the world to be stuck with in an insane asylum. Gertie was a mother through and through, which made the fact that her own son placed her in the asylum after she started seeing spirits all the more heartbreaking.

Gertie moved off into the back corner of the cell, babbling something to the wall. Reanna saw a stone wall; Gertie saw a gentleman to flirt with.

Holding back a head shake, Reanna watched as Gertie laughed. Gertie had estimated she had been in the place for eight years, give or take a year. In all that time, Gertie had never stopped seeing spirits, nor forgotten how to laugh or be kind. Reanna figured if Gertie had managed to keep all of those qualities alive in the midst of the filth surrounding them, then maybe being a spirit-seer wasn't all that bad. In wicked irony, it probably kept Gertie sane in the insane asylum.

And that had kept Reanna sane in turn.

The lock slid on the other side of the door, and Reanna braced herself as the door swung wide.

"Yer meal." Wally stepped in, setting two bowls on the floor in front Reanna. Gertie stayed in the corner. His ever-present leer was especially malicious this eve. Reanna kept her eyes down.

"I hear word yer gonna be got."

"What?" Reanna ventured a glance up at the brute. Then she shifted her head back down as quickly as it had risen. She had learned the hard lesson early in her captivity that it was best to stay quiet and have no eye contact with Wally.

He sneered a chuckle. "Got yer 'ttention, eh? Ye be lucky ye have a fine gentleman comin' for ye, ye wench, or ye be mine. He be payin' mightly for you to stay on the clean side of this place. On the clean side of me, or I be havin ye already."

"Gentleman?" Reanna asked, keeping her eyes down and her voice to a whisper.

"Fancy jacket, dark hair, gold tooth. 'e know ye well, 'e say. If 'e don't show, I might just break and have ye fir meself." Wally bent over in front of her, licking his pudgy lips and puckering them at her. Laughter at her repulsion followed.

The thin strand of hope snapped in Reanna's chest. Gold tooth. Mr. Nettle. Hell. With her father, at least she had a chance. A chance at what, she wasn't sure, but at least she had blood on her side. But Mr. Nettle—she was clueless. She didn't know anything of the man and had only met him twice. The first time she had barely remembered him, and the second time he had almost run her over. So why was he with her father now? Why have the least bit of interest in her?

Her chin hit her chest as she tried to make herself as small as possible in front of Wally.

After a moment, the brute stood, kicking over one of the bowls full of mush. He walked out without another word, the lock sliding into place.

Gertie waited a moment before she stepped out of the corner shadow.

Reanna sighed. "You can have it, Gertie."

"No, dove. Ye know we share it." She plopped down in front of Reanna and held up the full bowl to her.

Hands heavy, Reanna took the bowl and swallowed a chunk of the vileness that, at the very least, kept her alive. She held the bowl up to Gertie.

Gertie took it, but made no motion to sip. She was staring at Reanna.

"I don't like yer plan, dove. And I know ye be thinkin of doing it now." Her eyes were the clearest Reanna had ever seen them.

"From what Wally just said, I do not have a choice, Gertie. It is my only chance. I cannot let Nettle take me. Him, my father, I cannot let them do whatever they are planning. I have to get back to Killian. I have to."

Gertie shook her head, taking a sip from the bowl.

Reanna took the silent reprimand for what it was. But she had to do it, and she needed her friend's support. "You have seen Wally in the late evening round. He is slow. His eyes are blurry from the hours of cups he has been into. He trips every other time he comes in here. It is the perfect time. It is dark. And he is especially leering that time of night."

"But yer body, dove. It invites bad things to offer it up to him. If it don't work..."

"I can think of no other way to get out of the shackles, Gertie. And I have to. I have to get out of here. Before Nettle. I have to be gone before he comes for me. Nettle and my father put me in here, and heaven knows what they will do to me next. What they will do to Killian." Her throat thickened. "I cannot chance that."

~ ~ ~

"What does it say?" Devin stood at the sideboard, pouring himself a brandy.

Mid-pace, Killian snatched the letter from his desk and held up the vellum to Devin. Turning, brandy in hand, Devin took it from his friend, and downed a long swallow as he scanned the paper.

Devin's eyes rose from the words. "This is short. He wants to meet tomorrow, but there is no mention of Reanna in here."

Killian shrugged in the middle of his pace. "He must think it beneath him to actually mention her. Mention what he did. We both know exactly what this meeting is about."

"Do you know the place he requested?"

"It is an inn a short way into the countryside."

Devin drained the last of the brandy. "Do you trust him?"

"No." Killian stopped in the middle of the study, eyeing the paper Devin still held. "But do I have a choice?"

~ ~ ~

"You do remember where to go?"

Darkness had settled an hour earlier, but Reanna needed to repeat to Gertie the plan one more time. It was as much for her own nerves, as it was to assure her that Gertie knew what to do.

"Yes." Gertie nodded in the trace of moonlight.

"Are you positive? You remember the street, the house? To tell them that I specifically sent you. You can recite all of the children's names, if necessary." Reanna hoped Killian hadn't moved the children to the new house yet. Even if he had, someone should still be at the Brook Street townhouse. Killian would have seen to it. He would not have overlooked a detail like that. She hoped.

"You will stay there until I come? The children will love you, and your son will not be able to find you there."

"Aye, dove. I remember it all. Are ye sure ye want to chance this?"

"I do—"

The lock on the door clanked, interrupting Reanna's words. Gertie scurried into the corner and Reanna tensed, drawing upon every bit of nerve, every bit of courage she could manifest.

If this was the only way out, the only way to Killian, the only way to the children, she could do it. She had to.

Light from the hallway spilled in, along with the blubbering form of Wally balancing two bowls. He didn't trip on the raised stone like he sometimes did, and Reanna held her breath. He took another two steps forward, and the smell of gin washed over her. She exhaled. Good. She needed him drunk and clumsy for this.

She stood, crouching half over as the short length of the shackle on her wrist held her down. Wally pulled up instantly. She had never stood in front of him.

"What of ye, wench?" He dropped the evening bowls to the ground.

"If—" Her voice came out as a squeak, and Reanna coughed, opening her throat. "If I am to be taken from here tomorrow, then I would like my last night to be memorable."

Wally's hands went to his waist, blocking most of the light from the hall. "What say ye, wench?"

His words were slurred, and Reanna knew he was going to have a hard time following her logic. Best to make this as simple as possible.

"Memorable, Wallace. I am a virgin, and I would not like to die as one. I would like your assistance."

Eyes getting huge, he took a step toward her. "Ye ain't no virgin."

Reanna stood as tall as the shackle allowed, not backing down from the fists that were within striking distance. "No? Would I not know that, Wallace? Quite simply, the person coming for me tomorrow will not be letting me live long. I do wish to feel one of God's gifts before I die. And you are the only one here that can help me, Wallace."

Wally looked over his shoulder into the hall, then, leering, stumbled toward her. "God's gift? Yer a classy wench, ain't ye?" He apparently had forgotten all about Gertie, as he didn't even glance in her direction as he reached Reanna.

She took the weight of his hands, hiding her cringe as his fingers pawed her body up and down. The smell of gin only slightly cut the odor from his body.

She swallowed back bile as she put her free arm around his waist. He grunted in satisfaction.

Reanna craned her neck up at him. God forgive her for what she was about to say. "I want my arms around you, Wallace. I want my legs wrapped around you, riding you."

His eyes went wider. "Bloody fucker, ain't ye a piss whipper."

He reached under his shirt, pulling up on the thick chain that held keys. The chain came around his head, and he promptly dropped the keys on the stone floor.

He went to his knees, fumbling in the darkness.

Reanna stuck her free hand in his hair, rubbing. "Yes. Do it. Do it, now, Wallace. I want you. Quick."

He unlocked her ankle first and then dropped the keys three more times before he could free her wrist. The whole while, Reanna continued her prodding. As soon as the metal from her wrist clunked to the floor, he grabbed her by the waist, pushing her back against the wall. His mouth went on her neck, drooling or kissing, Reanna wasn't sure.

She let him paw at her body, taking his brutal roughness, moaning for effect, until she heard the iron click. His movement didn't pause.

Hands in his hair, she pulled up his head, looking him straight in his lazy eyes. "Wait. I want my dress off. I want your hands on my naked body." She slipped along the wall, but his hands followed. "Here, let me. You enjoy."

She bent over, grabbing the bottom of her tattered skirt as she slid further along the wall. She was just out of his reach, when Wally realized his leg was now shackled.

With a raging scream, he lunged at Reanna, grasping the hem of her dress and jerking it. Reanna fell, and Wally's fingers instantly dug into her ankle. She kicked, but his grip only tightened.

In the next instant, Gertie flew, diving at Wally's arm. Her teeth sank into his skin before Reanna could blink, and she was free, scrambling backward in the cell as she watched Gertie spit out what looked like a chunk of flesh.

Reanna and Gertie tumbled out of the cell, and Reanna jumped at the door, pulling it closed. She slid the long lock in place and grabbed Gertie's arm, pulling her down the hall, away from Wally's painful shrieks echoing against the walls after them.

Fortunately, shrieks were commonplace in the asylum, and Reanna and Gertie encountered no one as they stumbled barefoot along the corridors, eventually finding a door to the outside.

Night air, fresh with grass and trees, hit Reanna, and she almost froze she was so overtaken by the reality of open air around her. But Gertie kept pulling, and within moments, they were deep into the nearest tree line.

Both gasping for breath, Reanna stopped, wedging Gertie's fingers from her arm. "This is where we must split."

"But—"

"No. You know why." Reanna was glad she couldn't see the disappointment on Gertie's face in the dark. It would only cause her to reconsider what she was sure was the best plan. Reanna knew they would both be better off apart, blending in as best they could, once it was discovered they had escaped and searchers came.

Reanna also figured Gertie, especially, could blend into any environment with ease. People rarely looked directly at characters they didn't want to deal with. And Gertie's chances of disappearing—with her wild hair and constant talking to spirits—would be much better without Reanna.

She gave Gertie a quick hug. "I will see you in London. I swear. You will be careful?"

Gertie nodded. "Aye, dove."

"And if you are worried, or lonely, listen to your spirits. They will show you the way."

Gertie grabbed Reanna's hand, clamping it between both of hers. She brought it up to her mouth, giving it a quick kiss. "Aye. And I be sending some with ye, dove."

Reanna nodded, and Gertie dropped her hand, turning to disappear into the dark.

Spinning, Reanna took a deep breath, and began to run.

CHAPTER 23

"Reanna. Reanna."

Her name. Someone was calling her name. Killian.

She fought her way out of the darkness, out of the exhaustion from running half the night. A stick in her back, poking her. Something in her mouth. Grass, not hay, not dirt. She was still outside.

Before her eyes could open, she unconsciously began to smooth her hair, then realized the ridiculousness of it. No smoothing of her hair, rat's nest that it was, was going to help the appearance of a woman shackled to the floor for a month in a crazy house.

Her eyes cracked open and she rolled away from the stick, looking up.

Her arm went over her eyes, shielding them from the bright sun coming down on her. Her eyes went down. Feet. She looked back up.

"Killian?"

The figure moved out of from in front of the bright light, and the sun blinded her.

"No, Reanna. Not Killian." The figure bent, balancing on his heels.

She turned her head, her cheek resting on the grass. Was that the road she saw?

She blinked hard. She thought she was deep in the woods, well hidden from everything. It was fuzzy with the sun blotch in her eyes, but she definitely saw the shape of a carriage through the trees.

She closed her eyes, disgusted. Apparently, she was really bad at hiding.

The voice cut into her ears. "Killian does not want you, Reanna. He left you in that place."

Reanna blinked, looking up at the figure, willing her eyes to adjust to the light. She didn't recognize the voice. Slowly, the face came into focus.

Smiling. Gold tooth.

Nettle.

Reanna closed her eyes.

"Easy or difficult way? Your choice."

Reanna's mind went into a flurry. She knew what the difficult way was. And who knew where she would wake up. If she wasn't knocked out, maybe she could fight her way free when she got her bearings about her.

She opened her mouth, forcing air from her lungs. "Easy."

"Excellent. I was hoping you would say that. I do not want you bruised."

The sneer in his voice chilled her spine.

Bloody hell.

~ ~ ~

Water splashed onto Reanna's face.

"Wake up." Nettle's voice was in her ear.

Reanna's eyes flew open at the blast of wet cold.

She realized instantly that this was worse than the last time she woke up after being knocked out. This time her wrists were tied behind her back, a rag was tight across her mouth, cutting into her tongue and tied behind her head, and her eye was pulsating, pain reverberating through her head with the tiniest movement.

Trying to fight her way out of the carriage had not gone well. She wasn't good at hiding, and she was even worse at fighting. And now she was at the mercy of wherever Nettle had dragged her.

She realized she was on her side on a ratty bed, but only for a moment as Nettle grabbed her and pulled, dropping her to the ill-spaced wood planks on the floor. Cringing into a ball, Reanna gasped through the rag as it jarred her bruised eye, pain overwhelming.

Nettle knelt over her, voice in her ear. "You need to listen hard for Southfork's voice, Reanna. Listen closely. Closely. I believe it will clear up some delusions you have about your husband."

Eyes shocked, she turned to Nettle, unable to talk through the rag, but desperate at the same time. Killian was here? She had to get to him. She tried to sit up, avoiding Nettle's chest in her way.

He pushed her back down.

"Even if he did see you, he wouldn't recognize you like this, Reanna. You look like a rat catcher. And the things that are crawling all over you. I am going to have to burn my carriage." His mouth pulled back, menacing. "He does not want you, Reanna. No man does. And you need to hear this, so stop your squirming."

His hand went over her temple, forcing her head to the wood boards, pressing her ear to the sliver of space between the planks.

~ ~ ~

Killian walked into the inn.

Except for the few candles in the two front windows and a few lanterns by the entrance, the place was dark. Dark and empty.

As he surveyed the low-ceilinged room, his hand slipped under the front of his jacket to finger one of his pistols. An old inn, he saw from the outside that it was half-collapsed in the back. He had been told the place was still in business, but someone had clearly been mistaken. There were still chairs surrounding several wooden tables, but beyond that, the bar area looked deserted, no spirits, no glasses.

"You are late, Southfork, and I did not take you as a man who condones tardiness."

Killian eyed Halstead. He sat on the far end of the room, casual at a table. He had a half-full glass of brown liquid in front of him that he fingered, but did not grasp.

"I arrive when it is convenient for me, Halstead. Be grateful that I am here, even if it is only to allay you of some misconceptions you may have about me." Killian walked across the room, pulling back a wooden chair and taking a seat opposite Reanna's father.

Halstead's fingers moved from the glass, and he settled his hands across his stomach, clasping them. "I have something you want, Southfork, and I know you will pay dearly for it."

"I assume you speak of my wife?"

"I do. To the point, Southfork, you may have her back when my demands are met."

Face nonchalant, Killian threaded his fingers in front of his ribs, mimicking Halstead's posture. "Demands?"

"Yes. Simple, and not too much to ask in the current situation. I merely demand my wealth and status be re-established."

Killian sighed, shaking his head. "You are assuming, Halstead, that I have not enjoyed this last month without her presence. On that, you would be mistaken."

A thud from above drew Killian's attention, his eyes moving upward. "Is someone else here?"

"What? Oh. The noise?" Halstead waved his hand. "No. Not that I know of. This place is abandoned…unless…" His eyes narrowed. "Are you alone as requested?"

"I am."

Halstead relaxed slowly. "As you were saying, Southfork? My daughter?"

"Frankly, Halstead, I have been reminded that is easier to not have a wife underfoot."

Halstead laughed. "You were clever before, Southfork, when you ruined me. But you are clever no more. Your activities have been observed since the day Reanna left with me. You are not a man who has forgotten his wife. You are, in fact, a man that has done everything possible to find her. Even now you cannot hide your desperation." He leaned forward, elbows on the table. "I think you are now ready to negotiate."

"And you, Halstead, are a man that has made a serious mistake about his current position." Killian stood and leaned forward, knuckles on the thick oak table, leveraging himself above Halstead. "You can have her, Halstead. She means nothing to me, and you are now the lucky one that can deal with her and her myriad of problems."

Killian's words hung thick in the air, and the two stared at each other, seconds ticking by.

With a quick smile, Halstead pushed back from the table, going to his feet. "I am sorry you feel that way, Southfork. It appears my business here is done. I will give your regards to my daughter."

With a slight nod of his head, he stepped around Killian and walked to the door, whistling.

~ ~ ~

"Have you heard enough?" Nettle's vicious whisper sent hot air into her ear. He loosened his hold on her temple.

Cheek rubbing the wood floor, Reanna nodded. Numbness had set in immediately at Killian's words. Her whole world had just crumbled to nothingness, and she couldn't think past the blinding pain in her head, past her aching heart making it hard to breath.

"Good. I will never hear you speak his name again. Is that understood?"

Nettle gripped her upper arm, yanking her to her feet. She landed, leaning in to him, and he swore, pushing her from his body.

"You are still too filthy to touch in those clothes. We will fix that."

He yanked her arm, pulling her, stumbling across the floor and down a narrow set of rickety stairs.

Eyes shut tight against the horror in her heart, the reality of what had just happened, Reanna let Nettle lead her out into the darkness.

CHAPTER 24

"Stop."

Killian sank into the round-backed wooden chair, beaten.

In that instant, everything fell away.

Everything, save for the one thing that truly mattered.

"Stop."

Fingers on the door, Halstead turned back. He approached the table, left eye twitching as he advanced, sniffing the blood in the air. "You have reconsidered?"

"I have."

"What will you give for her?"

Killian took a deep breath, considering an answer he thought never to have to give. He had thought to get her back on his own accord. To find and save her by his own damn willpower. To not end up at the mercy of her father. What would he give for Reanna? The answer was simple, and he knew it before he took another breath.

"Everything."

A smile spread across Halstead's face as he retook his seat across from Killian. "I apparently underplayed my advantage, Southfork. Everything will not be necessary, for I do wish my daughter to be kept in fine fashion." His hand slipped under his jacket, producing a set of folded documents. He laid them on the table. "I think you will find my terms unfair, but I am not worried on that."

Halstead stood and went behind the bar, pulling out wax, a quill and ink, as Killian opened the agreement and scanned the papers.

Killian's face remained set, not hinting at the deplorable words he was reading.

As Killian finished the last page, Halstead walked back to the table and set the wax, ink and quill down by Killian's hand, and then he sat, fingers entwined under his chin.

Killian looked up at him. "I want her before I sign these."

"No. You still do not understand your current position, do you, Southfork? You will sign and mark these, and I will produce her. There is no other order of business."

Jaw clenched, Killian grabbed the quill and set ink to paper.

"I see you have your ring." Halstead melted the tip of blood red wax, and then pressed it onto the bottom of the document.

"I will get her immediately?"

Halstead nodded. "It is a short ride from here, and she is yours."

Killian took off his signet ring, and pressed it into the wax. The "S" entwined above the Southfork coat of arms appeared in the wax.

The deal was complete.

~ ~ ~

The bit of moonlight helped them travel fast on the roads, and within a half hour, Killian and Halstead were pulling up on their horses in front of a long, three-story stone building. Very little light shined from within.

Dropping from his horse, Killian's gut started to twist. "What is this place, Halstead?" The threat was clear in his voice.

"It was a safe place for Reanna. You will wait out here." Halstead started to the main door.

"Like hell I will." Killian hurried to the door, only a step behind Halstead.

The door swung open before Reanna's father could hit the knocker, and a small, hunched man appeared, lantern in hand. "Ev'ning, Lord Halstead. We were not expecting ye."

"No?" Halstead said. "Word was sent that I would be arriving to collect Miss Halstead this eve."

"Miss Halstead? But I thought ye knew…No?"

Killian pushed Halstead aside, bearing down on the man. "Know what, man? Where is she?"

The man took a step back, cowering. "She escaped last night, sir. Her and the witch. We have not been able to find them."

"What?" Halstead said from behind Killian.

Killian stepped over the threshold toward the man. "What sort of a place is this? Why would she have to escape?"

"We be an asylum, sir." His eyes flickered to Halstead and then back to Killian. "For the insane."

Killian spun in pure rage, his hand encircling Halstead's throat and shoving him against the wall of stone. "You put her in an insane asylum?"

Grasping Killian's hand, trying to free himself, Halstead nodded.

"Bastard." Killian tightened his hold to just shy of crushing the man's throat. And then, with more control than he ever thought possible, he loosened his hand. "I am going to resist killing you for the instant, Halstead. Resist until we find Reanna."

Halstead nodded vigorously. "I might know who has her. It was not the plan. But if she escaped and they could not find her, I may know. He was to check on her this morn."

Killian dropped his hand, breath seething. "You had better, Halstead. You had better."

~ ~ ~

Reanna stood in the room, watching the maid scurry in and out with boiling water to fill the tin tub that had been brought in. She stood, numb, not truly understanding what was happening around her or what she was doing. She just stood.

The tub filled nearly to the rim, the maid stopped.

"I be so sorry 'e make me do it, miss. The devil 'e is. So sorry. Please lord, forgive me."

Reanna gave her no acknowledgment, as the words meant nothing to her. Nothing meant anything to her.

The maid scurried out of the room.

Within a minute, Nettle entered. Head shaking, tongue tsking, he walked across the small room. It wasn't until he stopped in front of her that Reanna noticed the knife in his hand.

She knew she should feel panic. That a knife in his hand would harm her. But she couldn't conjure fear. She couldn't conjure anything in the gaping chasm that was her chest.

"You are disgusting, Reanna. The vermin on you. Your stench. We need to take care of all of that before I am to touch you."

Reanna kept her eyes on the steel of the blade. As much as her emotions were blank, her mind still worked, and she knew the threat the knife posed.

He stepped closer, keeping his body an arm's length away from her. Then he reached out, slipping the edge of the knife between her skin and her ragged dress, the peach color now indistinguishable from the dirt.

She didn't step away, didn't cower, and Nettle's eyebrow raised. "No cries for mercy? No begging? Interesting."

With a swift thrust downward, he cut through the cloth, through her chemise, and the whole of her clothing fell to the floor. His eyes ran up and down her body, and a flicker of disgust shot through Reanna's stomach. She wasn't sure she welcomed even the smallest modicum of emotion in this situation. Better to stay numb. To build a wall of indifference so high and wide against what was to happen to her, that nothing could get through.

"Some of you is clean. That is welcome." He took a step away from her, pointing to the tub with the knife. "Now get in. All of the vermin need to be killed."

Reanna glanced at the tub. The maid had just left, and she had been filling the tub with boiling water. She eyed the rising steam.

"No." Her head shook as she found her voice and her arms covered her naked breasts.

"I do not repeat myself, Miss Halstead. That is your only warning." His mouth pulled back, sneering out vicious words. "Now, get in the tub."

Reanna took a step backward. "No."

Growling, Nettle's arm snaked out, grabbing her by the hair, and he dragged her over to the tub. Reanna clawed at his arm, hellcat awoken. But Nettle easily outweighed her by double, and as disdainful as it was to him, he grabbed her arm, flipping her into the tub.

A quarter of the water sloshed out of the tub, but it did no good. Reanna's skin burst on fire. Nettle shoved her head under water, and she struggled, gulping in hot water, flames filling her lungs.

She broke the water sputtering, and Nettle allowed her a spasm of coughs before he sent her under the water again.

When she finally broke free to the air, he released her, shoving her head as he stepped away.

"That should kill the vermin. And wash with the soap."

A sudden banging of wood made his head crack upward, ears straining to the door. The bang repeated.

"Blast it," he muttered, snapping his hand to disperse the water soaking his jacket sleeve. He spun away from Reanna, exiting the room, closing the door behind him.

Her chest draped over the side of the tub, Reanna continued to hack coughs from her body, trying to expel the water in her lungs. Every nerve on fire from the scalding, her feet slipped frantically as she tried to gain footing and push herself out of the water.

With a desperate heave, she flopped over the thin rim of the tin tub. Hitting the floor, she panted, trying to quell the agony that had laced her skin. Every pore throbbed, and she rolled, trying to keep the least amount of her body on the wood floor.

It was in that agony, that she heard Killian's voice.

No. It couldn't be. It was her pain speaking insanity in her mind.

But then she heard it again.

Muffled, but she would recognize his voice in the bowels of hell.

He was here for her.

He hadn't abandoned her.

She opened her mouth to yell, but even in her haze, she knew her scream came out as a whisper. The scalding water had gone down her throat, stealing all sound.

She heard his voice again. But he didn't sound agitated. Didn't sound angry. And then a door opened and closed. Struggling to her knees, and then her feet, she tumbled to the window, falling against the windowpane.

In the light of the lanterns in front of the house, she saw two men on horseback, riding away from the house. No. God, no. He was leaving.

She banged on the glass with her palm.

They kept riding away. Reanna's head spun desperately, searching for something hard. A silver candlestick would have to do.

She picked up the heavy metal, stepping back from the window, and heaved it with the last shred of power she had.

It shattered the window, glass flying as the silver dropped through the night air. Rushing to the open pane, Reanna searched the dark woods for the horses.

No movement. All she saw was darkness.

She sank to the floor, despair settling into her bones.

He was gone.

~~~

Killian tore ahead of Halstead on the lane, reaching the main road, not caring if Reanna's useless father was still with him or not. He was going back to the asylum, and going to knock heads until he found his wife.

The side trip to the house of the man named Nettle was worthless. After seeing his gold tooth, Killian immediately remembered him from the London street long ago. But the man had been relaxing, half undressed when they banged their way into his home. Killian had discerned rather quickly that the trip was a diversion concocted by Halstead to get Killian away from the asylum.

A half-mile back to the asylum on the main road, a lone figure on a horse road toward Killian. When the man on the horse pulled up, stopping, Killian did the same.

"Where is she? Halstead did not produce her?" Devin's voice was laced with deadly concern.

Killian looked over his shoulder back down the road. Halstead was not to be seen. "He put her in the asylum up the road. She supposedly escaped last night."

"He what? The insane asylum?" Devin half stood in his saddle, anger overtaking.

"Yes. And she has not been found. Or so they claim. Did you see anything on your way here?"

Devin shook his head.

"Anything outside of the inn while I was in with Halstead?"

Head still shaking, Devin ran a hand through his hair. "No. There was a drunk and whore coming out of the inn, and that was about all."

"A drunk and a whore?"

"Yes. Why?"

"That inn had long-since been abandoned. It did not look like it from the outside, but there wasn't anyone in it. No one save for Halstead and myself."

"You don't think…"

"I sure as hell do. Where did they go?"

"Shit, Killian. It was dark. I didn't get a look at the woman—I only assumed it was a whore because of the bit of wild hair I saw, and she was stumbling. They left in a carriage. I followed it for a few minutes, and they disappeared down this road. So I went back to the inn."

"Bloody hell." Killian had already turned his horse and was headed back in the direction he came from.

"What about Halstead?" Devin shouted at his friend's back as he set his horse into gallop.

"Not worth our time. Not now."

Within minutes, they were tearing up the lane to Nettle's home. Riding straight to the stables, Killian didn't bother to dismount at the wide open doors. He pointed in. "Is that the carriage?"

"It is." Devin swore under his breath.

In a flash, Killian was pounding on the front door, pistol drawn in one hand, knife in the other. Devin was only a step behind him.

"Look." Devin whispered in his ear.

Killian followed his eyes to a silver candlestick lying in shards of glass. They both looked up, seeing the broken window above.

The door swung open at that moment, and Nettle had made no progress in either dressing or undressing since Killian had seen him minutes before.

Killian's knife was flat across his bare neck, shoving him back into the foyer before Nettle could get a word out.

"Where the hell is she?"

His back forced against the wall below the staircase, Nettle glared at Killian, eyes cold. "Do you mean Lady Southfork? We went through this minutes ago, Lord Southfork. While I was pleased to answer your questions a moment ago, I fear I am beginning to not look lightly upon your intrusion into my home. And my neck."

Killian pressed the blade harder. "My wife, Nettle. Or I will gut you where you stand. We know you have her."

"I do not have your wife, Southfork. I can assure you—"

Killian cocked his pistol, pushing it into Nettle's mouth, cutting him off. He eased the knife from Nettle's neck.

"Do you have him, Devin?" Killian asked, eyes not leaving Nettle.

"Yes." Devin stepped next to Killian, his own pistol trained on the man.

"He does not move a muscle." Killian put his knife and pistol back under his jacket, turned, and rushed up the stairs.

At the landing at the top, Killian made a quick assessment on which door led to the room that had the broken window. He turned the knob. Locked.

He took a step back and kicked the door in with his boot. Splintering wood was still falling when he saw Reanna. Naked, skin red, sopping wet on the floor. Even in his haste to get to her, he could see some of her skin starting to blister.

"Ree." His hands went onto her gently. She twitched, but didn't awaken.

"Bloody fucker."

Forcing the staggering rage out of his hands, Killian searched the room, seeing the rag she must have been wearing in a tattered heap. He grabbed a towel, setting it over Reanna's body. Snatching another one, he draped it over his arms and slid his hands under her, lifting her as he tried to cover her skin.

Within seconds, he was down the stairs, rage turning him cold with every step.

In the foyer, Killian handed her inert body softly over to Devin, who managed to keep a pistol trained on Nettle until Killian could turn around to face him.

"Take Ree out to the carriage and hitch the horses up." Killian's voice had gone detached, emotionless as he stared at Nettle. "She cannot ride on horseback to London."

Devin raised an eyebrow at his friend.

"Now, Devin. I will join you in a moment."

Without word, Devin backed out of the open front door to carry Reanna to the carriage.

Minutes later, Killian walked into the stables.

"It is taken care of?" Devin finished tightening the leather straps on the left horse.

"It is."

Devin stood tall. "Horses are ready. I set her on the back bench."

Killian jumped into the coach, drawing Reanna's limp form into his arms and spreading the towel along her body for maximum coverage. "Get us to home quickly. No heed to ruts or bumps. I will shield her."

With a quick nod, Devin closed the carriage door and vaulted up to the driver's perch, and set the horses to London.

CHAPTER 25

Reanna cracked her eyes, lucid for the first time since she had been dunked into the scalding water. She had vague snippets of memories. Killian holding her. Talking in her ear. Something gooey being spread on her body. Broth going down her throat. A soft bed—a real bed under her.

And now her head was being tugged at.

Her skin throbbed in pain, and she knew exactly what that was from. Scalding water. But what was that tugging?

She opened her eyes further.

Turning her head on the pillow, she was greeted with Killian, comb in hand, working through the matted nest that was her tangled hair. A smile immediately touched her lips at the sight of Killian's big hands holding her delicate tortoise shell comb, picking apart the tiniest snarl.

"Awake?" His eyes didn't veer from the knot of dark hair he had up to his nose, picking it apart single strand by single strand in the low light of the lamp by the bed.

She nodded.

"Awake and forming real thoughts?"

Her smile widened. "Yes. You found me. I thought…"

Her words fell into thick silence. At that, his brown eyes left the tangled hair, staring into hers. "You thought what?"

She closed her eyes, shaking her head at the panicked terror she had felt, the memory of it still so raw in her chest, it was hard to quell it. Hard to grasp she wasn't still being held by Nettle. "I thought you left me. I heard you. I saw you riding from his house."

"So you did break the window, didn't you? I came back, thanks to Devin. I had him waiting outside of the inn, and he saw Nettle taking you. He did not know it was you, at the time, and blast that, for what Nettle did to you. Are you in much pain now?"

"I will survive it. I stink, though."

Killian laughed. "Yes, you do. The doctor said this was the best concoction for the burns. He did not make apologies for the smell, though. But your skin is looking less red, and the blisters seem to be shrinking. So hopefully you will only stink for another day or so." He picked up a matted lock of her dark hair and started picking it apart. "One does get used to the smell. But I will be happy when you can get in a bath."

She chuckled. "Charming, you are." She watched him carefully extracting the lowest knot from the strand of hair. "You could have cut it. It would have been easier."

"I was not about to do that. As long as I can be looking at you, I have all the time in the world."

"Now that really is charming." She shifted her hand to rest on his thigh. The movement stretched her tight skin, but she didn't care. She needed to touch him, even if it was with just her five fingers. "Did Gertie make it to the Brook Street house?"

"Gertie? Who is Gertie? Your secretary said something about an older woman arriving there when he stopped by earlier, but I did not think to ask about it. I wanted to get back in here. Was that who he was talking about?"

Reanna breathed a sigh of relief. "Good. She made it. I was worried. She was with me in the asylum. She took care of me. She helped me escape. And then we split—I did not want her to get caught with me."

"You sent a woman from an insane asylum to be around the children? Why was she in the asylum?"

"Unfortunate choices by her son." Reanna recognized the concern in Killian's voice. "You forget I was in there, as well. Do not judge her by where she was forced to live. She is the kindest soul, but she sees ghosts."

"Ghosts?" Killian's hands stopped as he looked up at Reanna, eyebrow arched.

"Ghosts, spirits. She sees them. But they do no harm."

"You sent a crazy lady to the children?"

"Killian, she is far from crazy, and I take offense that you think that. Just because we cannot see spirits, does not mean they are not real."

"Do you believe in her spirits now, as well?"

Reanna's eyes flew upward, shaking her head. "It does not matter what I believe—it only matters what she believes she sees. And what Gertie sees does not affect her functioning or her interaction with reality. She just truly sees more people in a room than we do."

"But with the children? Are you sure that is wise?"

"She would never hurt or scare them. She knows how and when to be silent about what she sees. Especially after what her own son did to her. She has all this love to share, so I sent her to the children. They will adore her, and she will adore them."

Killian nodded. "All right, I trust your judgment. The children have been beyond crazy in missing you, as well. Aggie has been at the Brook Street house almost daily, trying to keep their minds off of worry and making sure all stayed in order."

"Will tomorrow be too soon to see them?" Reanna tried a beguiling smile, but knew by her cracking lips that it was probably quite hideous.

"Good try." He chuckled. "When you are in no danger of children bursting blisters when jumping on you, then I will let the little rascals near you. And not until then, no matter how big your eyes get at me."

She nodded with a frown. He was right, but she didn't need to like it. "Killian, you need to know something. I did not go with him. My father. I did not meet with him. I could not do that to you. It was Miss Collier—my god—Miss Collier—" She gripped his arm. "Killian, you need to get her away from the children. Right now, Killian, you have to—"

"Stop—I know. I saw it all. And Miss Collier is long gone. I was at the park across the street and saw exactly what happened to you, and then I was promptly knocked out."

"You what? No." Her hand went to his hair, searching for a lump or a cut. "Are you all right?"

He grabbed her probing fingers, setting her hand back onto his lap. "It was a month ago, and it only knocked me out for a moment. But in that moment, I lost you."

Reanna watched as his face flickered into darkness. A darkness that unsettled her deep in her gut.

"Killian, what you said at that inn."

His eyes flew wide. "You heard that?"

"I was above you. I could hear everything through the floorboards."

"Then you heard the deal I made with your father?"

She shook her head. "Deal, what deal? I heard you say you did not want me." She swallowed the lump in her throat. "That I was a burden."

"God, Ree, tell me you didn't believe it. That I would never..."

Her eyes dropped. "I did. You said it, and then...then...I guess I gave up. It had been so long since I had seen you. My mind, it wandered in the asylum. Reexamined. Questioned everything. Even things I thought were in the past. Everything just eroded. And then you said those words. I did not want to believe it, but it was my worst fear, and there it was—from your mouth to my ears. The very thing I dreaded more than death."

"The words were false, Ree. You cannot believe I would betray you so."

"I know. I knew it when I heard you at Nettle's." She looked up at him. "I think..."

"You are not a burden, Ree. You are my wife and the farthest thing from a burden. Never should you think that." His hand went under her chin. "You are my life. My everything. What you heard was me trying to maintain some sort of desperate upper-hand with your father. I needed to try every possible angle against him. Those words were false, and I had to force myself to utter such atrocities. Of all things, do not dare question the fact that I would lie to the devil and God above to get you back."

She sat up, panicked as his earlier words sunk in. "Killian—deal—what deal did you make with my father? Tell me this instant what you did."

Killian's eyes trailed upward to the grey canopy above as a sigh went deep into his chest. He looked at her. "I traded almost everything to get you back. Everything that is not entailed or in trust. The shipping companies. They are his."

"What? No."

"Lie back down, Reanna. It is done. I am at peace with it. You are here, and that is the most important thing."

"But no, Killian, this is outrageous—unacceptable—he does not get anything from you after what he did to me."

"Please, Ree. No. I am fine with it. I can rebuild what I need to. You need not worry on that. Please, just lie down. You need to rest. To heal."

"Killian, you cannot let him do this—"

"It is done." He cut her off, his voice raw. He leaned in, his fingers gentle on her temples, his breath caressing her face. "You…you are all that matters to me. I love you, Ree, and I would have traded the world for you. I would have traded heaven and hell, my life, my soul for you. So do not question what I did. It was my decision to make, and I stand by it."

Her breath hard in her chest, Reanna nodded, tears welling in her eyes.

He searched her face, his eyes landing on hers. "You gave me the life I never even considered, never knew existed, but always needed. I will never take that gift lightly, Ree. From here, until we die, old and happy, and surrounded by bundles of grandbabies. You are my greatest treasure. There is nothing that means more to me."

Tears slipped down, the salt burning trails in her raw cheeks. But the pain only made it real. She was here.

Home. Home with her husband. Her love.

It was real.

CHAPTER 26

A week later, Reanna's skin had healed enough from the stinky salve doctor Leiars insisted get slathered on every four hours that she finally got to take a bath. Miss Melby helped her dress in a serviceable slate blue muslin dress, perfect for getting dirty with the children.

After concurring with the doctor, Killian had given approval for a short visit with the children later in the day. But Reanna had some other business to attend to before they went to the Brook Street house.

She walked into the study, finding Killian behind his desk.

He looked up as her footsteps thudded on the new Persian carpet she had chosen months ago. "You, my wife, are the most beautiful sight I could ever ask for in the morning. Please tell me you are going to pull me away from this most tedious tally of numbers. I am available for whatever whim you have in mind."

Reanna laughed and moved to stand in front of the desk. "Excellent. I do have something in mind."

"Whatever you wish. With high hopes, of course, that your whim either includes locking the study door, or heading back up the stairs to my bed. Your smell was just enough to deter me for days, but now my hands are already itching to be on you."

Reanna smiled, putting her palms on the desk and leaning in. "We will get to that, soon, my husband. I promise. But first, where do you think my father is?"

Killian's face lost all playfulness. "Why?"

"He must be in London after the deal you made with him, after all he gained."

"Ree, do not think what I fear you are," Killian said, head shaking.

"Where, Killian? I will find him one way or another. He has what he wants, and he would not be so stupid as to harm me again. Not now."

"Ree, no."

"Yes. I am taking a carriage and going to find him. I was hoping you would come with me, but if you cannot, I understand. I will be home after I find him."

"No. Dammit, Ree. No." His hand slammed onto the desk.

Reanna jumped, but she held her feet in the same spot.

"What he did to you, Ree. What he set in motion. No. Forbidden." Killian stood, glaring down at her. "He does not deserve to speak to you ever again, Ree. Do not think to do this."

"Killian, I know. I know because I feel the exact way you do about him. But I need to see him. The last time I saw him, he was punching me."

Killian flinched at her words, and she could see rage pulsating along his jaw.

"So I need to end this, Killian. For me. For you. I need to see him. One time. If you do not allow me to go today, I will go tomorrow, or the next day, or the day after. You cannot keep me captive from him."

Reanna held hard against his glare, unflinching until Killian sank down, leaning back in his chair.

"Fine. I will have the carriage brought about. But I am coming with, and you will not be alone with him. I refuse that, so do not even ask."

She gave a crisp nod. "Thank you."

~ ~ ~

Walking through the building by the docks that held the main shipping offices, Killian paused outside the door of a large room.

Reanna looked up at him, her voice a whisper. "Is this it? This was where you did business here? So he is in there?"

Killian nodded.

Reanna's lips drew back in a hard line. "Good."

She took a step in front of him and walked through the entrance. Leaving Killian at the door, she rushed forward. In one short motion, she advanced at her father, drawing the dagger from her prettiest peach reticule. She had the blade long against her father's neck before her father, or Killian, could react.

Body contorted, leaning as far back from the knife as the wooden chair he sat in would allow, her father glared up at her, his hands gripping the desk. But he made no motion to try to rip the blade from her hand. The pressure she exerted, and the thin line of blood appearing above his cravat made sure of that.

"You are treading upon harsh retribution, daughter. Remove the blade from my neck this instant." His precarious position did nothing to curb his arrogance.

"I would have hoped your first words were an apology, father." Her words hissed out. "I would have, had I not experienced myself what you are capable of."

His eyes veered over her shoulder. "Southfork, remove your wife."

"I would prefer her not to be in your vicinity at all, Halstead, especially with a knife in hand," Killian said, voice measured. "But do not dare to think I would interfere with her wishes."

Reanna heard the door click closed behind her. Good husband.

She slapped down a set of folded documents, half out of her reticule, on the desk, capturing her father's attention.

"What are those?" Halstead asked.

"Everything you took from Killian, you will return. You will sign everything back over to him."

Her father scoffed. "I will do no such thing. Now, remove this blade from my body, daughter, or I will do it for you, and you will pay dearly for your insolence."

Reanna twisted the blade on his neck. "What do you think is going to happen to you if you take this knife from my hand and threaten me, father? Let me answer. Killian will kill you before you blink."

"He would not."

"Take a look over my shoulder, father."

Halstead's eyes flickered over her shoulder.

"Is Killian there, frightened, wondering what to do?" Reanna's eyes didn't leave her father's face. "No. Your threat was enough. He is standing there, murder in his eyes, waiting for me to move so he can step in and gut you, is he not? "

His eyes flew to Reanna's face. She could see his facade slip, cracking.

"I am the only thing right now between you, and death." Her hand slapped the papers on the desk. "So this is your option out, father. This is how you stay alive. You will sign these papers. And then we will have you escorted to the docks, and you will leave this land forever. Or I will save Killian the trouble and kill you with my very own hand."

"You would not dare."

"No?" She pressed on the dagger. "Tell me father, who inherits everything when you die? Have you thought to attend to that, or have you been counting your coins?"

His mouth clamped shut, face turning red.

"Yes, I thought so. I will get it all back upon your death. And if I get it back, Killian gets it back." She gave a slow nod. "That seems very fair. So enlighten me, father, why would I not hasten your death? Why do you think I am not as heartless as you? I am your blood."

"Daughter—"

"Sign the papers, father." Her voice was cold in its dead calm.

Murder set in his own eyes, Halstead glowered at Reanna, still attempting intimidation.

A long minute passed, and Halstead broke, his hand reaching for a quill. Reanna lessened her hold on his neck so he could lean forward and set ink to paper.

Setting the quill down on the desk, he leaned back, Reanna's blade still tight to his neck.

She held her free hand out. "Your seal."

He reached into his jacket pulling it from an inside pocket. Reanna grabbed it, ripping the chain apart as she yanked it from him.

"You will regret this, daughter. You will regret this."

"Doubtful." She leaned in, her eyes level with his. "Father. I am now done with you. Thank you for my food and clothes and shelter. Please consider keeping your life as repayment for services rendered."

She straightened, her eyes and blade not leaving him. "Killian, can you please open the door?"

Killian opened the door, and she heard two men walk into the room. Taking a swift step away from her father, out of his reach, she looked to door, pointing to the two burly men waiting.

"Father, these two will be your escort onto a ship that is about to set sail."

"But, daughter—"

"Get the hell out of Killian's office, father. Out of our lives."

He sat at the desk, not moving, scowling at Reanna until she flipped her wrist to the two brutes. They stepped in, each grabbing one of her father's arms, and jerked him to his feet. Halstead gave an undignified squirm until one of the men yanked upward, taking him off his feet. He landed, slumping in defeat as he stumbled out between the two men.

"Thank you, good sirs," Reanna said over her shoulder as they disappeared out the door. She was already busy setting wax and her father's seal to the papers.

The door to the office closed once more, and Killian was across the room to her in two strides.

"Good God, Ree. Why the hell did you think to do that?" He grabbed her, snatching her into his arms and enveloping her body. "And where the blast did you even get a blade—you near keeled me over in fear."

She let his solid arms shelter her for long minutes before she pulled her head out from his hold. Fingers pushing on his chest, she leaned back to look up at him, then tossed her father's seal onto the desk and slid her arms around his waist. "You are mine, Killian. And I protect what is mine."

He laughed, his chest shaking her. "I feel very safe. Safe on a whole new level. But do not ever do something like that again to me." His hand went to the side of her face, cupping it. "Hell, Ree, you are trembling."

She ducked her head, finding the crook in the middle of his chest. "It will pass. Just hide me again."

Gentle, his hand went to the back of her head, pulling her completely into him once more. He kissed the top of her head. "Are you sure this is what you want? He is your father."

"I want peace, Killian." She didn't lift her head from its cocoon. "Peace that can only be found with my father on a continent far, far away. I am sending him off alive. That is enough for me."

"Do you trust that—him existing somewhere without accountability?"

She turned her head to the side, tilting her chin upward, but keeping her cheek on his muscle. "I am sure you will take care of that, dear husband. I doubt my father will take two steps in any direction without a report coming back to you."

Killian smirked, landing another kiss on her forehead. "Already planning it out in my head, Ree."

Her shaking subsided, and without letting her go, he shuffled the two of them toward the desk. Keeping one arm tightly around her, he reached out with a hand to grab the documents from the desk.

"Where did you get these?"

"Miss Melby snuck in your solicitor to help me yesterday when you went to see the children. He delivered the papers this morning to her. I read them. They look like they are in order to me. Are they?"

Over her head, he scanned the documents. After a moment, he looked down at her, eyes in awe. "They are. How did you…" He cut off his own words, dropping the papers and rewrapping both of his arms around her. "You, my beautiful wife, have amazed me more than one man deserves to be amazed in a lifetime."

She looked up at him, light in her blue eyes shining. "It is a good thing you finally took notice of me, then."

Killian laughed. Pure. Heartfelt.

"A good thing, indeed."

EPILOGUE

"Can you wait just one moment?"

"If I must." The tip of Reanna's tongue slid out, grazing across her lips slowly.

"Debaucher. Do not make me forget this. I would have thought the past two weeks would have tempered your appetite for our bed." Killian leaned in to bite her lip, then squeezed and dropped her hand, darting into the study.

Reanna followed him into the room, sighing, and watched him go around the desk and begin to rummage through papers in a drawer.

He glanced up at her and chuckled. "The pout is effective, but this really will only take a moment, once I find the paper. I want to write down a note I had about Maggie while we were at the baptism. I think she would like a music box for Christmas, as she loves to dance, and if I do not write it down right away, I will forget." His head went down as he continued the search. "Use the moment to imagine what I am going to do to you upstairs."

Reanna laughed and went to settee, sitting. "Have I told you that you are an amazingly thoughtful man? A man who keeps an ongoing list of gifts for little children, I think, is hard to come by."

"You can thank me upstairs." Shuffling papers, Killian pulled several sheets with neat lines on them and set them on the desk.

"The baby is wonderful."

Killian nodded as he pulled a quill. "Yes. And handsome. But we are biased, of course. It would have been a perfect ceremony had Aggie's brother not toppled Aggie over. It was just a good thing Devin was holding little Andrew at the time."

"What was wrong with Lord Clapinshire? I know your shipping interests align, so you see him often. Is he always like that? He looked terrible."

"Clapinshire is usually not that drunk." Killian shrugged, dipping the quill into ink. "Devin has said he has been getting a little too accustomed to the bottle, these days. Apparently, Aggie is quite desperate to pull him out of his downward spiral."

"Sad. So sad."

A rap on the door interrupted their conversation.

"Enter," Killian said as he finished his note.

Ludwig opened the door, letter on a silver tray in his hand. "Please excuse the interruption, my lord. This missive just arrived, with a fervent plea to get it into the hands of Lady Southfork immediately."

Killian waved him in, and he came to Reanna, holding the tray before her. She took the letter, and Ludwig exited, closing the door.

Reanna opened the sealed letter, quickly scanning the contents. She looked up at Killian, odd crease in her brow.

"What is it?"

"It is my aunt." She shook her head, her eyes going back to the letter. "She would like us to host a house party for her with a just few, very specific she says, 'discrete and trustworthy' people."

"Bizarre. Why? I thought your aunt was one to never step foot on English soil again."

Reanna shrugged. "She was. I do not know what has changed. There are no details, just the request. And she asked for it to happen in a fortnight. She is travelling here even as we speak."

Killian tapped his fingers on the desk. "We will do it, of course. But we will have to delay the trip to Holloton with the children. I imagine we can convince Devin and Aggie to join us at Curplan Hall. Do you think that will suffice?"

"I hope so." Reanna lifted the letter from her lap. "It appears she has already invited two guests as well."

"She has? Slightly presumptuous."

"I know. But that is her. She is a bold, straightforward woman, my aunt Maureen."

"Who did she invite?"

Reanna shook her head. "She did not write their names. Nor did she say how long whatever she is planning will take. I am sorry this is upending our trip to Holloton with the children. They love being at the Charles Street house, now that they are settled, but they were still so looking forward to the countryside."

Killian set the papers back into the drawer, coming around the desk. "It is only September, so we have some time before it gets cold—we can still send the children up to Holloton with the nannies, and then join them after your aunt is done with our hospitality."

He moved to stand in front of Reanna, taking the letter and setting it on a side table. He grabbed her hands, pulling her to her feet. "Besides, now that the option is in front of me, I do have that copper tub at Curplan that I have been having especially wicked thoughts about enjoying you in."

Lascivious smile spreading, Reanna's hands went to his face, caressing the slight stubble along his jaw. "Speaking of wicked thoughts, my husband, my earlier imaginations had nothing at all to do with what you are going to do to me upstairs."

His eyebrow arched. "No?"

"No." Her lips went onto his neck, tongue tasting the salt of his skin. She spun them, then pushed Killian down onto the settee. "No, I would much prefer what I am going to do to you, right here, right now."

He grabbed her hips, yanking her down with a chuckle. She straddled him, hips circling as she grabbed his hand and moved it to the wooden armrest, guiding his fingers over the smooth curve.

Her teeth nipped his ear. "Sturdy, remember?"

"I do." Killian laughed, hands already working her bodice. "Heaven help me, I do, my love."

~ About the Author ~

K.J. Jackson is the author of *The Hold Your Breath Series* and *The Flame Moon Series*. She specializes in historical and paranormal romance, will work for travel, and is a sucker for a good story in any genre. She lives in Minnesota with her husband, two children, and a dog who has taken the sport of bed-hogging to new heights.

Visit her at www.kjjackson.com

~ AUTHOR'S NOTE ~

Thank you so much for taking a trip back in time with me. The next book in the *Hold Your Breath* series will debut in Winter 2015. Aggie's brother, Jason, has stepped forward to have his story told—and it should be interesting, what with his current despondent state. And, if you missed the first in this series, **Stone Devil Duke,** Devin and Aggie's story, is currently available.

Be sure to sign up for news of my next releases at **www.KJJackson.com** (email addresses are precious, so out of respect, you'll only hear from me when I actually have real news).

Interested in Paranormal Romance?
In the meantime, if you want to switch genres and check out my Flame Moon paranormal romanceseries, **Flame Moon #1**, the first book in the series, is currently free (ebook) at all stores.
Flame Moon is a stand-alone story, so no worries on getting sucked into a cliffhanger. But number two in the series, **Triple Infinity**, ends with a fun cliff, so be forewarned. Number three in the series, **Flux Flame**, ties up that portion of the series.

As always, I love to connect with my readers, you can reach me at:

www.KJJackson.com

https://www.facebook.com/kjjacksonauthor

Twitter: @K_J_Jackson

Thank you for allowing my stories into your life
and time—it is an honor!
~ K.J. Jackson

Printed in Great Britain
by Amazon

40661267R00159